Praise for *A Murder of*

"Cade charms his way into the reader's heart by being honest about his flaws and genuinely caring about the people he meets along the way. Besides, who could resist a guy with a wrinkly dog?"
 - Starla Pointer, *Oregon Wine Press review*

Praise for *A Walk of Snipes*:

"…the likable Blackstone, with a strong supporting cast, will keep fans of all genres coming back for more."
 - Joe Hartlaub, Bookreporter.com

"It only took me two days to read this book, it totally drew me in with PI Cade Blackstone being more involved with the story line this time then he was in the first book. He has evolved to a fuller "Character", with more things happening to him. Once again there were enough twists to keep me up late at night reading this book, and the added local Oregon spots made this fun for me, since I have been to many of the places listed and could picture them in my mind while reading the book."
 – Rhonda Birk, a reader

A SCREAM OF SWIFTS

Book 3: Mysteries With a Wine List

Kate Ayers

© Copyright 2016, Attempted Murder Publishing. All rights reserved.

Dedication

Unlike *A Murder of Crows* and *A Walk of Snipes,* which were dedicated to my golfing husband Jim, this book is dedicated to all of the victims of terrorist attacks around the world, both those left living and those who were taken from us. God bless every one.

Author's Note: *A Scream of Swifts* is a work of fiction. Names, characters and some places are the product of the author's imagination. The cities and towns in France exist, as do many of the businesses such as Auberge de L'Ile restaurant, Hotel Moliere, Le Vintage Bar, and the wineries. The town of Carlton also exists, in the midst of Oregon's wine country. It is a lovely place to visit, but most of the names mentioned in this book have been fabricated, including Fou Flamant winery. Any resemblance to actual persons, living or dead, is entirely coincidental. If you think you may be a model for a character, get over it. Not very likely. Read this book for what it is: A novel.

Swift: Among the fastest of birds, they are also highly aerial and love to travel. They can be found almost everywhere, but shy away from cold climates and islands. A group of swifts is called a Scream.

In Memoriam

I owe immense gratitude to Peggy Aitchison, my critical reader. Without her, this book would have turned out much differently. At the last, she suggested a better ending than the original one, although she never knew that. Most important of all, she was my dear friend for longer than I can remember. Tragically, Peggy died before the date of publication.

"Death never comes at the *right* time, despite what mortals believe. Death always comes like a thief."
— Christopher Pike, *The Last Vampire*

Rest well, good friend.

*

Chapter 1

It was a spectacularly bad start to a year. When the terrorists hit the tiny Charlie Hebdo newspaper offices in Paris on January 7, 2015, they hit a bit too close to home back here in Oregon, even though they were half a world away. Those of you who know me expect a smart mouth, but I have to be serious for a moment. You see, my girlfriend, Lauren Pringle, is a journalist, like the victims in France. Granted, she's not a satirist, nor does she work for a newspaper that insults the prophet Muhammad or any other religious figurehead, but she's in the business nonetheless.

Lauren's a crime reporter for the *Community News*, a well-run, albeit small, weekly periodical that covers the happenings out in Carlton, Oregon's premier wine country and my home for the past seven years. (In reality, she's the only crime reporter, since we don't get a lot of crime in our little town.) So, on the heels of the shootings, Lauren felt compelled to show her support for the fallen Parisians. That's how we ended up catching a flight to France in time to join the Unity Rally. I'll admit that it felt good, even though I'm not real big on reporters – other than Lauren, of course. They seem to be a strangely focused lot and the stuff they're usually focused on holds little interest for me. But showing support felt like the right thing to do.

Anyway, we found ourselves in the French capital early in January of 2015. And, really, all in all, it's a pretty good way to begin a new year, if you discount the reason that took us there. Paris is a city of exceeding beauty, a place that has lured me to it many times. I have, however, seen it in a better mood. Thus, after the Rally and three more days of watching the usually pompous, stoic city dwellers walk around in a somber fog, I suggested to

Lauren that we take in the sights a bit further to our south, say down around Montpellier or maybe, to begin with, the seaside village of Sete.

"Are you nuts?" she asked.

Yes, in fact, I was feeling somewhat nuts. Maybe a little restless and nervous, too, frankly, mostly due to the presence of an exceptional number of police types marching around the City of Light with a very visible display of armament. I thought that possibly towns closer to the Mediterranean might be slightly more relaxed, as in fewer countrymen accessorizing their outfits with pistols. And I had other reasons, too. Instead of voicing those, I answered, "No, really, it will be fun."

It took some convincing, I'll admit, but I used some skills I'd learned on a couple of my previous trips to France and Ms. Pringle finally acquiesced. We acquired a rental car, a dark gray Peugeot of all things, and drove to Lyon the first day, departing in the morning after the rush hour had abated. Or sort of abated. Well, it never really does, so we left earlyish, I guess I'd say. I also grumbled a time or two about the awful car, having been forced to leave my sexy yellow Lamborghini back in Carlton. What a comedown! I mean, being a fellow whose favorite holiday is Mardi Gras, dark gray really doesn't suit me, but then I'm not sure who it does suit. And a Peugeot? Even the name has no glamor.

Enough grousing though. After all, there I was, in the midst of one of the world's most beautiful countries, with one of the world's most beautiful women. Sure, that may be a slight exaggeration, but my girlfriend is what I'd call stunning. And I know others who would agree, like Rollie Hansen, a Carlton deputy sheriff once upon a time, but he's not worth talking about. So the trip was shaping up to be pretty darned fine. The only way it could have been any better is if my dog Jiggs and my macaw Irene Adler had been able to come with us. In fact, they are quite good looking, too. I decided to call home later and have a chat with the two of them. It would likely make all of us happier.

The bird and the Shar Pei had been entrusted to the temporary care of my new tenant, Jim Smith, a strange and secretive man who saved my life during an attempt to solve a missing person case. To help you understand, I am a private investigator, albeit a bit new to the game. I don't know Mr. Smith well, nor am I completely convinced of his even remotely honest nature, but my dog Jiggs has grown fond of him in the six or eight months since Mr. Smith has moved into an office down the hall from mine. I give a lot of credence to Jiggs' judgment about human nature. He's got a nose for it, you might say.

Irene, though, likes anyone who will talk to her so the bird's opinion is taken with substantially less weight.

Thinking of Jim Smith and my pets led me to the foolish notion of coming entirely clean with my girlfriend. I turned to Lauren as we cruised down the motorway along with what felt like three million French people fleeing Paris for country solace.

Naturally, I chose to ease into the naked truth slowly. "So we're only going as far as Lyon tonight. Great little city. And, hey, I know a superb place for dinner." I edged my phone toward her. "Here. Would you find Auberge de L'Ile in my Contacts? See if they can fit us in, like around eight o'clock."

The Ile is a rustic restaurant situated on an island – an ile – in the midst of the Saone River which would serve us a very expensive meal spread out over the course of approximately three hours. Ah, the French do know how to enjoy food, as do I. Lauren goes in more for vegetables, which some consider food, although, for me, the jury's still out on that. I suggested she call my favorite little hotel on the rue Victor Hugo, also, and book Room 43. It is best to be specific with the staff. That way, you get what you want.

I speak passable French (not really), but Lauren, ooh la la, she can do the language supreme justice. Thus, short moments later, some exquisite sounds emanated from the passenger seat of the Peugeot, ending with a melodic "Merci, monsieur."

I'm not convinced that Auberge de L'Ile actually had room for us so late in the reservation-making scheme of things, but we landed a table nonetheless, likely due to Lauren's beautiful and mesmerizing way of asking for it. Now it was time for me to fess up about the reason for taking our trip to the southern region called the Languedoc. Actually, the reason for taking the trip to France, period. "You remember Jim Smith, right?"

Lauren looked at me sideways, head tilted, a position I was able to see despite not glancing away from the road. That couldn't be good. But, then, almost any time Jim Smith's name comes up causes suspicion. With good reason. More about that later.

"Of course."

"Funny thing. Not long before we left, he reminded me about a wayward winemaker from Fou Flamant Wines back home.

"Crazy Flamingo Wines?"

My French isn't so good that I'd known that's what Fou Flamant meant, but okay. "Huh." Like beer crafters, winemakers come up with some, shall we say, unique labels. "Yeah, okay. Anyway, it's a fairly cool winery on the road toward Mac," I replied, using the local and familiar term for McMinnville, a midsize college town fifteen minutes or so from my house.

"Yes, I know. I've seen it."

"Ah. Good. Well, Jim mentioned that they're having some trouble lately."

"Is that so?"

"It is so." Actually, the trouble had started several months back and I had been dragging my feet about tackling the problem. It wasn't that I didn't want to go to France, all expenses paid – even though that part didn't really matter. It had more to do with getting a better handle on Mr. Smith and his veracity, something I was still working on, as mentioned earlier. But back to the trouble. "Yes, it seems that Fou Flamant's wine crafter has flown the coop, so to speak." I thought I had put that quite cleverly, with the avian reference and all, but Lauren seemed stuck on technicalities like me keeping secret reasons for the trip.

"I see. And where does Mr. Smith think that the wine 'crafter' has gotten himself off to?"

"Ah, coincidentally, we are heading sort of in that direction."

"Coincidentally."

"Well, maybe not so coincidentally." I am learning not to bullshit a reporter. It might have taken me three years to get this far, but no one said I was a quick learner. The good thing was that we now had reservations at Lyon's best restaurant – in my opinion – and a room at a four-star hotel, and I'd told Lauren the truth, or most of it. If you really thought about it, the trip to France was her idea. Or at least enough so that I figured to play that card and see how far it got me.

"If you'll remember, I did mention this back when Smith first moved into 86 N. Main." (86 N. Main is Blackstone Investigations' address. It's also a building that I own.)

Lauren turned to look out at the scenery. That could mean that she wasn't remembering events quite like I was. I started to think I might have to double down on this one.

"It's true. I even recall your reaction when I brought up the possibility of a case that might take me – us – to France. It had something to do with trying to understand how a snipe hunt works."

She couldn't help but smile at that. She had to admit I was right. Not only was I right, but that brought back memories of a very pleasant nature in which Lauren got the definition of a snipe hunt entirely wrong, but the way she'd demonstrated her ideas made me not care. So we drove along with visions of that day knocking around in our heads for several minutes, until we reached the outskirts of Lyon with its red-roofed stone buildings nestled among velvety rolling hills.

"But, to fully answer your question, it seems that one Monsieur Adrien Hatif, le winemaker –" I said this with my best accent "– was last headed to a little town about half an hour outside of Montpellier called Montagnac. Apparently, he took off last fall, for some vaguely stated family reason, promising to return in a couple weeks. Well, he extended his stay – another vague family reason – and now Fou Flamant wants answers. Actually, they want him back. Which brings this conversation back around to me. They have sent me, through Jim Smith, to bring him home to Carlton. So we'll be staying just down the road from Montagnac in a seaside resort, a killer cool spot called Sete. It's a quaint but popular town with wonderful views of the Mediterranean Sea. And we have reservations at a hotel called La Singulière, which way outshines the Whale Cape Inn on our coast back home. You'll love it." She would. La Singulière defined the word hospitality, something which had seemed an alien concept at Whale Cape Inn, a place we stayed while I investigated my last big case. But, first, we had a night in Lyon to enjoy.

We hid the Peugeot in an underground car park as quickly as possible. I mean, who wants to be seen in that boxy piece of machinery? Especially in a country as fashion conscious as France. Soon thereafter, we had checked into our room at the Hotel Hugo, or whatever it's called. I thought maybe I'd try to make up to Lauren after our little misunderstanding about the purpose of the trip. It took some doing, believe me, but we finally emerged from our suite wearing smiles.

Later, at Auberge, shortly before eight o'clock that evening, Gregoire, a waiter I knew from several previous visits, announced that he would be personally taking care of us for the next few hours. That was good news indeed. Gregoire had been there from the inception of the establishment, if my memory served me, and he knew how to optimize one's enjoyment of a culinary experience. From the look on his face when I introduced Lauren, he seemed to approve of my date. One or two other ladies had accompanied me to Auberge in the distant past, but if I had anything to say about it, Lauren would be the last. At age 36, I was beginning to feel the tugs of domesticity pulling at me. Maybe she was just growing on me, but even my wandering eye had started to stay home more. And, to be crystal clear, it was only my eye that still wandered.

Gregoire nodded and smiled widely as he brought out a tower of what he called *beignets d'herbes aromatiques et poivre rose*, paired with flutes of the house champagne, complimentary appetizers which greet guests in a casual seating area under a gnarly old tree outside the door of the three-story building. Since it was January, albeit a dry and warm one, overhead heaters were glowing to provide extra comfort and soft light.

I toasted Lauren in a flourish of Blackstone French. She frowned, which led me to believe that some of the silent consonants had been verbalized by mistake. That happens all the time with me. So I hoisted my glass toward the glorious crimson shutters of Auberge de L'Ile, smiled and then drank some of the bubbly. Nice, but I was looking forward to something a bit more on the bold, red side. Lauren, though, seemed quite content, with everything except my French.

After half an hour of this European style of warming up to the idea of bona fide dining, we were escorted to our second-floor table, a spacious round expanse of wood, one of only two in the room, the sparsity of which guaranteed that Gregoire would see to our every need, almost before we even knew we needed it.

The constantly changing menu at this place is poetry itself. A parade of extravagant dishes filled the next hour and a half. Then, just when I thought I could eat no more, Gregoire brought out a cheese board that looked as though he needed help carrying it. I'd swear the thing was three feet by three feet. But, then, it also had a selection of toasted breads and about a dozen condiment type things to choose from. And that was the lead-up to dessert.

Dessert deserves its own paragraph but I won't bore you with talk of dark truffles, rich cream puffs and finger shaped tiramisu. And no way would I mention the six flavors of gelato. There was much more, but we finally cried, "Uncle!"

- - -

Back at Hotel Hugo, the clock on the nightstand read 12:05, which meant that, in Carlton, the time was hovering around four o'clock in the afternoon. Jiggs normally took a nap about then, but when doesn't he? As for Irene Adler, she was unpredictable. So we took a chance and called home to find out how everyone was doing. Fortunately, Jim Smith was in his office. I could tell right away that he had Irene with him. She has a tendency to sing, especially when a telephone rings. And she has yet to master volume control.

"Hey, Jim. How are things over there in Oregon?"

"Fine, Cade. Real fine."

He didn't sound real fine though. I suspected my macaw may have been repeating her latest song, over and over and over. She does become fixated with a new tune. When she fell in love with "All About that Bass", I had to lock her in a room far, far away until she moved on to a less repetitive song.

"How are things over there in France? You are there, right?"
"Yep. Lyon, as a matter of fact. And things are excellent."
"Lyon, huh? Food city. Did you two have a nice dinner?"
"Oh, yeah. About three and a half hours of nice dinner."
"And wine, too, I'd say."
"Oops." I resisted the urge to burp and prove him right. "Is Jiggs around?"
"Uh-huh. I'll get him."

I pictured my dog lying in a pool of sunlight near Mr. Smith's south-facing windows, then remembered that it was January in Oregon, too, which meant that it would be another three months before anyone would get even a good glimpse of the sun. Anyway, in a matter of moments, I heard Jiggs sniff the phone, snort several times, and trot off. That's as much as I could have hoped for. I may have gotten in a greeting, but it's hard to remember now.

"So is that all you called for? To hear your dog sneeze into the phone and your bird screech out – what is that she's singing anyway?"

"Who knows? And, well, yes, that sort of is why I called. But, while I have you on the phone, may as well ask: Any new developments in the disappearance of M. Hatif?" Just as I enquired about the wayward winemaker, my eyes wandered across the room and I noticed Lauren unbuttoning the buttery silk blouse she'd worn to dinner so I totally missed Jim's answer. No matter; I don't think there was any news. But, if there was, I figured he could fill me in tomorrow, when we got to Sete. I told him I'd call again then, and hoped that conditions for concentrating would be better for me. Or not. These conditions looked pretty good. I hung up.

Chapter 2

Over breakfast the next morning, I mentioned to Lauren some of the possible side trips we might take in the next few days, depending, of course, on how elusive M. Hatif turned out to be. Really, though, considering that we were heading directly into the world's most productive wine region, I didn't think we could go wrong. But wine isn't the only good thing about that part of France.

I had chosen Sete as a base of operations mostly due to its outstanding beauty and setting perched directly on the Mediterranean, but it was also convenient – for touring and for my detective work. The address Jim Smith had provided as Hatif's place of residence, as mentioned before, was in a town called Montagnac, a village about the size of Carlton back home. But the Frenchman's uncle reputedly had a winery near tiny Loupian, between Sete and Montagnac. I hadn't gotten a good grasp on how close emotionally Hatif and his uncle were, nor whether this uncle was actually related. If not, there might be any number of uncles with wineries around. This was the Languedoc, after all. Prolific producers of the red stuff abounded. One of many reasons I loved it here.

Approximately forty-five minutes in the opposite direction from my business pursuits lay The Camargue, a river delta between two arms of the Rhone River. Being so close to this famous delta meant there would be no reasonable excuse to skip a visit. After all, why pass up a chance to ride exquisite white Camargue horses in pursuit of seeing the great pink flamingos during mating season? A flamboyance of them, as Cassandra York might have informed me. (An old girlfriend and current competition in the world of PIs;

nobody important. However, she had gotten me hooked on the bird group jargon, starting with a murder of crows.)

"Horses?"

My girlfriend looked skeptical, an expression that does not often cross her face. Except maybe when listening to some of my stories.

"Not just horses. *Camargue* horses."

"Oh."

My explanation didn't seem to persuade her. But, then, she hadn't seen these incredible creatures.

"Are you afraid of horses, Lauren?"

She made a pfft sound. "No."

"Uh-huh. Well, good." And unconvincing. "Anyway, we don't have to ride the wild ones, okay? They have tame ones, too. We can hire those." Her eyes got wide. I winked to let her know I was kidding. Not sure she believed that. So maybe we'd save horseback riding for the next trip to the Languedoc and this time take a carriage around the wetlands. I'd bring that up later, though. Her interest in flamingos and white horses seemed to be leaning toward apathetic at the moment.

We left Lyon behind, facing a pleasant four-hour trip with the very cool Hotel La Singulière at the end of it.

- - -

Right around noon, as we were hurtling down the A-9, my stomach began to growl. Well, naturally. My stomach is better than a watch for telling time. A few miles southwest of Avignon, we were perfectly positioned for a side trip to the Pont du Gard. The food in their little tourist cantina isn't especially good, but the scenery is out of this world. I mean, a Roman aqueduct from the 1st century? That's just slightly before Christopher Columbus was even dreaming about discovering our country, like 1300 years, give or take a few. And the Pont is still standing! In fact, it's still standing in remarkable condition. The iconic Portland Building is already in need of millions of dollars in repair, and it's only a little over 30 years old.

Explaining this to Ms. Pringle, I observed, "We would probably be wise to import a few Romans into Oregon for tips on constructing things that last."

Lauren groaned and rolled her eyes. As I've said before, she does that a lot.

There had been few cars in the lot when we parked, although I noted one followed us in rather closely. Europeans sometimes have a space invader issue, in my opinion. We stopped by the tacky little cafeteria and shelled out something like thirty euros for a couple of dried-out sandwiches before heading down a nice, wide path leading to the river Gardon. Lagging slightly behind, I admired Lauren's shape with each step, and the sway of her long blonde hair over that shape. I thought I could almost smell the lavender lotion that has recently become her signature scent, but it's possible I confused that with the French countryside.

All too soon, we reached the river and I reluctantly lifted my eyes from the view I'd been enjoying to the one I'd come down the trail for. Green, deep and flowing lazily, flanked by rugged rocks, that stretch of the Gardon can easily transport one back to the days of horse-drawn wagons. I love history. It gets my juices flowing. Pointing wildly, I gasped and exclaimed about a man with a spear wearing a toga.

Lauren's jaw dropped. I love to shock her like that, although I don't think she was looking at the imaginary toga-wrapped Roman.

"Oh, wow, Cade."

"Yeah." That's about the snappiest comeback I could think of, the grandeur of the Pont having rendered me nearly speechless.

Two other couples wrapped their arms around each other, apparently feeling the romance of the river much as Lauren and I. A lone figure stood off next to some bushes, speaking into a mobile phone. Now there was someone who didn't appreciate history. Or beauty. I made some clever remark to that effect, and then we didn't talk much for awhile, just munched, chewed and pondered the old aqueduct in quiet awe before starting back toward the car to begin the last leg of the journey to Sete. A little over an hour later, we got out of the car for the final time that day, at Hotel La Singuliere.

"Oh, wow, Cade," Lauren said again. Our position high on a hill overlooking the Venice-like town gave us a vast panorama. Gazing out over the small pool, we could see the canals of Sete below, along with its narrow streets leading toward the sparkling Mediterranean.

Registering took no time. Before going to the room, we stopped by the Concierge desk where we consulted a tall figure looking like a young David Niven about dinner reservations. Once I'd hauled in our bags, I discovered Lauren stretched out on a lounge made for one. I tried to work out a way to fit two onto it, but she was making it difficult, so I gave up and went outside to get the call to Jim Smith out of the way. When we connected, he sounded somewhat logy, and it occurred to me it was probably, like, 7:30 in the morning. Got to hand it to Irene Adler, she sounded wide awake in the background.

"Good morning, Jim"

"Yeah, hi, Cade. Doesn't your bird ever go hoarse?"

I thought that was funny, a bird going hoarse, and told him so. "Get it, Jim? Hoarse? As in h-o-r-s-e?"

"Yeah, yeah, I get it. Ha ha. Next time, I go to France and you take care of your own animals."

"But I'm the detective in this equation, Jim."

"Uh-huh. Right. Have you found M. Hatif yet?"

"Well, no, but I just got here."

"Where's *here*?"

"Sete."

"Yeah, like that explains anything. Where's Sete?"

I filled Mr. Smith in on our day so far, our location, and my plans for tomorrow, then asked him for any updates. This time, I listened to his answer. As suspected, though, he had nothing new to tell me. So far, my leads were slim pickings. An address in Montagnac and the name of an uncle's winery. The best news was that I was in France and had no plans to return to the drippy Northwest for another week or two, unless things heated up with Fou Flamant's winemaker. And right then, the Languedoc region seemed to be experiencing an early spring. That made my future look especially rosy. I hadn't seen the forecast though.

Jim laid the phone next to my dog, who had not yet risen for the day and I got an earful of extraordinary Shar Pei snores before Irene cranked up again and Smith cut the connection, leaving me to wonder how long my macaw might survive.

I wandered over to the pool with my map book and flopped onto a padded chaise. It's possible that I might have been pouting. Lauren didn't seem to be all that friendly, lying there on that lounge-for-one inside. The view over the Mediterranean, though, went a long way toward compensating for her aloofness. Despite the Sea's reputation as being a bit filthy, it shimmers and glistens and makes quite a breathtaking presentation, particularly in the splashy hour prior to sundown.

Thinking about planning the next day, I opened my Michelin atlas and ran my finger along the route toward Montagnac from Sete, quickly discovering that St. Martin de la Garrigue lie along the way, besides a few other interesting sounding wineries, like St. Martin de Graves. Ah, those lovely fairy tale St. Martins. But la Garrigue is especially interesting. (Unless you have tasted it or seen the chateau, I can't explain its appeal.) I circled its position on the map, anxious to share this news with Lauren. Actually, anxious to share anything with Lauren. What incredible luck this turned out to be, though. It would be even better if one of M. Hatif's uncles had some position of importance there.

Mr. Smith hadn't mentioned anything like that in his update, but I figured I ought to check it out for myself in order to claim to have done a thorough job. Yep, that's what I figured. And if not, we'd have to move on from la Garrigue to Graves. And, if no connection at Graves, well, the possibilities seemed to be endless. It had begun to look as though we might be in France longer than first anticipated, maybe a year or two. I went inside to tell my girlfriend about this great discovery and see if she might want to celebrate in some fun way. Turns out we did okay.

- - -

Terre et Mer was no Auberge de L'Ile, but few restaurants are. To its credit, its location near the water scored it some major points and our meals were executed quite professionally. After polishing off a bottle of the local red, Lauren and I laced our arms together and went for a stroll along the Canal Royal. It's a lively stretch of water and cobblestones with bustling cafes and bars, drawing in holidaymakers and locals alike. Next to us on the side not sporting drinking establishments, several boats floated lazily by, stirring up tiny waves to leave behind in their wakes.

"Oh, look!"

I followed Lauren's finger to the window of a shop displaying a variety of neon kites in all manner of shapes and sizes. Naturally, we had to go inside. As with most village shops, the place was small, but its inventory wasn't. There were kites looking like human and animal torsos and crabs and toons and octopuses – excuse me, octopi. Also whales, manatees, big and little circles, dogs (the French are big on dogs) and lizards and mermaids and, well, you name it, there was a kite looking like it.

Lauren twirled around like a child at Disneyland, her mouth open in a kind of awe. "Cade, they're beautiful."

I think the wine had gone to my head because I never say things like, "No, it's you that's beautiful," but I did. Fortunately, she got all mushy, which I really like. It's better when we're not out in public, though. Anyway, I covered my embarrassment by purchasing a corny keychain that had a miniature replica of an octopus kite with two-inch-long legs dangling from it and gave it to her as a token of something. Couldn't tell you what. I mean, it was an *octopus*, for God's sake. Well, maybe the next day would bring some better ideas. And some direction on how to find Adrien Hatif.

Chapter 3

The next day did bring some better ideas, although I swear I'd forgotten what day it was by then. There's something about the European way of life, the French way specifically, that relaxes a person almost to the point of uselessness. Triple that for the little towns in the south dotting the wine-soaked landscape. Just those few days in that laid-back atmosphere had muddled my brain such that I'd forgotten Jim Smith had given me an envelope containing what he considered pertinent information on M. Adrien Hatif, the missing person he'd shipped me off to the Continent to retrieve. Lauren actually brought it up. She couldn't see the logic in Smith sending me over with nothing more than my two thumbs to get me by.

As we indulged in a small feast of croissants with butter, honey, jams and cheeses and, of course, strong coffee, I spilled out the contents of the slender manila envelope. Three 5x7 photographs landed face up.

It was hard to conceal my surprise. "Huh. I would not have pictured our man looking anything like that."

Lauren reached across the table and twisted one of the photos around so that she could see it right side up, then touched her fingers to her lips. That made me want to touch her lips, too. Actually, a lot of things do that. Anyway, she blinked a few times and said, "Uh-huh."

"Uh-huh?"

"Uh-huh, I agree. He has a Rasta sort of look rather than a French winemaker sort of look. The dreads, the bright cape, the skin. What is that, almost cinnamon, do you think?"

"Good call." I peered closer at the image. Maybe I had thought he would be the stereotypical Frenchman from old films: a slight fellow with short brown hair, a beret and a twitchy little mustache, possibly wearing a billowy shirt, what some used to call a poet's shirt.

But the face in the photo was, yes, similar to the color of rich cinnamon, full featured, friendly, with eyes so dark you could fall into them. The Rasta feel came from the shoulder-length dreads and the woven cloth of his – what? How would I define that garment? Lauren had described what he was wearing as a cape. Possibly, but it was pretty long. Yellow, red, green, purple and blue. What shade didn't he have on? The man was a virtual rainbow.

It seemed that, with a character this, um, colorful, he shouldn't be at all hard to find. Right? For no discernible reason, I glanced around at the other diners in the room. It was absurd to think that M. Hatif would be breakfasting at Hotel La Singuliere in Sete along with us, but I couldn't help myself. As I did a quick scan, my eye caught that of another guest and it held for just a second too long for comfort. Did I know that man? When he broke eye contact, he left me with the uneasy feeling that it was with great reluctance. Almost like he'd been watching me. But that was just paranoid thinking. Probably more likely that he'd been watching Lauren. That made more sense.

- - -

The weather had done an about-face and reverted to full-on January, with low, brooding skies heavy with moisture that I hoped would stay up in the clouds. No hats had found their way into my luggage, an odd omission on my part, as I'm very fond of hats. Lauren, though, appeared to have brought along an abundant selection. Nonetheless, I suggested a quick bout of shopping, a pursuit I enjoy almost as much as Ms. Pringle does.

We retrieved the ugly Peugeot and set out for Montagnac, our missing person's current address and a village that should have taken a mere half hour to get to, had we been serious about timing. You might have noted by now that we are – or at least I am – fairly easily distracted. Especially by things like wineries, something we have a lot of at home, just not of the right sort to spark my interest. In the Languedoc, though, they have some real tasty wines, without the emphasis on expensive, temperamental pinot noir. Even with heavy, threatening clouds, that had the makings of a happy day.

Anyway, we arrived in Montagnac three hours into the afternoon, having discovered four delightful vintners along the way who offered degustation de vins, aka wine tasting. (I learn the important phrases in a foreign language first.) The French may have a reputation as being snobbish and unfriendly, but the country folk are most assuredly anything but. At least where we were touring. Again, maybe it had something to do with Lauren and her lovely way of rolling French words around in that sexy mouth of hers.

Everywhere we went, I smiled and said a cheery, "Bonjour." And everywhere we went, I got a look of unreserved confusion. Come on, it's not that hard to say. How wrong could I have gotten it? But when Lauren said, "Bonjour," well, even I could tell the difference. No way could I mimic her, though. *C'est la vie.*

On our way to Adrien's – temporary, we'd been led to believe – residence, we pulled out a photo of M. Hatif at each of the wineries. The staff showed genuine interest in looking at it, but there was no flicker of recognition from any of them. One interesting thing did happen, though. As we were about to leave St. Martin de la Garrigue, Lauren elbowed me, a bit sharply I thought.

"Ow."

"Cade, look. That woman over by those barrels."

I turned toward where Lauren was gesturing but caught only a glimpse of the backside of a brownish-red-haired lady of indeterminate height and age, considering she was in motion and I couldn't see her face. She rapidly ducked through a door which closed with a decisive clank.

"What about her?"

Lauren shook her head. "Nothing, I guess. She just – well, she seemed to look up suddenly when you said Adrien Hatif's name, but it was probably coincidence."

Well, I don't believe in coincidence, and Lauren knows that, but I do believe in mistaken interpretations and this certainly sounded like one of those. Besides, it appeared as though there would be no way to confirm or disprove our theory anyway. The woman had disappeared into the depths of the winery, and even Lauren's beautiful way of speaking would likely not get us into its private parts.

I sighed, feeling the mellowness that winetasting brings with it, and paid for the six bottles of la Garrigue's Bronzinelle blend I'd formed an immediate flavor bond with. Reluctantly I said, "We really must get on to Montagnac now."

Darkness would be descending upon us in under three hours, probably closer to two. With the already dim skies, the drive back to the hotel would be much less fun, especially since the wineries would be closing around 4:30. Besides, if we hoped to catch M. Hatif at home, this could be our best bet. Not sure why I thought that, but I didn't believe he was currently working for any of the chateaux in the area. Someone over the course of the afternoon would have known that. And if he was just hanging around the Languedoc on a lark, he probably would be getting ready for some later evening plans. At least, that's what I'd be doing. But then I'm not a lost Rasta French guy. Nor, frankly, am I frequently correct. (I am still quite new at this detecting stuff.)

We motored into Montagnac, a rather disappointing town if you compared it to the utter enchantment of its surrounding siblings. As one saving grace, it did have a nice building with a spire on it, situated in what I pinpointed as the center of town. Probably some old abbey. Almost every little community around there, no matter the size, had an old abbey. Montagnac sat mostly on the flatland rather than aspiring to grow itself into a hill town, an aspect that I find much more ambitious and exciting. I mean, winding up narrow, twisty, cobbled streets, like the ones in Sete, really gives a driver some thrills, not to mention the occasional dent or mangled side mirror.

We located M. Hatif's building relatively easily in the grand scheme of things and, to my delight, discovered a parking place directly in front. At least it was an unoccupied piece of ground big enough to pull the ugly Peugeot off of the road for a few minutes.

Hatif's rented flat looked as though it had been built right about the same time as the Pont du Gard had been, 1st Century. Looked like it might have been built by the same crew even. Okay, I might be exaggerating. It could have been 4th Century. Not to split hairs, but it looked damned old.

I stared up at the two-story façade and observed, "Damn, this place looks old. Do you think it's safe to go inside?"

Lauren rolled her eyes at me, once again, although I think it was the first time that day.

Jim Smith had supplied an address, but no key, of course, and a knock on the door produced no Adrien Hatif. My deduction about this being a good time to find him home turned out, as often happens, to be incorrect. I looked around. "Do you see a manager's apartment anywhere?"

She did not, as there was only one door in sight and a staircase at the end of a short corridor. Perhaps the manager lived upstairs? That would certainly be an odd arrangement but, as I've said before, Europeans do things differently than we Americans do. I took a quick run up to the second floor, finding just one other door, but got no response from knocking on it either. I noted it did not say "Manager" or the French equivalent, whatever that might be, so I assumed the building was run by off-premises management. Coming back downstairs, I saw my girlfriend try the knob on our quarry's door and push. It gave inward.

"Oops," Lauren covered her mouth with both hands.

I uncovered her mouth and gave it a giant kiss. "Nice." Then I *accidentally* bumped up against the door, causing it to swing inward further. "Oops," I echoed. Donning some gloves that I save for inside exploring, I rubbed them over the doorknob to smudge Lauren's prints in case anything more criminal than snooping had occurred in there.

My eyes swept the room, noting how tidy it was, and empty – at least empty of living beings, including those of the plant world. "Wait here."

"Not a chance," Lauren said.

The woman never takes me seriously. I rolled my eyes at her this time, but it did no good. She followed close on my heels.

"Don't touch anything."

M. Hatif's apartment appeared clean, lived in and set up for the long run. Photographs of the family kind sat on the top shelf of a small bookcase. Most people don't unpack those sorts of things unless they plan to hang around for a while. This surprised me considering that Hatif's trip to France was supposedly a quick visit to catch up with the family news. A wedding or a graduation or something? Yeah, yeah, he had overstayed his welcome if that were the case, having arrived several months back, but, still, maybe he got sidetracked. I know how that goes. Happens to me all the time. And, well, there are a lot of French women here to be distracted by, and French women tend to be sexy, at least by my definition. Believe me, I know a lot of men who would agree.

Anyway, I digress. The largest of the family photos stretched across more than half of the shelf, showing Adrien's entire extended family from the looks of it. I saw a younger version of himself flanked by an older couple who must have been mom and dad, plus what appeared to be a set of twins, three more men – brothers, I guessed – and a woman who could have been anywhere from 25 to 35. They all had skin in variations of Adrien's cinnamon, and all of the guys wore brightly colored clothing, except for one.

I pointed and said, "That one must be the family lawyer."

Lauren groaned.

Another picture showed two men beside a wine barrel, hands around each other's shoulders, big smiles. I wondered what that was all about. They might be family, too, but it was hard to tell because of the photo's size and the fact that it was in black and white. The same held for the logo on the one wine bottle that was visible in the picture. Minuscule. No way could I read it. The other pictures seemed as though they might have been of previous classmates engaged in various pursuits with M. Hatif. A canoe featured in one, a statue in another, bicycles in two of them, and a pretty girl in every one.

Wandering around, I picked up a couple of personal trinkets but felt no spark of connection to them nor any sort of clue where they might take me. His bedroom looked typical for a twenty-something male. A few clothes strewn here and there, the wardrobe doors gaping, shoes tumbling out. (Nothing in gray, black or brown, though, but fabrics in hues that would make a reggae mama proud.) The bed was made, although not well, and a book lay open, upside down, on one pillow, with a well-worn dust jacket. The title was in French, so I didn't catch it. In the kitchen, the elfin refrigerator held food which had not had time to grow mold, leading me to believe that the apartment's resident likely still resided there.

A shallow wooden bowl on a sofa table held some envelopes, so I rifled through those. Sam Spade never let an opportunity like that pass, and he always found something useful on one of the pieces of paper. Maybe I'd get lucky, too. A majority of Hatif's correspondence turned out to be bills, I discovered, with Lauren's help. But two of them were handwritten – a pure rarity these days – and looked personal. One was an old-fashioned party invitation from someone named Yvette. And one was from a winery called Arrogant Frog.

Lauren jumped when a loud bump sounded from above us, like something heavy hitting the floor. I grabbed several quick pictures of Hatif's mail with my iPhone, then snapped several more shots of Hatif's flat for later review. The apartment was fast growing dim and I had no desire to turn on lights, nor to leave fingerprints behind. As noted, I'd taken precautions already with my ever-present gloves. When we heard another clunk from overhead, we knew it was time to leave.

Looking at my watch, I sighed. It was already past four o'clock. If Arrogant Frog's hours were like the other wineries we'd visited, we would be hard pressed to get there before the tasting room closed, since it appeared, from the address on the envelope, to be further up the road near the next town (one with a name that did not sound at all French), Pezenas. Oh, well, it gave us a good destination for the next day, unless that day turned out to be Sunday. I still was a bit in the dark on that.

Taking a last quick look around the flat, I ushered Lauren toward the door. She gave me no resistance. I guess she doesn't like breaking and entering all that much, even though we technically did not break before entering. But we didn't want to have to explain the subtle differences to the French gendarmes.

On the street again, a gust of wind tugged at Lauren's faux fur coat, revealing a hint of her left thigh. I eagerly watched for more, but it must have been a lone rogue breeze. She adjusted her hat, which caught my attention, too, since it sits on top of a generous heap of vibrant blonde hair. She stopped suddenly and let out a squeak.

"What?"

"That woman!"

I reluctantly looked up and saw, again, the backside of a brownish-red-haired woman, maybe the same brownish-red-haired woman from the last winery we had visited. I saw a glimpse of a profile before she turned and hustled along the curb then disappeared around the corner.

"Here." I tossed Lauren the car key and trotted up the street toward the intersection, shouting, "Yvette," just in case I got lucky. As I rounded the building, I knew the chase was futile. Montagnac may not be exactly a bustling town, especially in that neighborhood, but it has many alleys and porticos that a fleeing figure can dart into. Besides, who knew if that really was the woman we had seen at la Garrigue winery earlier? It did not seem very likely. In fact, it actually seemed wholly ludicrous to think that she might have followed us. That's why I didn't try very hard to find her. In retrospect, I probably should have.

Chapter 4

As anticipated, we reached Arrogant Frog in time to watch them close their large, ornate iron gates. We admired the Baroque A and F inside of a circle, each on one side, unfortunately from the wrong perspective – streetside. While I puffed out my cheeks in frustration, Lauren giggled at the life-size – life-size as in six feet tall – frog standing on its hind legs holding a tray with a bottle of red wine balanced upon it, positioned beside the stone wall flanking the narrow lane inside the property. I'll admit it did have a way of changing the mood.

"Well, damn, guess we'll have to come back tomorrow."

"What a pity."

I was happy to note that Lauren was finally catching on to the benefits of a case that would require us to tour around the French countryside and stop at wineries yet another day.

"Uh-huh. A pity." I glanced around. "Hey, doll, as long as we're this close, would you like to take a peek at downtown Pezenas?" The part of the village that we could see from outside the Arrogant Frog winery showed promise, so I hoped she would say, "Yes." She did.

We drove deeper into the village and located a spacious car park across from what appeared to be a charming row of well-patronized bars and restaurants. (You might have noticed that I tend to like that type of establishment.) Before we chose one in which to indulge our culinary cravings, though, we decided to amble through the narrow back streets and wandered in and out of tiny shops for a little over an hour. I found a hat suitable for Cade – one which would have turned Sam Spade green with envy

– but then noted that the sky had finally lifted, probably because I had now prepared myself for precipitation. Still, I imagined that the chapeau looked damned fine sitting with a slight rakish tilt on my curly dark hair. (Very Spade-like.) I modeled it for Lauren. She snickered. Not really the reaction I was going for.

Shortly after 6:15, we trekked back toward the plaza we'd seen when we first arrived and came upon Le Vintage Bar de Vins. Besides the obvious agreeability of the name, hanging next to their door they had a banner emblazoned with the phrase "Je Suis Charlie" (*I am Charlie*), referring, of course, to Charlie Hebdo, the newspaper that had been attacked a week and a half earlier. In our travels south, this sign of solidarity had greeted us often along the way, although we were pleased to observe the display of fewer firearms as we got further from Paris. Even so, the country remained tense. We stood, motionless, for a moment of silence in remembrance of the fallen journalists before entering the bar.

Their sandwich board, situated in a strategic place on the bricks outside of the bar, is what ultimately enticed us inside. Its listing of tapas sounded incredible even by French standards. Already, musicians were setting up on a tiny stage and nearly all of the tables were full. The wine list featured mostly local vintners, as one would expect, but that list encompassed an enviable variety. Who would think a town like Pezenas would have such a rich heritage in the grape? Probably everyone around there, frankly. Anyway, I ordered a bottle of a deep, inky red blend from Domaine St. Hilaire, whose chateau, the waiter said, was just around the next set of curves had we driven on through the town. Lauren set about choosing a selection of tapas, the descriptions of which made my stomach gurgle in keen anticipation, reminding me we had skipped the lunch part of the day due to the overabundance of croissants and cheese at the breakfast part of the day.

As we waited for our food and drink, I let my eyes roam through the crowd. The French are so enjoyable. Mostly because they so enjoy entertaining themselves in a rich and decadent fashion. On the road into town, we'd seen a McDonald's and I nearly rear-ended the car in front of us. Come on, the French shouldn't even think of eating stuff like that. They have no reason to. No offense to McDonald's, but it's not French cooking. I'd say the same about Burger King, Jack in the Box and Carl's Jr. They had no business being in a country that had such a delicate palate. Sorry, I'll get off my soapbox. But, seriously.

That evening, the crowd in Le Vintage Bar was an eclectic bunch. Besides French, I heard English voices, Aussies, Germans, and even an American or two. At the table next to ours, a raucous group of Brits were busily hoisting their drinks and having an animated political conversation, peppering their comments with "Bloody hell" and the occasional "Bollocks!" The man most fond of this word sat facing our table and carried a startling head of white hair and bushy eyebrows, thick eyeglasses and an ever-present impish grin. He had about twenty years or so on me, yet he looked like someone I'd like to get to know. It must have been that grin.

I turned my attention back to Lauren, where it belonged, really, although it was now split between my girlfriend and the events of the day. "Do you really think that was the lady from la Garrigue winery there outside of Hatif's flat?"

Lauren's expression looked pensive. On almost anyone else, it's serious. On Lauren, it's sexy. However, many things are. She answered, "Seems like a stretch, doesn't it?"

"Yeah, it does."

"But that hair...it's pretty distinctive. Not many people have ginger hair."

"Ginger?" I'd been calling it brownish-red. Only to myself, apparently. I suppose I hadn't realized there was such a fine distinction.

"Of course it's ginger."

"Right."

Whatever it's called, ginger hair can be purchased off of grocery store shelves in the States. I know about these things because I dye my hair on holidays like Halloween and Mardi Gras. Clairol has three or four shades of the ginger. And that's just Clairol. I commented something to that effect.

"No, Cade, you miss the point. It wasn't just the color; it was the whole look."

I'm sure I've mentioned at least once before that women are an enigma to me. She was talking about the whole look? All I saw was a woman in motion with longish brownish-red – I mean, apparently, ginger – hair. If there was a style, I didn't catch it as it flew through a winery door one time and around a street corner another. If that was even the same woman.

I sighed in concession. "You'll have to explain."

"Simple. The woman at la Garrigue has massive amounts of hair, hitting her probably about mid-shoulder blades. It has some natural curl, is coarse, thick and well cared for. It's an expensive do."

"Huh. How did you see all that in just a split second, Sherlock?"

She tipped her head back in triumph and said, like it was obvious, "I'm a woman." Well, that *was* obvious, but, I mean, that wasn't really an answer. At least, not to a guy. But then women often don't make any sense. My last missing persons case had involved a man on a ski lift who pushed me off the chair as we rode over a rocky chasm. After thinking about it for a while, Lauren had acted like I'd made the whole thing up. Now I ask, does that make sense? I didn't understand why he would do such a thing at the time, but I did know that I hadn't leapt off a moving chairlift just for the hell of it. Fortunately, though, I had managed to delay my landing until there was something soft – well, soft*ish* – to land on. However, it had left me with a cranky ankle that kicked up trouble now and then. And from the dull ache now, I guessed it wasn't real crazy about cobblestones as a walking surface. I took a drink of wine in hopes of placating that ache, and maybe finding a hint of man logic in Lauren's explanation.

We spent more time than planned at Le Vintage, eating up – literally – their tres bonne, as they say in Pezenas, tapas, and didn't really talk any more about the ginger-haired woman or speculate about whether her name might be Yvette of the party invitation. We did learn that the white-haired Brit at the adjacent table was named Jack, and his fondness for "Bollocks" sort of rubbed off on us. In fact, we probably used that word in a sentence about thirty times on the way back to the hotel, which we reached around 10:30 that night, just in time to call home and chat with the recent partners Smith & Jiggs.

As usual, Jiggs had little to say. Nothing, actually. More like a pair of snorts. At least, I hoped they were snorts. Jim Smith, though, had a lot of news. The wine country west of Portland seemed to be currently going through a teeny crime wave. Over the span of two nights, three or four cars had been torched, one along with its garage in Cornelius, a strip of a town that merges itself into Forest Grove, where Cassandra York, the old girlfriend I mentioned earlier, has her PI offices. The others were random victims that appeared to be opportunistic. In other words, they were just in the wrong place at the wrong time. The entire area remained on edge. Smith, though, didn't care about his vehicles. Somehow, cars just came to him as if by magic. The man is a puzzle. And probably a crook. That can be useful in my line of work. I planned to keep him around. So far, our "relationship" had been a symbiotic – and deniable – one. Smith rents a room in my building – for free, having saved my butt last year – and I occasionally avail myself of his services. Without asking questions about how he gets the results he gets. And trust me, the man gets results. I like having him around. And now I looked forward to hearing what he found out about these car arsons. No doubt, he would have news the next time we spoke.

Chapter 5

The next day turned out to be Sunday, chilly and slightly misty, but now both Lauren and I had hats. We slept in, although some of the time wasn't taken up with actual sleeping, then we slowly dressed each other for the weather. As usual, she ended up looking a lot better than I did. Breakfast was a leisurely affair, once again involving croissants and jams, but also dried meats, fresh fruits and, of course, a selection of pungent cheeses and strong coffee.

I was feeling lazy, but Lauren's boss had called and left her a message sometime during the early morning hours, saying they needed her back at work, so we stepped up our tourism plans and crammed a week's worth of sight-seeing into very little time, like hours. Fortunately, the flamingos and Camargue horses cooperated with our abbreviated schedule, making dramatic appearances along the delta, or whatever the French call that part of the south, in a timely manner. We had to forego the carriage ride through the wetlands, though, but I promised her we would return one day and do it up right. She didn't seem too disappointed.

The white horses of the Camargue are actually gray, due to their black skin beneath their white hair. Okay, technically, I suppose that makes them a number of colors beyond gray. But besides the surprise of their color, their size also shocked me. I expected grand wild horses of terrifying height with thundering hooves to be galloping around the marshlands, their heads fierce visions of streaming manes and flaring nostrils, but these fellas were little. All in all, not the prettiest things either, but to their credit they did appear quite sturdy. When it comes right down to it, though, I don't think that's an adjective I'd like people to settle on when describing Cade Blackstone, but it's the best I could come up with for the Camargues. Still, an ancient and noble breed.

The flamingos were a different matter altogether. Noisy and boisterous, their pink legs made an impressive show, as did their plumage. They were nearly as tall as the Camargue horses, too. About a third of the flock (which, as I said, is called a flamboyance, but it feels weird to say a flamboyance of flamingos despite Cassandra York's edification on that subject) stood confidently on one leg, leaving the other one bent, adding a plethora of angles to the scene. We watched, ourselves perched on a sheltered vantage point, for nearly twenty minutes, as they honked and flapped and took flight just long enough to feel air beneath their wings before settling into a fresh patch of water. I was so engrossed in the spectacle of nature I forgot to pay attention to what went on around us. The hairs on my neck tingled at one point, leaving me to wonder whether we were being watched. I'd have to be more vigilant from here on out. It has always paid to follow my gut instincts.

Mid-afternoon, we stopped in the little bayside village of Marseillan at La Cabane, a café well known in the area for its mussels. Happily, they lived up to their reputation as we stuffed ourselves almost to the point of bursting. At some point while Lauren sopped up the last of the salty broth with crusty bread, I thought I caught a glimpse of the man I'd made eye contact with the first morning at Hotel La Singuliere.

"Excuse me one moment," I said, dropping my napkin onto the table.

Lauren looked puzzled, but with her mouth full, she was unable to speak as I hurried after the retreating figure. By the time I reached the café door, there was no one in sight. How could he disappear so efficiently? The streets had people on them, sure, but none of them resembled the man I was looking for. It was almost as if he'd jumped into the canal. At least no ginger-haired woman was lurking on the cobbles. Not yet anyway. I returned to the table and pretended the trip had been a sudden need to visit the men's room. I don't think Lauren bought it, but, again, *c'est la vie*.

It had been my hope to spend a couple of nights with her at the Hotel Rive Gauche in sweet little Marseillan. Unlike lofty La Singuliere high on its perch, the Rive Gauche sits right down close to the water, giving its guests the feeling almost of being on a ship. This charming town of just over 10,000 is quiet, especially in January, with the most disturbing sounds being those of fishing boats motoring by. But that, too, would have to wait for another trip. Damn the *Community Press*. There were so many wonderful things to see and do here, and now Lauren had to go home. Why did Carlton have to experience a mini crime spree just now?

Then I brought myself back around to the purpose of my visit to France. In reality, having Lauren leave could turn out to be beneficial. At least, I tried to tell myself so. She had become a distraction. Hell, she began as a distraction and only grew to be a bigger one with the romance of the Mediterranean lapping at our hotel door. I had been commissioned to find Adrien Hatif, and it had started to look as though it might be more difficult than I had at first thought. And possibly more dangerous if there were people following us. Of course, that might just be my imagination. But, if not, I couldn't risk any harm coming to my beautiful blonde girlfriend, even though she does know how to handle herself in a crisis.

"I wish you didn't have to go," I said, meaning it more than I wanted to admit to myself.

"No more than I." Lauren cocked her head and put on a pout, an expression which never looked good on Cassandra York, a previous girlfriend I've mentioned a few times, mostly because she's a rival PI out in our Northwest wine country, and still a pain in my ass. But on Lauren a pout is about as sexy as a pout can get. So now my earlier thoughts that we should squeeze in a bunch more touring over the course of the afternoon turned to different thoughts. Lauren's look seemed to suggest that she agreed. In the end, we didn't tick off any more sights.

- - -

The next day felt terribly sad without Lauren. I mean, I had no one to bounce things off of, and I'm not just talking about ideas here. Early that morning, as in pre-dawn, we said a very physical good-bye at the Montpellier airport. I watched until her plane safely ascended the southern French skies. By then, the roads around the moderate sized city had already come to life. I negotiated my way along the lagoon via secondary highways then crossed over to La Languedocienne, a cool name for the highway that passes by loads of wineries, and I passed by them with a wistful regret.

"I sure wish Lauren was here," I said to the empty passenger seat, and it had only been half an hour since she'd left. The days ahead threatened to grow very long. France is for lovers. Being alone there felt awful. No Lauren, no Jiggs and no Irene Adler. In fact, Irene hadn't even spoken to me the last couple of times I'd called home. That would have to be remedied soon. Meanwhile, I brought my thoughts back to the road.

Before I could say "Montagnac", the outskirts of the little town loomed once again. And, once again, the same spot outside Hatif's apartment awaited the ugly Peugeot, leading me to believe it wasn't really a parking spot at all. Well, it had worked the previous visit, so why not again today? If anyone challenged me, I could always claim ignorance. Clueless tourist. I pulled over and got out.

Inside the ancient building, M. Hatif's door was closed but still unlocked. Either the man was extraordinarily trusting or he had not been home since Lauren and I paid him a visit two days ago. With my gloves already pulled on, I pushed inside. The only sounds emanated from above in a loud and robust manner, as though someone were engaging in a highly enthusiastic preparation of breakfast. Which reminded me I had skipped mine. My stomach growled and my feet led me to the refrigerator. No, of course I didn't eat any of the man's food. I thought it prudent, however, to check whether new provisions had been laid in or old ones cleaned out. As far as I could tell, all looked as it had on Saturday. Including the mold status.

M. Hatif's mail appeared the same, too. In fact, peering closer, I noted the most recent date was 7 *Janvier* (January 7) the day of the Charlie Hebdo shootings. Nothing in over a week and a half? Maybe he had gone away for a holiday? No, wait, that's what the trip to France was supposed to be. Or was it? Did I actually know that? If no luggage showed up in the bedroom, other options would have to be considered. I made my way toward the rear of the flat, paying attention to details along the way and snapping more photos with my phone.

The generous bedroom held little furniture; in fact, just one chair and a full size bed. A small wardrobe sat adjacent to a tiny depression in the wall that seemed to serve as a closet. Hoping they could tell me something, I began patting down shirts and exploring pockets.

Fully engrossed in my search of Hatif's clothing, I did not hear the man behind me until he slammed my face into the back wall.

"Ouch!"

He'd grabbed my arm and had it wrenched behind my back, plunging me even further into a pissed-off state than I had been. I mean, come on, that hurts. Then my nose started to bleed, just a trickle at first, but soon it would gather speed and ruin an excellent Tommy Bahama shirt. That pushed me over the edge. I kicked backward and connected with his shin. He hadn't been expecting that, lending weight to the notion that he was a pure amateur at this sort of thing. Also lending weight to the notion that we were now even.

"Ha! See how you like that." His grip on me loosened and I spun around, my adrenaline spiking, ready with fists up. Probably not my best stance, since I am not well trained, but I am trained nonetheless. Fortunately, better trained than my attacker. I whirled around and faced a man who looked amazingly like Adrien Hatif of the pictures I'd seen; yet this wasn't Adrien Hatif. A brother? It was difficult to get a good look, as he was hopping on one leg and holding the other. While he did that, I warily stepped over to the bathroom, situated a little to the left of the closet I'd been rifling around in, and filched a towel to press against my bleeding nose.

As I did, he recovered well enough to hit me with a barrage of French questions. Or at least, I think they were questions. I held up the hand not occupied with stanching blood flow and said, "Je ne parle pas francais." *I don't speak French.* I have learned this sentence in every language, along with the words for foods I don't like and how to say *bathroom.* What else do I need, really? I already know the word for *wine.*

Chapter 6

My attacker turned out to be an excellent source of information once we patched up our respective wounds. My face would be bruised for a few days and his shin would ache but neither of us had sustained any permanent damage. We dusted ourselves off and introduced each other, breathing more heavily than usual; at least, I was. According to him, before me stood Michel Hatif.

"You one of the twins?" I'd seen the pair of identical twins in the bookshelf photo on my first unauthorized visit to the apartment.

"No. That's Rayce and Patric. They are older than me."

His English was remarkable, thank God, since my French had gone home with Lauren. "Man, how many of you Hatifs are there?" In fact, my English was turning out to be not so good either.

Michel smiled, and I could see the family resemblance to Adrien without ever having met Adrien: The mocha skin, the dreads, the wide mouth full of big, white teeth flanked by deep dimples. "Six boys and our baby sister Aimee."

I whistled. That's a pile of kids to be raising. "Your mom wanted to keep trying for a girl or what?"

This time, he laughed outright, a deep, hearty sound. "Oui, something like that. Hey, my parents, they are French, you know. When they are not dancing, they are romancing. Henri and Simone Hatif, they are two beautiful people."

Well, they certainly made beautiful babies, although I didn't voice that opinion. Instead, I probed for more history. As you've no doubt heard me say before, I like facts. They can lead to clues. "Dancing?"

"Dancing. Father is a winemaker by day, but he wasn't named Henri for nothing."

My expression must have given away my confusion, for he laughed again and then explained, "He was born in Toulouse, not too far from here. It is a town of many dancing halls. My grandmere, Dominique, very much was interested in Henri de Toulouse-Lautrec so she named her first son Henri, like the very famous painter. My father grew up there, dancing every chance he found. One night, he met my mother, out dancing. He right away fell in love and they married. They are beautiful lovers. They make beautiful family. And my father Henri is excellent winemaker. He continues making the wine with his brother, my Uncle Vicente."

Which direction should I go from here? There were so many questions screaming to be answered after that short explosion of words. I just started asking whatever popped into my head. Michel answered every one with equal passion.

I discovered that Arrogant Frog was a winery the elder Hatif brothers – Henri and Vicente – patterned their first joint venture on, whimsically called Le Chat Cachemire, which loosely translated to The Paisley Cat. And I also discovered that the Hatif family history might take a bit longer to chronicle than either Michel or I could afford that morning. I hoped he would be willing to share his contact information with me along with more of his time in the upcoming days. And I wanted to meet Simone and Henri, the beautiful mere et pere (mom and dad for those of you challenged, like me, in the French language).

But there were more pressing issues right now than the genealogical events of several decades past. Issues such as the reason for his younger sibling's return to France a few months back, which became clearer now, talking to Michel, where, before, it had been murky at best. Even Jim Smith had merely tossed about vague possibilities, like maybe a family wedding, some friend's graduation, an important funeral. It was none of those. No, apparently a young woman from the other side of Montagnac whom Adrien had been seeing – rather a bit more than seeing, it turns out – had surprised him with the news of a baby boy. And she swore that Adrien was the boy's father. There was no doubt.

"Is her name Yvette, by any chance?"

"Yvette? No. Why do you ask?"

"No reason. What was her name; do you know?"

"Oui. Chantal."

So who was Yvette, sender of the party invitation? Michel gave no indication that he recognized the name.

"Okay. So a woman named Chantal tells your brother that he has a son. Just like that?"

"Oui."

"And Adrien comes home."

"Oui."

"Just like that?"

"Oui."

"Hm. So let me get a feel for this. He leaves a great job he's had for – do you know how long he'd been in the US?"

Michel shrugged. "Maybe more than one year."

"How did he find that position; do you know?"

"Ah, yes. Adrien saw ad in *La Revue du Vin de France*. Every month he reads *La Revue*. He sees it, he tells me. So happy."

"Okay, so he is excited by this winemaker job, gets hired, works there for at least a year, seems to love it but he leaves it and doesn't go back? Makes no sense." I scratched my head to help me think. "He's stayed here over three months now. He's rented an apartment." That was the part that absolutely flummoxed me. It sounded so permanent. "Did he plan to make a life with this Chantal? Get married?"

Michel shrugged again. Maybe I had thrown too many words at him. Or it's possible he really did not know.

"Have you met the boy – what's his name?"

"Pierre. Yes, I meet Pierre. He is cute kid, as you say."

"Did Adrien do a lot with Pierre? Pierre and Chantal?"

Another shrug, accompanied by a sheepish smile. Could it be that the two brothers weren't all that close? Had some kind of rift occurred in the Hatif family? Maybe it was time to find out. "When did you last see Adrien?"

For the first time since we'd shaken hands, Michel looked less than happy. His eyes angled down toward his shoes. "Christmas."

That was over three weeks ago. But, then again, the holidays are a notoriously busy time so that didn't really tell me a whole lot. "Was Pierre with him?"

"No."

"Did he bring Pierre over to the house before?"

Michel frowned as though puzzled by the question. Maybe it had been badly worded.

"Did Adrien ever bring Pierre to meet your parents?"

"Oh, no, monsieur."

Hm. He's here three months, has a son – granted, a surprise son – who he is supposedly happy about, but doesn't bring him around to meet grandma and grandpa? An odd prickling sensation crept up my spine.

"Did your parents know about Pierre?"

Michel lifted one shoulder, dropped it.

"Ah." I scratched my head. "Okay. So, did Adrien mention any plans to go away when you last saw him?"

"No."

He had gone back to looking at his shoes, which, while nice, weren't so nice as to merit that much attention. I asked, "So how was Christmas? Did you all have a good time?"

"Oui." He hesitated. "Ah – oui. Yes."

We stood for a few ticks in awkward silence before my patience ran out. I had gotten up way too early and finished my last cup of coffee far too long ago to abide any bullshit. "Look, Michel, I know you have very little reason to trust me, but I am trying to find your brother. You haven't seen him for – for weeks, and I think you're worried. Besides, his empty, unlocked apartment strikes me as pretty suspicious." I stopped to let that sink in, praying that it might frighten him into talking. "Anything you can tell me about his life might help. Especially his recent time in France."

Those shoes still held him rapt. He shifted from one foot to another before looking up. Any trace of a smile had vanished, along with his dimples. "Okay. Adrien – Adrien is the baby in the family, after Aimee. He, as you say, has mother wrapped around her tiny finger."

"Little finger."

"Yes. So the other boys, especially Rayce and Patric –"

"The twins?"

"The twins. The other boys, mostly Rayce, get a lot angry at him."

"Ah, sibling rivalry."

"Pardon?"

"Nothing. Go on. Something happened at Christmas?"

"Oui. Yes. I am not sure what caused it, but some shouting and pushing happened."

"Who?"

"Rayce mostly, but Patric and Chanler little bit, too."

"So the twins and – which one is Chanler?"

"Chanler is brother just older than me." Michel's eyes grew wide and he frowned. "Rayce, he try to hit Adrien. Then Uncle Vicente step in to stop it. Rayce has very bad temper, says things he shouldn't."

"Did you hear what they were saying?"

Michel shook his head. "No. I hear many bad words." A brief, almost embarrassed smile flitted across his face. "And I hear something about wine, but there was drinking." That shoulder rose again.

Wine? Well, of course there was wine, but why talk about it? Everyone around these parts had wine. It was a given of everyday living here. And one of the top reasons I favored vacationing here. The significance of that statement would have to be sorted out later though. Maybe the other brothers would be as willing to talk to me as Michel here. Unless, of course, they had something to do with Adrien's disappearance. Then, well, things could get messy.

"Anything else?"

"Maybe I hear Chanler mention Chantal."

"Adrien's girlfriend?" Or was she his ex-girlfriend? Had she moved on to Chanler Hatif? Or maybe she moved *from* Chanler to Adrien to begin with? Now *there's* a motive for conflict. I think Shakespeare wrote a play with a plot like that.

"Oui, but I am not sure."

"Is that all, Michel?"

"Yes. My uncle step in then. Everyone walk away. Adrien left."

Boy, that statement couldn't be more true. Adrien had indeed left. But had he gone missing voluntarily or did someone make him go missing? And more importantly, where had he gone? Yeah, I know, that's what I was here to find out. I had a few more questions and I hoped Michel had the answers.

Taking a deep breath, I said, "Okay, people disappear for all sorts of reasons. Number one is money, to escape debt. Was Adrien in trouble with anyone over money?" I let my eyes sweep around the room and my brows arched all on their own. "From the looks of this flat, he wasn't living high off the hog."

"High off the –"

"Never mind." Apparently his English didn't extend as far as American idioms. "Did Adrien owe anyone big money?"

"No. I mean, I don't think so."

"How about drugs? Any problem with drugs?"

"No, monsieur, I don't think so. Not that I see."

"Okay. No drugs. So, the boy. Did he seem okay with having a son or did he maybe want to escape daddyhood?"

Michel shook his head. "He talks like he is happy about it. Chantal can maybe say."

"Yeah, maybe."

Why else did people flee? Love triangles? Bad marriage? None of those seemed to apply here. There were probably a gazillion good reasons to skip town, but I couldn't think of any more just then. I moved on to something else. "Have you talked to Adrien since Christmas?"

"One time. Last week. He text. We are supposed to meet for coffee this morning but he does not show."

So that explained Michel's presence in Adrien's flat.

"You say he texted?"

"Oui."

"You didn't actually speak to him, then?"

He blinked several times and appeared to be concentrating. "No. Text."

Damn, that meant it could have been anyone. Didn't prove it was Adrien who sent the message. "Merci, Michel." I thought for a bit longer, wondering what new direction to take next. I had seen no suitcase in the closet before Michel smashed my face into the wall. I could have missed it, but the space was so small it seemed unlikely. That could mean Adrien planned a little getaway from Montagnac. Probably nothing of any duration, since there were no packed boxes or even empty ones waiting to be filled. Another factor that spoke against a long-term departure was that his apartment did not look like he had left for good. Shirts still hung on the clothes rod, pants were draped over the bedroom's single chair, all manner of personal items lay strewn about the rooms as though their owner would be back any minute now. Could be he just needed some time and space in order to wrap his head around the idea of playing papa. After all, that is kind of life-changing news.

We walked into the living area and I gathered up the mail from the table, replacing it with my business card. If Adrien Hatif did show up, that would give him an indication of who had snatched all of his bills and letters and he could give that number a call. In fact, I really hoped he did, and damned soon.

Michel watched as I did this, but made no comment, just picked up a hat which looked too small to fit on the tangle of dreads atop his head. He left his own note beside my card.

I asked, "Can I buy you a cup of coffee?" It seemed only fair, after having kicked the crap out of his shin, to make an offering of some sort. But he shook his head.

"Thank you, no. I should speak to Chantal."

"Chantal?"

"Oui."

"You are going there now?"

As if my question made him doubt the wisdom of this choice, he glanced at his wristwatch. "Oui. Yes."

He'd nearly made it through the door before I snapped out of my stupor. He was going to visit Chantal! This was an opportunity I did not want to miss.

"Wait, Michel."

He turned, looking quizzical, and maybe a little concerned.

I scratched my head, groping for the right approach, not wanting to sound like the brash American I am often accused of being. "Um, listen, can I come with you?"

"Oh," he smiled again, appearing relieved. "Of course. Come."

I trailed him as he walked outside and up the street in the direction of my Peugeot. I began to wonder whether he wanted me to drive until I saw a different sort of Peugeot parked beside mine. This one had only two wheels, though. I groaned, involuntarily. The idea of straddling a French motorbike, holding onto Michel around the waist as we hurtled through the cobbled streets of Montagnac sent shivers up my spine. Had I signed on for this when I agreed to look into bringing M. Hatif back from France? Possibly. Probably. I swallowed and cringed.

"Desole' – sorry, I have only the one –" He pointed at the helmet in his hand. Oh, good, ever so much better: I'd be hurtling through narrow, cobbled streets on a motorbike with no helmet. I hoped it wasn't a good day to die.

Chapter 7

After a terrifying six minutes that felt like sixty, Michel jerked the Peugeot to a halt at a curb in front of a fairly modern building which looked as though it housed half a dozen of what we at home call garden apartments. It was a pleasant surprise since garden apartments hadn't appeared to be very popular in the area. But, then, I hadn't seen much of Montagnac on our way across town, mostly due to the back of Michel's helmet being the prominent part of my view. When my eyes were open, that is.

A woman I assumed was Chantal stood just inside a wrought iron gate, waving languidly at us. A tiny human clutched at her billowing pants, hiding his chubby face against her leg. Michel must have called ahead to let her know we were coming, although I had heard nothing of any conversation over the roar of the motorbike engine, despite my lack of a helmet. Michel confirmed my guess that this was Chantal and I stuck out my hand to shake hers, forgetting the custom in this part of France was the three-cheek kiss, even if it's just a three-cheek air kiss. I waggled my fingers at the little person, which made him shriek and bury his face again.

Once the awkwardness of the greetings was out of the way, Michel embarked on a chat with Chantal involving many fluttering hand gestures while I took in her physical appearance. She was nothing remotely close to what I would have expected a man as strikingly good-looking as Adrien Hatif would be attracted to. The prettiest part of Chantal was her name. Not that she was bad looking; simply plain. Where Adrien's skin was a deep cinnamon, Chantal's tended toward a flat milky white. She had a turned-up nose, which might be considered cute although it extended just a smidge too long. And I didn't know whether she usually had a healthy head of shiny hair, but at this point it could only be described as mousy brown, somewhat limp, with a lazy curl that fell to her shoulder and puddled there without style.

I heard Michel say my name.

"Pardon?" I said, trying to put a French spin on the word.

Chantal looked at me with eyes the color of romaine lettuce. Well, there was something a little special in that shade of green. Maybe that's what had captivated Adrien. I mean, the woman had a nice body, somewhat tall and angular, but nothing remarkable. Me, I go in more for curves. And blonde hair.

Michel said, "M. Blackstone, you had some question for Chantal?"

"Ah, merci. Um, yes. When did you last see Adrien?"

He translated, so I guessed she did not speak any English, which seemed fairly odd for a person of her age. The young people of Europe are bilingual at the least, English being a requisite second language. Her answer surprised me, too. According to her, it had been around three weeks since she had seen Adrien, or shortly before Christmas. Hadn't the man come over specifically because of Chantal and little Pierre? Wasn't that what Michel had told me? I also wondered why he didn't stay with her if that were the case. I must have voiced that out loud, for Michel began speaking to her as soon as I finished with that thought.

"Chantal is sharing apartment with her friend Marie from her work. Adrien did not want to make – you say – the waves." He smiled, showing off his cavernous dimples again. Damn, those Hatifs could exude charm without half trying.

"Has she heard from him during that time?" Three weeks is an eternity when you're in love. How could she stand not talking to him, not seeing him, not touching him?

"She says no."

"Did he say anything about taking a trip? Going away?"

Chantal shook her head as Michel asked this.

Huh. I tried a different angle. "Was Adrien happy about the boy? Was he pleased to meet Pierre?"

When Michel translated this question, Chantal's face lit up and a broad grin spread across it. With Adrien and Chantal as parents, this child would have a killer smile. "Oui." Well, I knew that meant "Yes," and the young woman's expression said it as well. It was an expression that said she truly believed Adrien was excited about having a son.

How had she delivered the news about Pierre to Adrien? Had they kept in touch? How old was Pierre anyway? He looked like he was no more than a year, if that.

After much back-and-forth, Michel gave me a synopsis. Pierre had just celebrated his 11-month birthday. So he had been born about February 20 by my calculations. Apparently, Chantal had spotted Adrien on Facebook. His profile had presented itself in one of those "People You May Know" windows. She sent a Friend request, he accepted, and then she dropped the Pierre bomb on him. Well, it probably went down a little more friendly than that. Anyway, they reconnected, he returned to France, and now he seemed to have gone off somewhere else. I was no closer to an answer than I had been when I got there.

"Merci. Thank you." I had one more avenue to explore, but it wouldn't be a pleasant one. Apologizing in advance, I asked, "The last time she saw him, or one of the last times, did they argue, by chance?"

Michel drew in a sharp breath. He obviously did not want to translate my query. Then he sighed and rushed ahead.

Chantal blushed and looked away. That was all the answer I needed, but I hungered for the down and dirty details. "Michel, see if she will tell us what they argued about."

He looked at me as though I'd asked him to negotiate a price for the kid.

"Please, Michel. It could be important. We want to find Adrien." I used that ploy again. "We *all* want to find Adrien."

He puffed out his cheeks, then I heard a flurry of French. Chantal shook her head. Michel tried again, but Chantal waved him off. Tears streamed down her face, and it grew a splotchy red. Did she look angry or embarrassed? We didn't get a chance to find out. She scooped up little Pierre, turned and fled into the apartment, closing the door with a bang behind her.

Chapter 8

After Michel delivered me back to my car, I checked my messages, noting that Jim Smith had called. Excellent; I had some updates for him. It puzzled me, nonetheless, since by my calculations it had just barely passed 7:00 a.m. in Carlton, long before the time Smith generally even considers turning on his phone. Well, he asked for it. I hit "Call Back".

As the call went through its journey to the cell tower to the satellite to another series of towers, or however that works, I let my eyes wander around the quaint little street. In fact, the streets of Sete were much quainter, if that's a word, than those of Montagnac. But my business seemed to be centered around Montagnac and, since I had taken a liking to nearby Pezenas, I'd come to the conclusion that maybe it would be better for me to transfer my French headquarters – aka "hotel" – from Sete to Pezenas. Without Lauren and without the need for the Camargue horses – or the flamingos, for that matter – to be in close proximity, it made far more sense. I still planned to check out the winery supposedly owned by the uncle in Loupian, but that was almost as close to Montagnac as it was to Sete, so that was a moot point. I'd take care of the moving details later.

Meanwhile, a shapely figure caught my attention. Something about her struck me as familiar, but that could have been that she had a nice figure and I like nice figures. But wait. Was her hair ginger? Before I could make up my mind, she disappeared around the side of a stone building and I heard Jim Smith grousing about the early hour from across the ocean.

"Hey, Jim. Good to hear your voice."

"Yeah, right."

"How are things in beautiful Carlton?"

"Marvelous. Enough with the small talk. What have you got to tell me?"

"Good news."

"I hope so."

"Yes, indeed. Lauren is on her way home as we speak."

"Hallelujah and praise the lord."

"Didn't know you were a religious man, Jim."

"Neither did I. Where did you get this – this oversized parakeet anyway?"

"An exceptional little book shop in Ashland, as a matter of fact."

"Should have left the horrid thing there."

At this point, the background noise defined itself and I recognized Irene Adler's singing.

"Sounds like Irene's learned a new song."

"Hmpf." At least Jim wasn't the sort of man to get rich with colorful words. Irene did a fine enough job of that for the both of them.

"Anyway, Lauren's plane gets in late this afternoon, like around three your time. She'll probably pick up Jiggs and Irene right around happy hour."

"I'll need a good, stiff drink by then."

I thought of a few fun remarks but decided Jim might not be in the right frame of mind. Irene seemed to have worn his patience to a frazzled thread. The bird has a way of doing that. So, instead, I filled him in on my morning's activities, including the part about searching Adrien Hatif's flat uninvited and kicking the living daylights out of his brother's shin. Jim Smith has a super loose interpretation of what constitutes breaking and entering. It works out real well that way. My news mellowed his attitude, so I figured Irene might survive until Lauren made it by to collect her and Jiggs. In fact, Smith sounded like he'd worked himself up to a fine mood when I hung up.

Next on my agenda was a quick trip out to The Paisley Grape, or whatever that winery had been called that Adrien's father Henri and uncle Vicente joint ventured initially. I got out my local map, which included the vignerons of the region, including Le Chat Cachemire. Cat; it was The Paisley Cat. Anyway, it looked to be only about half an inch on the map, so it couldn't be more than about five or six miles, right? I fired up the Peugeot and rolled out onto the cobbles.

After something like three miles, an interesting roadside business caught my eye: what appeared to be a rental car agency, but with a twist. An employee – identifiable by the nametag bouncing along on his left lapel – had just gotten out of a Ferrari. A Ferrari that was parked next to an Aston Martin which was next to a Porsche next to a BMW next to a Jaguar next to a

Maserati. I braked, hard. What, no Lamborghini? Nope, not one Lamborghini in sight. Still, a Ferrari or an Aston Martin would be a fine second choice and worlds better than the Peugeot I was currently driving. So that's how I found myself, a short half hour later, driving the twisty French roads in a red Ferrari Spider. Cute car. It was a good first step toward making me feel more at home, although the passenger seat still lacked my trusty sidekick Jiggs, with his wrinkled blond face and flapping jowls that perfectly fit his arrogant attitude. Or Lauren. Yeah, Lauren, who kept me much warmer at night than Jiggs. I sighed, admitting to myself that I missed them all.

The Paisley Cat had been a half-inch away on my Michelin guide, but that stretched into sixteen miles and two villages over, appearing finally on the apex of a slight ascent outside of a tiny berg called Alignan du Vent. I rounded a corner – at a brisk speed, tires gripping with a last-minute fierceness I'd been missing in the Peugeot – and saw a lane leading to an old stone building that resembled a smallish deserted castle. I say deserted because ivy had nearly reclaimed it for Mother Nature, giving it the appearance that no one had inhabited the place for many moons, like numbering in the hundreds.

Nonetheless, exiting the car, I called out, "Hello? Hello!" Smart, huh? Anyone inside would have long ago heard the growl of the Ferrari as it rumbled up the drive. I'd given the engine one more testosterone-laden rev before pulling the car up to what I'd assumed must be the main entrance. In a sweeping survey of my surroundings, I gauged that no one had a clue about my presence. Checking my phone out of habit, I registered that it showed no bars of service. That sent an ominous chill up the back of my spine. There's almost no place in Europe that doesn't get excellent cell phone service. Here, no bars? Unheard of.

Naturally, I went ahead and tried the front door. Locked. And not only a locked door, but a locked door looking like something from a medieval fortress; one of those massive wooden things with huge triangular pounded-metal hinges that clamp onto the door with dinosaur jaws, or something resembling them. That should have been my cue to leave. Cade Blackstone, though, does not give up so easily. Oh, no. I searched the front of the castle/winery, poking my hand into the ivy to probe for secret passages, I guess. And – success! The third window to the left of the door was not only broken, but missing entirely, leaving me scratching my head at the lax security the Hatifs practiced, both in their homes and their business. Okay, in their defense, this didn't look like it had been a business for a while. In fact, I wondered whether they even still owned the building.

I stepped back to take in the scene. Not a soul in sight. Quiet as a churchyard, save for the cry of a nearby mourning dove. The low hum of car engines from the distant road traveled across the fields, but nothing else. The Paisley Cat sign still hung straight as the day it was put up, directly above the fortress door. And somewhere under the ivy there probably lurked a tiny notice announcing the tasting hours, which of course didn't matter to anyone anymore. A couple of wine barrels posed artistically in what had once passed for the yard.

"Well, are you going inside or not?" I said, surprising myself with the sound of my own voice.

Stepping through the window, the scent of fermented grapes hit me immediately. Wineries don't give up their aromas without a fight, and for this I was immensely pleased. But another odor mixed with the grapes, and that one wasn't so pleasant. Distinctive and unmistakable, that coppery smell came from some sort of blood. Fairly fresh blood, too.

My phone may not have had any bars of service, but the flashlight app still worked, although it couldn't illuminate fast enough nor brightly enough to suit me. Holding it high above my head, I swiveled it around, noting with dismay that it fell short of reaching the corners of the cavernous room. Some broken cask bits and pieces littered part of the floor, and a dark substance pooled around a small pile of boxes in one of the far shadows. Was that the source of the smell? And did that pile consist entirely of boxes or was there something else in there, too? In the low light, one or two of the shapes seemed to be moving, and a few looked as though they might once have been alive. As these thoughts raced through my mind, something dive-bombed me through the air, a whiffle grazing my head. It flew off, screeching.

"Damned bat." Harmless, sure, but I don't like being startled.

Off to my left, I thought there was the vague shape of a door hanging ajar. A sliver of the outdoor light filtered in. Maybe the clouds were contributing to Le Chat's eeriness, for the light had an ethereal quality to it and lost strength a few feet inside as though encountering resistance. A puff of air blew my shirt sleeve, like the building was breathing on me. A scream split the air. If I hadn't instantly recognized it for the shriek of some crazed bird, I'd have been running for that door. An entire flock of birds swarmed in and flew up into what might have been rafters, if the place had rafters. Trying to calm myself with a deep inhalation, I swept the beam of the flashlight further to the side away from the opening.

"This place doesn't look like it's seen a human this millennium." What was it that Michel had said about the winery? That his dad and uncle partnered in winemaking here, yes, but how long ago? Well, I couldn't remember that Michel had named a specific time. Obviously, it had been awhile. So what had happened to the business? And what had taken place here to leave behind that sinister smell?

As that question entered my mind, the smell seemed stronger all of a sudden and goose bumps formed on my arms. Now I really wished Jiggs were with me. Not that he's much of a guard dog, but he does pretty fine when it comes to intuition. In fact, he'd have probably turned tail already and run by now. I figured maybe that was the best course of action for me, too, so that's just what I did. In my rush to get out, I could've sworn I heard footsteps pounding the floor behind me.

Chapter 9

Thankful that I'd dumped the ugly Peugeot in favor of, well, pretty much anything really but particularly the muscly red Ferrari, I sprinted for it as though chased by demons. In fact, I may well have been. The sounds that followed me through the deserted winery could only have come from dark spirits. Okay, possibly wind. The nearby town name, Alignan du Vent, translates to Alignan *the Wind*, which explains the incessant howling around that entire area. Anyway, in my haste to get back out the window, I ripped a nasty gash in my left hand on a jagged remnant of glass. Certain more suspicious souls might have suggested that the possessed old building took a bite out of me in my frantic attempt to escape. Whatever the cause, it hurt like a son of a bitch.

When I reached out to open the car door, my hand left a smear of blood on the handle, which brought me up short. The rental contract probably excluded spills of red bodily fluids on the upholstery. That presented a small problem. Fortunately, Lauren had forgotten one of her scarves in the Peugeot, which I'd only discovered in the transfer over to the Ferrari at the car hire. I grabbed it and wrapped it around my hand three times, apologizing to my girlfriend for ruining one of her favorite accessories.

"Sorry, Blondie. I'll buy you a new one."

The car roared to life and I accelerated down the driveway, almost launching onto the highway before I came to my senses, remembering that real drivers are probably a larger menace than winery ghosts. Especially if the winery ghosts are imagined, as the ones chasing me likely were. (Most of the drivers on the French roads are real.)

As I drove – at a speed pushing the car's abilities, and mine – toward Sete, my mind whirled. Should I call the local police? I mean, that smell had to be blood, didn't it? Does deer blood have the same coppery odor as human blood? Could there be an explanation as simple as that? Of course. It could have been a deer. Or a raccoon. Or a rabbit. I sometimes overreact. Yet I'd hate to underreact at just the wrong time.

The combination of those thoughts made me wish that Harry Blackstone (Dad) were here. Captain of the San Francisco Police Department, retired. He'd know what to do. If I went to the cops now, what would I tell them? Bigger question, how would I tell them? They speak French; me, English. It certainly wouldn't do to have them misunderstand. That presented a conundrum. At least, to me.

Instead of solving the immediate problem, I spent the remainder of the day packing everything I'd brought and bought and transferring it to Le Grand Hotel Moliere in Pezenas. Mundane tasks make avoiding hard decisions easier to avoid, so switching rooms became the task of choice.

I'd picked the Grand Hotel Moliere because I'd read on some website that Pezenas called itself "the town of Moliere". With that kind of synchronicity, how bad could it be? Besides, the hotel's location was ideal, at one end of the plaza that had Lauren and me instantly taken with this ancient little village. In retrospect, maybe that would turn out to be not so smart, since I already missed her more than I cared to admit, and she hadn't yet actually touched down back in Oregon. Maybe, once settled in my room, after a nice, lonely dinner, I'd call and at least hear her voice. And Irene's. Best I could do. Jiggs doesn't speak much over the phone.

Around 6:30, after I'd unloaded my bags into a surprisingly large suite overlooking the crescent plaza, I ventured over to Le Vintage Bar de Vins once again. No band this evening, so a lot more tables were free and the place was quiet almost to the point of somberness. Fine by me. My emotions, and the length of the day, had caught up with me. Tapas and a few glasses – or, better yet, a bottle – of good red wine was just what the doctor ordered. Dr. Cade, that is.

I selected a small table reasonably close to the entrance, where the light could shine in enough to chase away some of the shadows. Darkness did not feel like my friend. Once comfortable, I glanced around. A familiar shock of white hair caught my eye. It was English Jack, the fellow with the bushy eyebrows and the impish grin I'd noticed with his friends the first night I'd been in Le Vintage Bar. He was probably a regular patron, and probably expecting his friends. The table he now sat at would easily accommodate six –

eight if they squeezed, and Europeans seem to be mad about squeezing a lot of bodies into small spaces. I had liked Jack's face immediately. Plus, the man spoke English. Wouldn't it be nice if it turned out that he was a retired bobby or something? Scotland Yard detective? I could run my problem by him.

Raising my arm slightly, I called over to him. "Hello, Jack. How are you this evening?"

That grin. "Bloody fine. You?" His eyebrows rose when he saw the bandage on my hand. Well, it is quite the conversation starter. Then he squinted at my face and I remembered my unintended encounter with the back of Adrien Hatif's closet wall earlier in the day. Jack must have thought me extraordinarily prone to accidents or else unable to control my fighting instincts. Either way, it didn't seem like the best of indications to strike up a friendship. But the grin never left his face.

"Looks as though it might not have been your best day, eh?"

"It has been somewhat eventful."

"It appears so. Buy you a drink?"

"Thank you." I walked over his way.

Jack motioned to the waiter, who had a mere three tables to attend to at this point, and asked me what I wanted. I ordered a glass of the St. Hilaire, the same wine that I had enjoyed with Lauren two days before. While waiting for it to arrive, I asked, "You aren't by chance a retired policeman?"

"What? Me?" He made that tiny, two-letter word stretch into three syllables. The Brits do have a way with the language. He burst into a laugh so jovial that I don't know how he avoided knocking over his table. In fact, from the strength of his protestations, I began to hope he wasn't one of the area's most notorious criminals.

"Sorry. It's just that no one's ever accused me of being a policeman before. Don't have the muscles for it." He patted his robust stomach. "No. I'm more of a numbers guy."

It was my turn for arching eyebrows.

"All legal, pal. Nothing shady. Chartered financial planner, actually. Rather boring." He motioned to the empty chairs. "One of the lads is ex-police though. Ian. If you've got a legal question, he's your man. Come on, have a seat. He'll be right along."

I smiled as the waiter brought the wine. And maybe I looked troubled, for Jack turned serious. "Does your wanting a policeman have anything to do with the state of your face and your hand there?"

"Oh, um, no. I mean, maybe. I don't know."

"Well, that's settled then." The cocky grin had returned. "Say, where's that beautiful blond I saw you with?"

"She had to go home."

"More's the pity."

"Yeah."

I took a large sip of my wine, which went down quite well. Maybe it was the soothing qualities of the deep red St. Hilaire that emboldened me, but the story of my entire day came gushing forth, from dropping Lauren at the Montpellier airport to M. Hatif's unlocked flat and the misunderstanding with his brother Michel to the funky smell at Le Chat Cachemire and my panicked exit through the overgrown window. In the telling, it sounded like quite the adventure, and somewhat fantastical.

By the end, Jack's eyes had grown as large as dinner plates, magnified further by his thick glasses. He whistled, then waved at the waiter. "You're going to need more of the red stuff, as you Americans say." He pointed at my glass. "Garcon, une bouteille, sil vous plait."

"Oui, monsieur."

I couldn't tell whether he merely liked to drink or my story had impressed him to the extent he felt it called for copious quantities of wine. Seeing how this evening had started, the coming days might answer that for me.

As the waiter left on his mission, I turned back to Jack. "Of course, I didn't really see anything. It was very dark, but that smell –"

"Very wise not to call the local gendarmes. Probably just a hare or goat. Unnerving though, eh?"

I agreed. A hare or a goat sounded logical, or maybe I just wanted to believe that. Unburdening had left me spent, but in a nice way. The wine may have been working some magic, too.

"I would suggest, though, if you do tell anyone, that you leave out the bit about breaking into the fellow's flat." He winked. "Ah, here comes Ian now. And I see he's got Kellen with him. Can't tell who's behind Kellen."

He put a hand out as I rose to leave. "No, stay. There's plenty of room. The lads'll love you."

The "lads" swarmed the table in a flurry of accents, all appearing to be in their 50s, but none seemed to mind a 36-year-old American at their table. We numbered seven by the end of the evening, which went on far longer than I should have let it, but it's possible I worried that the winery ghost had followed me back to town and I didn't want to walk back to my hotel alone. In the dark. Naw. It probably had more to do with the fact that Lauren would be sleeping in Carlton while I curled up alone in a queen-sized bed in a hotel named for Moliere. And a little bit may have depended on the fact that the English and the Scots kept the table well supplied with good wine.

Chapter 10

By the time I returned to my room that night, it was a wonder I could even fit the key into the lock. Those Englishmen had a sneaky way of buying rounds of drinks or bottles of wine, or whatever they were buying, without my knowledge. At one point, the St. Hilaire ceded the table to some excellent Armagnac, which went down way too easily. Something else probably came after that, not sure. Once we said good-bye, I may have taken the long way back to the hotel, because it felt like I walked for twenty or thirty minutes, and I'm pretty sure Le Grand Hotel is only six doors away from Le Vintage Bar. Huh. It goes without saying that I did not get the chance to call Lauren and tell her good night. Not sure the words would have sounded anything like they should have anyway.

Breakfast the next morning was a painful affair. Food looked and sounded awful, but my stomach revolted at the idea of settling for coffee all by itself. I nibbled on a trio of pastries that the kitchen staff assured me were not too sweet, and some soft, inoffensive cheese. That did the trick as well as anything could, considering. Then, with eyes at half-mast, I stumbled back to the room for another splash of cold water on my face. While I was busy toweling off, my phone rang. Caller ID said "Lauren Pringle". I hesitated before hitting "Answer".

"Good morning!"

Wow, wasn't she the chipper little bird? Whatever happened to a thing called jet lag?

"Hello, dollface." My Sam Spade imitation popped out unbidden as it often does when I'm hung over. "How was the flight?"

"Oh, Cade, it was a total disaster. The layover in Amsterdam stretched into six hours which meant, of course, that I missed my connection in Detroit."

"Ugh. Couldn't happen at a worse place. You did get Jiggs and Irene though?" I had my fingers crossed, although it seemed ominous that I wasn't hearing any singing in the background. "Lauren? You did pick up Jiggs and Irene, right?" Apparently that wasn't the correct follow-up question, as she clicked off. I'll admit, it may have come across as insensitive. I called her back.

"Hi. It's me. Sorry, I had a rough night." Rather than explain about the English and the Scots, I said, "I miss you."

She sighed. "Thanks. Miss you, too. I just now got home. I'll get Jiggs and Irene in the morning." In the morning? Oh, right, the time difference had slipped my mind. Nine a.m. here meant midnight where my girlfriend was. I groaned and prayed Jim Smith hadn't offed Irene Adler. "I only called so you wouldn't worry."

Worry? I'd have figured she was tucked in hours ago, but then I wasn't exactly in any shape to worry. Or even think, for that matter. Then her tone struck a chord in my brain, which was slowly waking up. "Worry?"

"Oh, Cade, you haven't seen the news, have you?"

"Um, no." A sense of urgency was creeping up on me.

"You need to turn on your TV. There was a horrible crash at Schiphol Airport. That has to be why my flight was delayed for so long."

"Oh, God." I sat down, hard, on the edge of the bed. "Casualties?"

"Yeah. It was pretty bad."

"Terrorists?"

"They don't think so. Authorities don't have answers yet though."

"Oh, doll, I'm so sorry. I mean, I'm happy you're home and safe."

"Me, too." She yawned. "I'm home, and I'm absolutely exhausted. Love you. Only wanted to tell you that, and that I'm safe. Good night."

"Good night," I said, to a dead phone. Lauren had probably barely managed to hit "End" before lapsing into a deep sleep. What an awful day for her. Flying has become a crapshoot anymore. In fact, the odds of winning a jackpot in Vegas seem better than the odds of having an uneventful plane trip. I let myself fall backwards onto the pillow, where I stared at the ceiling for several long minutes. My breakfast threatened to come back up, and I was unsure whether that had more to do with Lauren's shocking news or my hangover. While waiting for the nausea to subside, all sorts of thoughts ran through my mind, most of which revolved around why I was in the south of

France all by myself. Lauren had inadvertently reminded me that life is short, and also that I ached for her. Terribly. This was a new feeling for me. Not necessarily an unpleasant one, but a new one.

"Let's get this thing done." I didn't exactly jump up, but levered myself onto one elbow, assured myself that the food was stable in my stomach, and then finished the job of becoming upright. Outside, light snow flurries had begun falling and now danced at the window, filling me with second thoughts about having traded in the ugly Peugeot for the sexy Ferrari.

"Well, I guess we'll find out how she handles in tricky weather," I said, with little confidence, since snow is a rare commodity around Pezenas. I shrugged into my mid-thigh coat and wrapped a cashmere scarf around my neck.

Reaching for the car key that had wedged itself in the depths of my pocket, my hand closed around a piece of paper. A name and what looked like a phone number were written on it, although European phone numbers look quite different than American ones, but that was my best guess. Now who had given that to me? It probably was no big mystery, at least last night, but since I could recall so little of last night, it had become quite the mystery this morning. The scribbling looked like it said Gilles LeDuc. Maybe it was a restaurant. Grille? Perhaps one of the Brits had recommended a good dinner place. No reason to keep playing a guessing game, though, when someone at the other end could clear up my confusion. I punched in the numbers.

"LeDuc Agence, Gilles ici."

Huh? "Um. Je ne parle – "

"Ah, American. LeDuc Detective Agency. Gilles speaking."

A detective agency? Why? I scoured my brain for a clue, but nothing was coming back to me. Who had given me this name?

"Hello?"

"Um, can I call you back?"

"Certainly. Ian said I may get a call from an American today, but it sounded like you fellows had some fun last night. Gather your wits and we can talk later." For the third time in just a few minutes, the phone went dead as I held it to my ear. Gather my wits, indeed. My confessor was Ian, huh? What had I told him that made him suggest a local detective? No way would I call this Gilles fellow back until I had the answer to that figured out. And considering how my head felt, that could be a while. But at least part of the mystery had been cleared up.

Keys in hand, I locked up the room and made my way carefully toward the car. The snow hadn't increased in intensity, for which I was grateful, but the temperature had certainly turned frigid, making me glad I had dressed for the weather. My plans for the day included a trip to Loupian, to the Brazen Grape or Musty Vine or whatever the winery was called where Adrien's uncle worked currently. Names kept escaping me (including, on occasion, my own). Thus it was fortuitous that I had it written in my notes. If there was anything I'd learned from Capt. Harry Blackstone – dear old dad – it was to take good notes. His kid listened well.

As for driving in that part of the world, well, it can be dicey even on the best of days. And, since that part of the world rarely sees much in the way of snow on its pavement, driving promised to be even dicier. But French motorists pretty much stick to the rules. It would have helped, though, to know what those were. I had a vague notion. Fortunately, the Ferrari got us to Loupian with no major incidents, despite the number of motorists sliding around us in directions not meant to be travelled.

It turned out that the winery name was actually Proud Swan (or, in French, Fiers Cygne). Their hours for tasting were flexible during the low season and, during a light snowstorm, they became almost nonexistent. But if someone walked through the door, out came the tasting glasses, along with smiles and salutations. French winemakers are a very amiable bunch. On that cold January morning, I found myself the only person besides the skeleton staff of winery workers inside the Fiers Cygne winery.

M. Vicente Hatif was easy to spot, prominently displaying the family dimples and cinnamon skin. Those Hatifs are a smiley lot, I'll say that for them. Vicente greeted me with verve (and discreet alarm at the state of my bruised face) then toured me around the place before pouring several generous glasses, which, on almost any other day, would have been welcomed with equal verve. At least I could appreciate the color, and I tried to work up some compliments about the nose and the complexity and whatever other tasting flattery I thought would go over well.

Being one of the front men in the business must have gone a ways toward sharpening Vicente's English skills, for he spoke exceptionally well, an asset not to be taken for granted in a man of his generation. He expounded for several minutes about the brix and the terroir and some other technical wine terms. I half listened, half thought over how to finesse my questions about his nephew.

Swirling a cabernet sauvignon in a large Reidel glass, I asked, "You last saw Adrien when?"

Vicente took a moment to consider. "I saw him Christmas Day but he last worked 24 December. Christmas Eve."

"He worked here?"

"Oui." He nodded.

I didn't realize the young man had taken employment in France. I mean, he already had a job at Fou Flamant. Back in Carlton. This new piece of information added weight to the idea that he planned to stick around his homeland a bit longer than most of his friends in the States thought.

"Um, okay. When was he scheduled to work after that?"

"He should have come here 27 December but he did not arrive."

"Did Adrien have a good attendance record?"

"A good –"

"Sorry. Did he always arrive for work?"

"Oui. Always."

"And he didn't say anything about taking time off or going away?"

"No. No, nothing."

"How about the other men? Did Adrien get along with them?"

"Oui." Vicente's dimples deepened. "The men they like Adrien very much. He is good with the wine." He kissed his fingertips for emphasis.

"Any close friends here?"

He smiled and shook his head. "He likes all the same."

I shifted gears, taking him back to Christmas Day at the Hatif family home. "Michel told me about an argument, I believe with Rayce?"

Vicente's face fell and he directed his gaze toward his shoes, much like his nephew had. Perhaps that was a special French diversion tactic.

"M. Hatif?"

"Oui."

"Can you tell me what it was about?"

"No. Rayce gets angry much time. They had been drinking wine, maybe too much. Rayce say some things, like Rayce maybe thought Adrien had best present."

"Best present? Best Christmas present?"

"Oui."

"Was he right? Did Adrien have, um, best Christmas present?"

"Maybe." Uncle Vicente looked up at me from under his brows. "I give Adrien promotion."

"A promotion for Christmas?"

He grimaced. "Oui."

I winced along with him. That was something that probably did not belong under the holiday tree. "I don't think I want to know the answer to this. Does Rayce work here, too?"

"Oui."

"Sure he does." That can't have made for a merry old time on Yule Day. "Okay. So there's a bit of a ruckus, and –"

"Ruckus?"

"Sorry. The boys have a little fight," I put up my fists to demonstrate. "And you broke it up?"

"Oui."

"And then what?"

"Adrien goes away." He pinched his nose. "No one sees him since."

"No one sees him, no one hears from him."

"Oui."

"Since Christmas Day."

"Oui."

I patted him on the shoulder to suggest that I didn't think him a total idiot. The man felt bad enough, plainly.

Back in the car, I placed a call to Michel. Thankfully, he answered. The day wasn't fit for man nor beast to be out and about, though, so it shouldn't have come as a surprise. I hoped it was a good time to meet Mom and Dad. I had more questions. Michel said he would like to go with me, let him call ahead and then come pick him up. He gave me his address, made the necessary arrangements, and soon he was sliding into the passenger seat of the Ferrari. He wore a huge grin as he caressed the dashboard like it was a woman's, um, cheek.

"Much better car than yesterday."

Was it just yesterday that I traded off the Peugeot? My head still pounded from the long night.

I agreed, saying "Oui, much better." I couldn't resist showing him how well the Ferrari handled in snow. The rear end held until I took a corner a bit hot. I backed off, thinking it would be best not to get too full of myself. He'd been enjoying the beauty of the Italian car, but then caught a glimpse of my bandaged hand.

"What happened, M. Cade? Please, I didn't –"

"Oh, no, Michel. No, this wasn't you. You just –" I gestured at my face. The bruise had darkened pretty dramatically overnight. He gasped.

Laughing, I said, "No worries, Michel. It's just a bruise. How is your shin?"

"My shin?"

"Leg. How is your leg?"

"Oh, is fine. But you don't look fine. Your hand?"

I gave him the short version of my trip to Le Chat Cachemire, leaving out the part about the winery ghost. After all, I wanted him to take me seriously.

"Just a tiny warning, monsieur, Maman will fuss." He pointed at my injuries and shrugged. "It cannot be helped."

Being fussed over by a French mother did not sound like the worst thing that could happen, actually. A small part of me sort of looked forward to it.

- - -

M. and Mme. Hatif lived in a detached home on five hilly hectares (which is equal to something like twelve and a half acres) a short mile north of Montagnac. Built of the typical gray French stone and accented with the Provencal blue shutters, the cottage-like structure overflowed with country charm. The window boxes added to the home's ambiance, although I had to try to imagine how striking they would be in another couple of months. Right now, the few plants still alive were the hardy holdovers from last fall, and they looked beyond ready for spring weather to rejuvenate them. The Ferrari's tires crunched on frozen gravel as we pulled to a stop before a minuscule gate in a low wooden fence that outlined a small yard, seeming dwarfed by the sizable property. Blades of grass struggled to peek through the snow. In another hour, the ground would be completely white if this storm didn't ease up.

Michel walked ahead of me to a scarred red door, which looked as though it might have protected six generations from the elements. He led the way inside the house, which was warm and glowed with soft, golden lights. Aromas of baked bread filled the rooms. My mouth watered.

Henri Hatif, shorter and stouter than I had envisioned, came forward with his hand extended. "Welcome, monsieur. Welcome." His wife, Simone, was close behind. A beauty even at the near side of fifty, she greeted me in the traditional fashion and, yes, began fussing over my cuts and contusions.

Once assured of my general good health, they stood with smiles so big it seemed they would swallow up all of the air inside the home. And a bonus, at least for me, was that behind Mme. Hatif trotted a Springer spaniel, tail aloft and waving. He wore a smile that proved him an authentic Hatif. He ran immediately to Michel, with an excited whine escaping him each time he took a step. He twirled and rubbed his head against Michel's leg. It's only by some miracle that he kept himself on all fours.

Michel kneeled down and engulfed the dog in a hug, then scratched his ears before introducing me to Chirac, the youngest member of the family, at just seven. "He shares a birthday with the former president. Not the year, of course," he explained. "But that's how he got his name." The elder Hatifs smiled and nodded. I leaned in to pet Chirac, too, and was rewarded with more wags. Chirac's energized presence made me yearn once more for Jiggs.

Henri and Simone asked about my stay in their country, followed by an apology for the despicable weather. "This is very rare." The couple offered me everything except the deed to their land. It seemed almost impolite to question them about their son, and I hoped they understood that my motives were pure. No one wanted Adrien to come to a bad end, and any aid in finding him could help avoid that.

I eased into the subject of Pierre. Michel had told me that he wasn't sure his parents knew about the boy. The look that passed between them was all the answer I needed. How could Adrien have kept their grandson a secret for the, what, three months that he'd been here? Four?

So my next question didn't need to be asked: Had they met Pierre? Obviously not. But how about Chantal; did Henri and Simone know Chantal?

"Ah, yes. Very beautiful girl," answered Mme. Hatif. Her husband nodded and, then, realizing the import of my inquiry, stopped and pursed his lips. "Chantal? Chantal is mother?"

"Chantal, yes. Oui." I confirmed.

Whether this news pleased or upset them was not apparent. Both Hatifs held their emotions in check. They probably wanted to speak in private, not in front of an American detective they didn't know anything about. Made sense. So I'd discovered that Adrien's parents knew nothing about their grandson. Unfortunately, I came away no better informed about Adrien's whereabouts than when I'd arrived, nor directions the search should now take, for they told me nothing new that Michel or Vicente hadn't already said. Nonetheless, I was glad I'd come, and I wanted to remain at Cinq Chenes (the name of their petite estate). The hotel suite that awaited me back in Pezenas no longer held any appeal. It was merely empty and impersonal space. The Hatif place was full of old family memories and decades of comfort. It made me once again pledge to find their youngest son, even if it was a pledge made only to myself.

Chapter 11

Michel and I parted, me intending to drop by the hotel in Pezenas, him off to do who knew what. I realized that I had never taken the time to read through Adrien's mail. Since my clues had winnowed down to pretty much nothing, it felt like that should be my next logical move. The party invitation from Yvette had piqued my curiosity. No one so far had the slightest notion of who the woman was. That puzzled me. His family claimed no knowledge of anyone named Yvette. No one at any of the wineries I had visited showed a hint of recognition when hearing the name. And now, thinking back on the invitation, I could not remember the particulars, like date, time, location, so I wanted to take a closer look.

As I walked by the front desk of the Grand Moliere, I thought I noticed the hotel clerk smirk, but maybe it was just my guilty conscience. That guy couldn't have been on duty when I came in at – what time had it been anyway? I gave a pleasant nod and strode through the tiny lobby, trying to look purposeful. And sober.

On the second floor, the maid had just finished with my room. Did I imagine a look of disapproval or was that my guilty conscience again? Had someone started rumors about me during the morning? I smiled at her as I squeezed by in the narrow hall and closed the door behind me. Adrien's letters remained tucked inside a zippered compartment of my suitcase. It's not that I didn't trust the hotel's staff, but it didn't seem wise to leave temptation languishing in plain sight.

In Adrien's flat, it had struck me as old-fashioned that Yvette had sent a paper party invitation, but she had. Most of my friends send evites or a casual email saying, "Come on over for BBQ ribs next Friday night." This didn't say anything like that, but it did say the party was Wednesday. (Yes, I actually know the days of the week in French.) I checked my calendar. It showed Wednesday as tomorrow. Excellent. I had an invitation to a party tomorrow night, which gave me time to recover from the impromptu party with the Brits last night.

The rest of Adrien's mail appeared routine: Bills, advertisements, bank letters. I stuffed it all back into my luggage. Looking at my watch, I noted it was half past one, too early to call home. I leaned back and closed my eyes for just a minute. When I opened them, the clock on the nightstand read 2:36. How had more than an hour gone by? I shook myself out of that comfortable slumber.

Slowly, bit by bit, snatches of the previous night crept into my consciousness. I thanked whatever gods might exist that Le Vintage Bar did not feature karaoke, as I thought I remembered those of us at our table misbehaving badly enough without tossing in that indignity. Don't let anyone ever tell you that the British are proper. Oh, no. It's that accent that fools you. It makes them sound so classy, almost stuffy. Not so. They are a raucous bunch of wonky chaps who love to spend an evening cheering on some daft cow who's arguing politics with a couple of nutters. Or something like that. Anyway, I had gotten well and thoroughly pissed, which is their way of saying stumbling drunk.

But now I recalled Jack's friend Ian informing me that I would be requiring local help if I wanted to do any investigating around these parts. That meant I must have spilled my entire story, even though it was my original intention to keep things under the radar and unofficial. Just some guy having a friendly look around. Well, that didn't work out so well, now, did it? Anyway, Ian, being former police – although not in this country – had a bit of expertise and I probably should take his advice. In that case, M. Gilles LeDuc might become a close companion in the upcoming days. This is something the French detective explained when I called him again later on that day.

"Ah, M. Blackstone, you have gathered your wits, no?"

Not really, but I said I had nonetheless.

"You see me in my offices. We discuss your case. Say, 4:00?"

"Sure." Calling it a case was giving it a status I didn't think it deserved. In all likelihood, Adrien Hatif had had a spat with his brother or his girlfriend or run out on them and his newly discovered kid, or maybe he simply decided he wanted to take a tour of Croatia, but I hadn't elevated that set of circumstances to what I'd call an actual case. Europeans do things differently, though, as I've mentioned, so I'd play along. Meanwhile, LeDuc had given me time to try and get my headache under control and check in with Michel once again. Maybe he'd heard from Adrien, rendering the meeting with M. LeDuc a moot point.

Oddly, Michel took so long to answer that it almost went to voice mail, but he picked up a split second before the ring tone cut off and answered, sounding slightly testy.

"No, nothing from Adrien. But Rayce had some things to say."

From Michel's inflection, I gathered whatever Rayce had to say might well fall under the category of unfriendly. My head throbbed once more.

"Okay. Let me hear it."

"I cannot repeat it. I will just say he does not want to speak with you."

Usually it takes at least *one* face-to-face meeting or at minimum a few words over the phone for me to piss someone off. This was a new record. I pinched my nose. It hurt and felt good at the same time.

"Fine. Why care what happens to his brother?"

"Excuse me?"

"Never mind." I was too hung over to worry about diplomacy. "Do you have time for a quick coffee? I can come right over."

He hesitated for two beats before saying, "Okay. I will be ready."

"Merci, Michel." I clicked off. My day felt well mapped out. After coffee, there would probably only be about enough time to run back to Pezenas for my appointment with PI LeDuc. Meantime, maybe Michel could give me some background on their childhood years, fill me in on the brotherly dynamics and how the sister fit in with all those boys. I wanted to understand the animosity between Adrien and Rayce. The rest of the Hatifs, those that I had met anyway, seemed to be a laid-back, genial lot. What had set Rayce on a course against his sibling? Hopefully, I would find out in a few minutes.

Shivering in anticipation of what awaited me outdoors, I wrapped my scarf tighter around my neck, steeling for the playful breeze that had kicked up in the last few minutes. "Playful" was a strong euphemism. Back home, we'd call it bracing and still be giving it a gentler term than it deserved. Light snow flurries stung my face as I walked to the car.

Michel said he knew of a tiny café that he swore served the best espresso in the village of Montagnac, which sounded like just what I needed, particularly if, by "best", he meant "strong". As we entered, he spoke some rapid sentences to a person I assumed was the proprietor, then guided me to a secluded table where I perched on a well-worn wooden bench. An oil painting of a cat peeking around a flower pot hung on the wall. An overweight woman placed a platter of French pastries in front of us. From the measure of her girth, it appeared she sampled her work generously and often. I hadn't thought my stomach ready for more food, but the aroma coming from the overflowing plate convinced me otherwise. I reached for one of the beignets. They were still warm. And tasted like a slice of nirvana.

"Thank you for introducing me to your parents, Michel. And to Chirac."

He smiled as he smeared a dab of jam onto a croissant.

"It is good family."

"Yes. Good family." Despite my muddled brain, a reasonably cogent question occurred to me. "Does the whole family live around here?"

"No. Yves has home in Italy. Cortona. And Chanler lives in Spain."

The Spanish border is only a few hundred kilometers by car from Montagnac. But Spain is a good-sized country and precisely where Chanler lived might make a difference as to whether Adrien would have run off for a quick visit. I inquired as to which town.

"Figueres."

"Ah, the home of the Dali museum."

Michel appeared impressed. "Oui." Figueres was not merely the home of the Dali museum; it was where Salvador Domingo Felipe Jacinto Dalí i Domènech, first Marqués de Dalí de Pubol, known to the world as Salvador Dalí, was born and where he died. In all honestly, I could understand wanting to live there; it's a beautiful town on the northeast coast of Spain, a hard-to-resist area, and approximately three hours' drive from Montagnac. Definitely nearer than Cortona, Italy.

"Do you think Adrien might have gone to visit Chanler?"

Michel looked startled. "Oh, no, monsieur. No."

"Why not?"

"They were not so close. I cannot imagine it."

"How about Yves?"

"No."

"Has anyone called Yves and Chanler to check?"

He shrugged and pulled out his phone. "We can be sure like this, no?"

I admire a decisive man. Unfortunately, the two calls proved that Adrien had not gone to visit either of his geographically distant brothers, leaving me stuck in the same old quandary. I sighed, feeling adrift once more. "Maybe if you just tell me about your family, that might help."

Michel raised his eyebrows.

"Please. See, I don't know where to go from here. Give me a little understanding of who the Hatifs are."

He flashed the trademark smile. "You want to know who are the Hatifs? We are the Swifts!"

"The –"

He cocked his head and laughed. "Yes, the Swifts. It is nickname, monsieur. Hatif translates, in English, to hasty, literally, which is like fast or swift. And some people around here call us Swift, like the bird. The swift is a dramatic bird. And then there's a black swift, which is even more dramatic." He flashed a huge grin, showing off the family dimples, and flapped his arms, which I thought a bit over the top. "The nickname started long ago. Some family member was called Vite, which in French means fast. I do not know why he was named this. But nickname is like Swifty in your country. Then, his son had same name. People started calling us Swifts. And it also came partially from our winemaking. My family always get the bottles done first. Even bad years. We always have. No one knows how we do it. We just do. Magicians, no?" He shrugged, a French national gesture, seemingly. "And we do it better than everyone. It makes the other winemakers crazy. Some do call us crazy." Michel bit into another beignet, leaned on one elbow, and looked at me with mahogany eyes that beamed sincerity. And a touch of craziness.

"Huh, the Swifts. Clever." I'd actually seen those birds, and Michel could be loosely viewed as its avian counterpart, maybe, but my mind doesn't really work that way. I prefer facts over these ethereal concepts, so I decided to pursue some. "How did your family get into winemaking?"

"Ah. My grandfather – that would be Cedric – his father made the rum. And his father also. They made the rum. In Martinique." He looked at me with questioning eyes. "You know Martinique?"

"Yeah, lovely island in the Caribbean." A little piece of France floating in the sea off the coast of Venezuela.

"Yes. Martinique. Very beautiful. There they made the rum. But Cedric did not like living on an island and did not like the rum. So, when Cedric hears of the winemaking in France, at young age – sixteen – he comes here." Michel paused as if to give me time to appreciate the human wonder that was his grandfather. "He had big success and, after few years, he meets my grandmother, Dominique." He looked sideways at me. "It was a little scandal. She has the white skin and he has the dark skin, so a scandal, but not so much a scandal as in United States back then. No. So they married, and soon along come two boys. Et voila! The family of Swifts begins."

"How many of you children joined in the wine business?"

"Ah, the wine business. My father and Uncle Vicente make the wine. Very good wine. Magnifique, as we say here. They start when they are teenagers. Build several wineries. Then sell. Last is Le Chat Cachemire, where Adrien wanted to work. But Adrien was only one interested, at first. Then Rayce. Then me little bit."

"So why did Adrien go to America?"

Michel blushed and ducked his head. "I think papa sees conflict between Adrien and Rayce. And sees much opportunity in America. Maybe he teaches him what he could. Maybe he wants him to learn more. Besides, he and Uncle Vicente sell Le Chat. Papa works on his own now. Vicente is winemaker at Fiers Cygne."

"The Proud Swan."

"Oui. You know?"

I shook my head.

Hardly anyone had mentioned the sister in all of this. Where did she fit in? It seemed to be a family overwhelmed by boys. I had to ask.

"What about your sister? What does she do? Any interest in the winery?"

Michel looked at me as though I had brought up the subject of an alien. "Aimee?"

"Yes, Aimee. What does Aimee do?"

"Aimee is – what you say – lawyer."

"Is she married?"

"No. Once, but no more."

"Children?"

Michel's eyes dropped to the table. "No, no children."

"But she wanted children?"

"Oui."

"That's sad."

"Yes."

The subject seemed to be a delicate one, judging by Michel's instant loss of humor. I wanted to probe deeper, but thought it best to postpone that for a while.

"I assume she never wanted to work at Le Chat Cachemire."

"No."

"But you did, a little bit, you said?"

"Oui. Little bit." He shrugged again. "Adrien was so good at it."

As I sipped my espresso, thinking what to ask next, Michel glanced around the minuscule room and I thought I heard him say, "Shit," which sounds less like a curse word in French. A woman who I figured could only be

Aimee from the hair and dimples was striding with purpose toward our corner table, a determined look on her face. She stopped a mere two inches from Michel's toes and launched into a harangue of French sounds. For once, I was happy I didn't *parle francais*. The two of them exchanged words in a burst of emotion for the next three or four minutes, Mlle. Hatif occasionally pausing long enough to glare in my direction. Each time, she received my most innocent and engaging smile in return. However, it did not appear to soften her mood. When she had finished whatever it was she had set out to do, she turned on her heel and marched off.

    I cautiously asked, "Your sister?"

    Michel nodded.

    "I take it she is displeased."

    He nodded again. "Oui. I must go."

    "Oh, um, yeah, sure. Let me drop you by your flat."

    "No, is not necessary. Thank you. I can go myself."

    With that, Michel left the table, waved to the fat lady, and disappeared out onto the snow-covered streets. What had upset Aimee so? And how did she even know Michel was having coffee with me in the little bistro? Where was Lauren when I most needed her? She always had logical answers. Me, I sat there with more questions than I came in with and a headache that had intensified.

Chapter 12

Shortly before the appointed hour of 4:00 p.m., my GPS guided me seamlessly to the LeDuc Agency. The French detective's office reminded me of that of Blackstone Investigations back home in Carlton, although mine overlooked the main street of town. It was hard to tell whether his did or not; the village streets were all winding and approximately the size of golf cart paths. None appeared to be a major thoroughfare. Gilles LeDuc himself was something of a disappointment, too, sort of like the town streets. I suppose it was unrealistic to expect the man to look like Sam Spade, one of my fictional idols, but did he have to resemble Danny DeVito? That was a long way off from my visual ideal of a Languedoc PI. Okay, he didn't really look like DeVito. Just the fringe hair, big crooked smile, funky glasses and stocky build. But the Frenchman was at least an inch and a half taller than the actor; probably close to five foot two. To his credit, he dressed in a rather elegant manner, and it appeared he favored vests. I instantly liked his face, weathered and full of expression, with eyes that danced, even when he said a simple "Bonjour."

On the wall behind his desk was an impressive array of certificates. However, I had no idea what they were for because all of them were presented in his native language, thus foreign to me. They looked official, though. He motioned me into a sturdy oak chair, which didn't come anywhere close to being comfortable. I guessed that he wanted his clients to get to the point, dish out the facts and leave. That might be a good strategy to remember.

"So M. Blackstone, you have come to France to work on a case."

I cleared my throat. "More like a trip to see if I can find a friend for a friend."

He steepled his hands and rested his chin on them. "I see. So it is not a case per se." He let me think that over for a few moments. Why was I stalling? Probably because I don't work well with others. Jim Smith is the exception, and I don't really work *with* Jim. Jim occasionally does some odd job to aid me in an investigation. Some odd job that might not be exactly legal. Let's say that Jim has his ways of making things happen and I don't need to know the specifics. But M. LeDuc could probably be of service, especially since I didn't really know my way around the French legal system, not to mention the French countryside, which was currently turning into a winter wonderland.

I scratched my head. "Well, it's complicated."

"Ah, oui, complicated. Explain, please."

So I laid out most of what I knew, including the upcoming party at Yvette's, maybe hoping he would volunteer to act as my date. He did.

"What time is this party tomorrow?"

I told him and suggested I could pick him up at nine o'clock.

"Excellent. We will start our search for this friend of a friend then."

M. LeDuc stood and I realized our meeting was over. We shook hands, and that was that.

- - -

Later, shortly before stepping out for dinner, feeling ravishingly hungry since I'd ingested almost no food except for the excess of baked goods, I telephoned Lauren.

"Good morning." I heard a yawn before she'd awakened enough to answer.

"Good morning."

"Hope I didn't wake you. You sound groggy."

"No, I'm up but still working on my first cup of coffee. Watching the early news." There was a quiet lull before she continued, "The crash at Schiphol killed thirteen passengers."

I whistled. And thanked Providence that Lauren had not been on that flight. I said something to that effect.

"Yeah, me, too. Wish you were here." The pout in her voice transmitted clearly over the airwaves, reminding me of how sexy was the mouth that produced that pout. "When can you come home?"

"Well, about that. I finally have a possible lead."

"What?" I could hear the investigative reporter in Lauren waking up.

"Remember Adrien's mail? There was a party invitation from a woman named Yvette?"

"Uh-huh."

"The party is tomorrow night. I'm going."

"O-kay. And how is this going to help? You don't seriously think Adrien will be there?"

Put that way, it did sound silly. Stranger things have happened, though. "Uh, probably not. But it's the only lead I have so far." I filled her in on my recent activities, from my chat with M. & Mme. Hatif out at their Cinq Chenes estate to Michel's recitation of the family history. She agreed that there didn't seem to be anything in all of that which sounded suspicious or like it led anywhere.

"Any more sightings of the ginger-haired woman?"

"No, but it's snowing so sightings of anyone on the streets are scarce."

"Oooh, I'll bet it's gorgeous though."

"Yeah."

By then, my news was depleted, but Lauren had some other news, hers being more local, and more disturbing. Ex-Deputy Rollie Hansen had left several notes taped to the front door of my house, a big federal style thing a short distance outside of Carlton, notes with large block letters spelling out URGENT in red permanent pen. (He always tends toward the dramatic.) I already knew he wanted to get in touch with me because of the numerous calls to my cell phone that had gone unanswered. I mean, I rarely answer calls from Rollie when I'm in Carlton. Why would he think I'd pick up while enjoying a spin around France?

Anyway, Lauren had peeked inside one of the notes to see what the emergency might be. Apparently, Cassandra York had dropped off the radar for a few days recently and Rollie was worried. Well, the tall redhead had her own ways of introducing drama into the lives of those around her, so she probably was punishing her boyfriend for some personal slight, real or imagined, with her version of the silent treatment. She'd be back; she always was. Besides, I had my own missing person case to deal with. And I was thousands of miles away. What did he expect me to do?

My attitude, while admittedly callous, seemed to put Lauren off, which surprised me. I'd have thought that me chasing after an ex-girlfriend wouldn't exactly thrill her. I made some noises that showed appropriate concern about Cassandra's safety and promised to see what I could find out. Then I turned to a subject that actually interested me.

"One more little request. Jiggs and Irene?"

"That's two things." She sounded a tiny bit irritated.

"Uh-huh. You'll be sure to pick them up?"

She mumbled something unintelligible, for which I should probably be thankful.

I smooched loudly into the phone and rang off with a quick, "Thanks, doll," before she could get huffy. I view confrontation as something to be avoided. Also, my appetite had grown into a monster, threatening bodily harm if I didn't take care of it soon.

Reaching for my jacket, I caught an image of myself in the mirror and decided that, while improved significantly since the morning, a splash of cold water and a quick comb through my hair couldn't hurt. And come what may, I told myself, definitely avoid Le Vintage Bar just in case the British had invaded once again. I'd noticed a pleasant-looking café just two doors down from the hotel. It appeared to be fairly empty every time I passed by but, as long as they served identifiable food, they had my business for the evening.

- - -

Okay, that little café just two doors down from the hotel sits empty for a very good reason. Their food is ghastly, a fact all of the locals must be well aware of. And now I was, too. It had seemed impossible that a French chef could create anything bad, but this place must have been run by a team of decorators unfamiliar with the workings of a stove, as it looked adorable from the street and the stuff they served was artfully presented. But something got lost in the transition from raw ingredients to finished dish. Dinner last night was awful! Awful as in I left hungry after shelling out 36 euros, not including wine.

So, this morning, I wound through the tiny streets behind Le Vintage Bar until I found a bustling establishment so crowded that it had to have great food. Still, I made my breakfast choices carefully. As I ate some cheese and a pastry and sipped strong coffee, I thought of the day ahead. It occurred to me that I had no plans until it was time to pick up Gilles LeDuc for Yvette's party at 9:00 p.m. But the coppery odor out at the abandoned Le Chat Cachemire winery had been nagging at me for almost two days now. No way was I going back out there on my own though. So I wondered whether M. LeDuc could be persuaded to come along, and maybe even bring Ian, his Scottish friend who had recommended him as we shared an embarrassing amount of alcohol. Never hurts to ask, I thought, pulling out my phone.

LeDuc listened quietly while I explained the situation, then I heard him rifling through what must have been an appointment book.

"Ah, oui. It seems that I have a light schedule today." We set a time for me to pick him up. "I can talk with Ian, ask him to accompany us."

I thanked the French detective and rang off. Ten minutes passed and the restaurant was emptying out and my coffee had run dry a while ago, so I joined the exodus. With a couple of hours to kill yet, I wandered through several stores in old Pezenas, scoring a scarf for Lauren to replace the one that got ruined when I ripped my hand open on the winery window, and three thick, warm sweaters and another pair of gloves.

As I was paying for the last of these, LeDuc called me back. He explained that Ian sent his regrets but he was currently touring some guests around the picturesque fortified town of Carcassonne, some hour and a half away. Probably best, since the Ferrari seated only two anyhow.

I stopped for another coffee just to ensure that my hangover from yesterday stayed away, then made the journey back to my hotel room where I packed away my new sweaters. I rebandaged my hand, bundled up, and grabbed my hat. I even remembered to stuff my new gloves in my jacket pocket before heading out to pick up the detective.

- - -

The stout DiVito look-alike waited by what passes for a curb in Pezenas, wearing a heavy wool coat and Burberry ascot and hat. I tooted the horn so he knew it was me in the red Ferrari. He opened the passenger side door and leaned in.

"Nice car. Detectives make more in America than France."

I didn't want to go through the whole explanation of how I'd inherited from my Uncle Cliff because of a heroic deed I'd performed in saving his beagle Bagby. (Heroic in Uncle Cliff's eyes. The real story is that I had thoughtlessly grabbed the stupid creature out of the jaws of a pit bull, earning myself a nasty bite and an obscene sum of money.) So instead, I said, "It's been a good year."

"Ah. Oui, a good year." He eased himself inside and we pulled away.

While driving, I noticed LeDuc glancing over at me a couple of times, almost sneakily.

"What?"

"Your hand, monsieur."

Well, he had been kind enough to ignore the condition of my face, so it seemed like a reasonable concession to explain at least that part of my recent calamities. Again, I left out any mention of winery ghosts.

I found that trying to retrace my steps from two days ago was tricky at best. Sort of like returning to the hotel after drinking with the British; the route

I took turned out not to be the most direct one. However, we arrived without incident, so I marked the trip as a success.

Le Chat Cachemire looked like a scene from a postcard with its fresh coat of snow. There were no tracks on the lane leading in nor any on the walk up to the massive door, which, today, inexplicably, opened with ease. That should have been a welcome development, seeing as how we didn't have to gain entry by way of an ivy-covered window that had glass shards lurking in the frame, ready to rip flesh. Instead, it felt ominous, like the old building was laying a trap. Why had it been stubbornly locked on my previous visit and not today? Had someone been here in the meantime?

I pushed on the door and it swung open slowly but without resistance. The creak of the hinges sent shivers down my spine, the kind that fingernails on a blackboard will cause. We inched inside, me at least on tiptoe and high alert; Gilles with a cane I'd not noticed earlier. Still, my companion walked with a sort of unflappable attitude. Also, he had come prepared with a torch (flashlight to us Carltonians), while I once more relied on my phone app. Things inside looked much as they had before. Smelled much as they had, too, except that the coppery odor had grown stronger, almost overpowering, and had an underlying rankness to it.

We stood for a moment, back to back, shining our lights around us. Mine didn't penetrate far into the dark, but having the large main door open helped dispel some of the gloom. The pool of liquid by one of the many piles drew LeDuc's attention.

He motioned. "Monsieur?"

I nodded, unsure whether to trust my voice.

Careful of his footing on the cluttered floor, he picked his way over toward the dark puddle and the lump beside it.

"Oh, merde."

His voice trailed off, low and breathy. I shook myself out of the momentary stupor I'd fallen into, wrapped my jacket more tightly about my chest, and joined him.

Looking down, I moaned and turned away. "Ah, crap."

My eyes watered. I rubbed them, then pinched my nose with both hands. I hadn't realized how much I didn't want this to be what we found. A deer, a fuzzy rabbit, even somebody's sloe-eyed dog, although that would be almost as bad. But not this. The body lay curled around a sack of some sort, as though he had been trying to protect it when he died. If it was so important, why hadn't it been taken? An answer occurred to me but I didn't want to acknowledge it. Remembering the locked door the day I arrived (today, unlocked), an eerie notion swirled in my head. Had my arrival frightened off the killer? I certainly wasn't quiet about my entrance. A Ferrari rumbling up the gravel driveway, an American yelling "Hello!" And hopping through a busted-out window. And, inside, the onslaught of birds that had swooshed in could have masked the sounds of a man fleeing in the darkness. I hadn't seen the giant door open, nor any light rush in, but my focus had been toward the back and the lump lying in the pool.

Goosebumps ran up my arms and neck. Surely my imagination was running away with me. Surely this man had been dead long before I'd come visiting Le Chat Cachemire. Right? Whatever the truth, the fact remained that this man had been dead and lying here when I wandered through on Sunday. Maybe a ghost had chased me out after all.

LeDuc and I stared at the body of what was likely once a transient. Drab, tattered clothing made it impossible for it to be Adrien Hatif of the rainbow cape. And this corpse had no dreads, but he did have white skin. At any rate, we had found the source of our odor, and it wasn't Adrien Hatif, so I could rest easy. I guess. Still, the question remained: where was Adrien Hatif?

Chapter 13

The discovery of a body took up the rest of the afternoon, with the police interviews and reports and such. Thankfully, it seemed that Gilles LeDuc had a sterling reputation with the area law enforcement, which rubbed off onto Cade Blackstone. He made sure everything was in order by the time we left the Case of the Wandering Winery Waif in their capable hands. I hurried back to the Grand Hotel Moliere for a quick change and discovered a few spare minutes for a call home. Nothing new there, but it felt good to hear their voices. Lauren's and Irene's, that is. Jiggs was snoring.

By nine o'clock Wednesday night, when I rolled to a stop in front of the LeDuc Detective Agency, the snow had stopped falling, leaving a downy blanket of three inches covering everything. Temperatures remained cold, though, feeling like it was somewhere in the upper 20s, although my Smartphone readout had switched to Celsius and I don't do the conversion so well. The door to Gilles' building opened and the little man slipped out, looking rather Holmesian in a tweed coat and cap. (It wasn't quite a deerstalker but close.) And, thank God, he had no meerschaum pipe nor magnifying glass. I guessed this was LeDuc's version of party attire. He carried his cane which he thrust inside the Ferrari before lowering himself onto the seat.

The detective assured me he knew how to get to the address printed on Yvette's invitation, so I deprogrammed the GPS and listened to the Frenchman's directions. When he wasn't giving instructions to turn right, left or continue straight through a roundabout, he was enriching me with a wealth of other information, mostly of a historical nature about the area and its residents. On first glance, he had seemed a brusque and abrupt sort of man. Our initial appointment had appeared to be one sided, and then he'd ended our meeting quite suddenly. But, this afternoon, on the drive out to Le Chat Cachemire, he had become downright chatty, and the trend was continuing into the evening.

"So, monsieur, you say your case involves the Hatifs."

"Yes."

"Henri and Simone Hatif."

"Uh-huh."

"Called around here the Swifts."

"Yeah, I heard that."

The little fellow actually chuckled, something I didn't think the French capable of. Knowing it's risky to take eyes off the road, nonetheless I couldn't help myself. I glanced his way, my mouth falling open. It must have been the shocked expression on my face that made him chuckle some more and he said, "It is a small community. Especially when one works in the wine business."

Well, that made sense.

"Hatif wine is legend around here. Have you tried it?"

I admitted that I had not. He recommended a specific vintage of Henri's current winery (I'll admit to having forgotten the name already), a tasty mourvedre, and suggested a similar year of Fiers Cygne also, maybe as a comparison of the brothers' styles. Whatever his reason, I promised to try them both, and I meant to keep that promise. After all, it involved red wine.

"You have met M. & Mme. Hatif?"

Yes, I told him, and their dog Chirac, at their home Cinq Chenes.

"Ah, Cinq Chenes. Five Oaks. You know it was owned once by an American?"

"No, I did not know that."

"Oui. An American gangster."

"Bugsy Siegel?"

"Bugsy –"

"Forget it."

"Americans have funny names."

He didn't think Swift was funny? I let that slide. "You were saying?"

"Mme. Hatif is quite a beauty, no?"

I agreed.

"Henri is a lucky man."

Where was he going with this? "Yes, Henri makes superb wine and has a beautiful wife. But I don't see how that helps me find their son Adrien."

"Ah, Adrien. Nice boy. Very wild when younger. But why not? The girls, they like him. Maybe that is how they get nickname Swift, too." He laughed at his tiny joke.

"What about the other Hatif children?"

"Ah, oui. All the boys are very handsome. The young ladies chase after them. They were heartbreakers, as you Americans say."

"And the girl? Aimee?"

"Aimee." He hesitated, glanced out his side window. "Aimee. Aimee was difficult girl."

"In what way?"

"Too smart. Pretty in odd way, but angry all the time. Aimee was a rebel."

"How did that manifest itself?"

"Pardon?"

"How did that come out?"

"She was all the time protesting, protesting. She was sent home from school often because of things she says. She had trouble making friends. But she could get other students to join her causes. Today she is lawyer."

"Yes."

"Did you meet?"

"Yes. Well, not exactly." I summarized Aimee's appearance at the bistro the afternoon before.

He laughed. "Sounds like Aimee."

We approached a roundabout and LeDuc guided me to the second exit, then had me take the third exit of the one immediately after that. An ugly blocky building loomed too close to the street for my American sensibilities, and it was there that he suggested I find a place to park the Ferrari; we had reached the address. An even smaller street intersected at the end of the building. I turned the corner, then pulled up onto the narrowest sidewalk I've ever seen, mimicking three other cars in what apparently was legal street parking. LeDuc assured me the Ferrari would be safe there. Now all we had to worry about was gaining entry to the party we were hoping to crash.

"You worry too much, monsieur."

As it turned out, he was right. Instead of going to the trouble of inventing an elaborate story to get Yvette to let us in, Gilles simply knocked on her door and, upon hearing no response but loud laughter inside, led us through as though we belonged there. It would have seemed to me that, with the memory of the attack on the Charlie Hebdo offices in Paris so fresh, that the entire country would still be on edge, but apparently the youth of France wasted no time getting back to their carefree lives. I suppose the term *laissez faire* isn't popular in this country for no reason.

M. LeDuc had thought to bring something for the hostess, which earned him a smile from the young woman that he gave it to.

"Is that Yvette?"

"Oui."

"Huh. How did you know that?" There were close to twenty-five people mingling in the cramped flat, over half of them women, and LeDuc instinctively had picked out this woman as Yvette.

"Just look at her. She is comfortable here. The way she moves, the way she stands, all of it proves it is her home."

Maybe I needed more time in the detective business, because, put that way, it was easy to see that the woman Gilles had approached was the apartment's resident, i.e. our hostess. She stood with her arms clasped behind her body, head high, surveying the roomful of guests.

Gilles held out a glass of something red to me, then wandered toward a table laden with food. Inspecting the myriad dishes left me perplexed; none appeared remotely familiar, although, because they were French, most were beautiful and intricate.

"Didn't Yvette ask who we are?"

"No, monsieur. We bring a gift."

"Ah," I said, pretending wisdom. I took a sniff of the stuff in the glass Gilles had given me.

"By the way, M. Blackstone, do not drink that."

The aroma emanating from the liquid was not remotely identifiable, except that I could be certain it was not wine. I let my eyes roam around the room, peering over the rim of my glass as though enjoying a sip from it. Never having met Adrien left me at a disadvantage, knowing how much of a chameleon some people can be. I'm something of an expert at disguises myself, especially in the area of hair colors and styles, and especially during the weeklong celebration of Mardi Gras. But for a man like Adrien Hatif, distinctive characteristics like massive dreadlocks and deep dimples would be hard to camouflage. Of the men in the room no one came even close to a possibility. I commented as much to Gilles.

"Then we need to ask some questions, no?"

"Yep, that's Plan B." I navigated through a sea of bodies over to Yvette, who was only then extricating herself from a conversation with two women who appeared to be under age and over drunk, swaying and giggling, rubbery knees buckling. Gilles trailed behind at a distance, then stopped nearby. Yvette smiled at me, yet remained on her guard.

"Bonsoir, mademoiselle," I said, hopeful that my accent didn't suck, although it would hardly matter, for I now needed to switch to English as I had depleted my French unless we were to talk about wine, foods I don't like or the location of the bathroom.

Gilles angled closer, but said nothing.

By now, Yvette had begun looking over my shoulder at her other guests. I took a deep breath and leaped in. "Mademoiselle –" It occurred to me I did not know her last name. It had not been printed on the invitation. Well, why would it? Adrien would know who was inviting him to this party. "Um, Yvette, my name is Cade Blackstone. My friend and I have come about –"

She put a hand up and shook her head. "No English."

Really, no English? Was she pretending ignorance or did she really not know my language? I glanced over at Gilles, who relented and came to my rescue. He did the introductions and then the two of them had an exchange of words, but the only ones I understood were "Adrien Hatif". By the way Yvette was shaking her head, I could tell that our trip was pointless. As Gilles continued his questions – what more did he have to ask anyway? – I slipped away, thinking I might actually try to find the bathroom.

European flats aren't set up like American apartments, so the first door I opened turned out not to be the bathroom, but a bedroom. And an occupied one at that. Two men looked at me, clearly startled, their expressions turning from shocked to hostile. I said, "Excusez-moi," shut the door and ran over to Gilles, pushing my way rudely through the crowd.

"We must go, Gilles. *Now*."

The cool little man did not hesitate. The slamming of a door in the back of the flat may have helped spur him into action, too. We made record time getting out to the car, skidding once or twice on the icy sidewalk but staying mostly upright. Our pursuers were less fortunate. Both of them went down, giving us the edge we crucially needed. M. LeDuc's short legs moved with lightning speed in his race for the Ferrari. I clicked the key fob, we hopped in and drove off as fast as I dared on the treacherous roads.

Mercifully, the car handles well on snow. I prayed I might have an advantage, too, since I'm used to driving in these conditions, especially up to the ski slopes of Mt. Hood back in Oregon, and the south of France rarely sees even a dusting of the white stuff, so hopefully anyone trying to follow wouldn't have the skills to keep up.

A time or two I thought I saw headlights approaching in the rearview mirror, but then they turned off. Gilles and I didn't talk until we reached the Pezenas town sign, and then LeDuc merely said, "Straight on."

I slowed further, although my heart continued to pound. When I got to the LeDuc Agence, Gilles motioned me ahead. He directed me to a narrow lane and then another. We took four turns before he had me stop beside a door which I thought might lead into the world's smallest garage. While the Ferrari idled, he went in and opened the door, backed out an ancient Saab, then motioned me inside. I understood: the Ferrari would be mothballed for a while until we figured out what was going on. It's too high profile.

Once my car was safely hidden in the garage and I had gotten into the passenger seat of the Saab, we discussed our options. First, we needed a place to go where we could talk about what happened. I felt a compulsion for familiar surroundings, so we ended up at Le Vintage Bar.

Even though it had gone half past ten, Ian and English Jack sat at one of the few occupied tables, having a rousing discussion over the local mayor. I looked at Gilles and raised my eyebrows as an inquiry. In answer, he limped toward their table, relying on the aid of his cane, pulled out a chair and sat heavily into it. The waiter reached the table before I did, which meant that drinks weren't far behind. For that, I was more than thankful. I had heeded Gilles' warning about the red stuff in my glass at the party, and now I wanted some red stuff in a glass that I could actually drink. Hopefully, soon, we would have a chance to work out our next move.

For the next hour, though, we sat, the four of us, sipping nice wine and trashing the village politicians. All in all, a lovely way to pass an evening, except for the fact that my curiosity was demanding much of my attention. But at our table, the argument raged on.

Jack was on one side of the political fence, tossing out comments like, "The sodding bloke's blinkered," while Ian magnanimously gave the mayor the benefit of the doubt. "Ah, come on, Jack. He's trying to save the citizens money. The town doesn't need another fountain in the park." And on and on it went. Shortly before midnight, Ian and Jack wobbled to their feet and gave a salute, which we took as a good-bye gesture. One of them was singing "Candle in the Wind" as they wove out the door. It frightened me to think they might try to drive.

Watching them made me wonder why I'd trusted them, or at least Ian, to steer me to Gilles LeDuc, although LeDuc came across as the sanest of the men I'd met so far. I turned back to him, noting color had returned to his complexion and the muscles of his face had relaxed. He still held onto his glass by the stem with both hands, as though fearing it might try to bolt if he didn't keep a good grip. His gaze appeared to have turned deep inside. He shook himself and looked directly at me.

"M. Blackstone, tell me now what went on at Yvette's."

I pressed my eyes closed and tilted my head back. The panic had given way to a subsequent calm, although M. LeDuc appeared spooked still. "When you were asking Yvette about Adrien, I could tell she didn't have a clue where he was, so I went looking for the bathroom. I accidentally opened the door to a bedroom where two men were busy doing some kind of a deal. Not sure what, but the look on their faces warned me to get the hell out of there."

"Very wise decision."

"Thank you."

"Do you know who that was?"

"No idea."

He glanced around, lowered his head and whispered, "Fabron Gauthier."

The name meant nothing to me, although the effect it had on M. LeDuc was transformative. He hadn't been tall in his chair before, but now he had shrunk to near midget proportions.

"Fabron Gauthier?"

"Shh!"

His paranoia was becoming infectious. I whispered, "Who is Fabron Gauthier?"

"Big drug dealer."

"What?"

"Oui, monsieur. He runs drug business in Languedoc."

"This was the guy at Yvette's party?"

"Oui, monsieur."

"Are you certain?"

"Oui. He is very – how you say – distinctive."

"And you saw him when?"

"Just before we turn the corner to the car."

"Which one was – ah, you said distinctive. White blond hair and eyebrows, pale face, skinny. I saw that much before I ducked out the bedroom door."

LeDuc was nodding enthusiastically.

"But what would Gauthier be doing at a neighborhood party in little Montagnac?"

"No good, you can be sure of that."

I scratched my head. "Damn. Was Adrien involved in drugs? Everyone I spoke to in his family swore he wasn't."

LeDuc just raised his eyebrows, like he might be looking at the most gullible man on Earth. "Yeah, yeah. Who would admit it? Who would *want* to admit it?"

We both took a drink of our wine.

"So what was that red stuff Yvette was serving there at her place?"

"We don't want to know."

"Yeah, you're probably right." I looked at my watch. "Yowza."

"Monsieur?"

"Oh, sorry. I just didn't realize it had gotten so late. I should be going." I tipped the last of the wine into my mouth, wistfully savoring its richness, before placing the empty glass on the table.

"Where will you go?"

"I have a room at the Grand Moliere Hotel, just across the plaza there."

He shook his head. "You should not stay in the hotel. My flat is a short distance from here. I have an extra room."

"Are you certain?"

"Oui."

I considered his words. My mind wasn't working all that well, due to lack of sleep, abundance of wine, and fear, but I made a decision anyway, hoping it was a good one. "You're probably right. But I need to get my things."

"Be careful, monsieur. Go quickly. I will wait here."

"Yeah." I squared the tab with the waiter, took a glance over my shoulder at Gilles, and stepped out into a night that had grown darker than any night ever before it.

Chapter 14

Outside, the streets appeared innocent, but snow can cover a multitude of dangers. My senses were on high alert, even after three glasses of wine. There's nothing like fear to keep oneself sober. Europeans tend to stay out later than we do in Carlton, but Pezenas on that winter night had shuttered its doors. A few lights burned in nearby windows but otherwise the town had an abandoned feel. It was with sadness that I contemplated leaving Le Grand Moliere, if for no other reason than its name. And it had such a royal mien. Now, passing through the lobby, the same clerk I thought had smirked when I walked by earlier was on duty at the desk. His expression looked exactly the same, so apparently he wore an eternal look of disdain.

We took care of the business end of things before I hustled up to my room, keeping watch on my surroundings. I checked to be sure that my door had remained locked and unmolested. It had. Inside, the room had not been ransacked. It seemed that my imagination had run away with itself yet again. Nonetheless, knowing that M. LeDuc was waiting at Le Vintage Bar to take me to his flat, I rapidly tossed in the few clothes that had escaped my suitcase during my short stay, gathered up the papers I'd been poring over earlier, and scouted around one last time for anything I might have forgotten. Then, my hypervigilant side kicked into gear and I stepped over to the window. Peering out onto the plaza below, I noticed two figures milling around in the snow. From my perspective above, it was difficult to determine their heights. And both appeared bundled up, so Gauthier's distinctive white blond hair was not in evidence. Still, could it be the men from the party? Certainly not. I backed away, slowly.

Down in the lobby, the clerk had become engrossed in some computer work. I caught his attention from the safety of the staircase. I'm sure he thought me mad, but then I'm sure he'd already reached that conclusion from my behavior of the other night. Reluctantly, he crept over. Somehow I managed to convey my interest in a back door. He let me know that the hotel didn't have a back door but it did have a side door. Not quite as good, but it would have to do. I pressed a five-euro note into the clerk's palm and slipped away down the short hall in the direction he had indicated.

Shadows engulfed the doorway, which spilled out onto an enclosed patio shielded by bushes of some ilk. I took a step outside and the snow crunched beneath my feet. I cringed. "Shit." Risking a peek around the side of the Moliere toward the center of the plaza, I cursed again, under my breath. The two figures had not moved. They couldn't be Gauthier and his sidekick. How was that possible? Come on, the splashy Ferrari was nowhere in sight. I wasn't even sure they had seen us speed off in the sexy sport car so how could he know what to look for? Maybe he identified the car by its engine sound? More likely he had eyes on the streets everywhere. But, if he'd followed LeDuc and me here, he must have super powers. Still, no reason to take unnecessary chances.

Across the plaza, I could see Le Vintage Bar. Problem now was just how to get there. I backed away from the corner of the building and explored the patio for another exit. About a hundred feet along, it opened onto a parallel street behind the hotel, a very dark street but deserted. Logic told me that following it to the left would eventually lead me around to the bar, or at least the bar's backside. I struck out, hopeful that Le Vintage Bar, unlike Le Grand Moliere, had a back door.

Within five minutes, I was setting my suitcase and shoulder bag on the chair next to Gilles LeDuc and heaving a sigh of relief. Bringing him up to date on the latest news, he did not appear pleased, although he did not appear nearly as ruffled as I might have expected. Giving him the credit he's due, the little Frenchman had some very sneaky ways about him and, before long, we found ourselves in a cozy apartment on the fourth floor of a restored building the equivalent of about eight blocks from Le Vintage. Neat, like its inhabitant, and small, it nonetheless had everything one needed, and the added benefit of Old World character.

LeDuc had offered a spare room, and indeed he had one, albeit my master closet at home was double the size. Beggars can't be choosers, though. Now I don't mean to sound ungrateful, but how had things gone downhill so fast? This morning, I was a carefree American PI taking a look around for an AWOL winemaker. In my experience, winemakers aren't usually huge troublemakers. And then I went to a party in a cherry red Ferrari. Bam! Now I'm hiding in a fourth floor walkup with my means of transportation threatening to be a drab green Saab that looks as though its owner bought it in 1974. Tonight, I can touch the four walls of my room from my perch on the single bed, where this morning I arose from a European queen sized bed in a hotel named Le Grand Moliere. Worst of all, men with evil intent are on the lookout for me, and I don't even know why. Or how to tell them, "I saw nothing. Nothing!"

After I deposited my bags in the tiny room, M. LeDuc suggested we retire for the night. Perhaps the situation would appear clearer in the morning. I agreed, but first I needed to call Lauren. A few minutes past one a.m. made it shortly after four p.m. on the West Coast.

Lauren wasn't home yet, but she answered her cell phone, like always. That's almost a given, considering she's the *Community Press* crime reporter in Carlton. "Hi! I've been wondering what happened. How was Yvette's party?" Ms. Nose-For-News was positively rubbing her hands together in anticipation. A natural-born journalist.

"Exciting!"

"Yeah?"

"Yeah. But you pegged it: no Adrien." I figured she didn't need to hear about Fabron Gauthier and his henchman. They were, after all, irrelevant to my case. At least, I hoped so. And the details of the after-party hours would only cause her needless worry. That's what I told myself, and prayed that she never found out what happened. She tends to get irritable about things like that, especially when omitted. I smoothly changed the subject.

"So how are Jiggs and Irene?"

"Fine."

"More important, how are you, dollface?"

"Fine."

Fine. I got the distinct impression that I should have asked about her before asking about the dog and the bird. Well, there was no fixing it now.

"Any more messages from Deputy Hansen?"

"Actually, yes and no. I am, right this minute, investigating a story about a car that was reported abandoned two days ago. I mean, someone reported it two days ago, but it's been here longer. It appears to be Cassandra York's."

That sounded ominous. Even for Cassandra, that was more drama than she would normally infuse into a situation. I sat on the mattress and leaned against the wall.

"Where are you?"

"Out at the end of a remote road called Carpenter Creek, sort of off of Stringtown Road. You know, around Dilley."

Yeah, I knew the area, and I also knew that Cassandra would pass by Dilley whenever she traveled from her office in Forest Grove to, well, most parts south on Highway 47, parts like Carlton and McMinnville. But I could think of no reason for her to detour onto a rural road, and certainly no reason to abandon her car at the end of it, even to make Rollie suffer, although that ramped up the fun factor for her somewhat.

"What does the car look like?" I was curious about its position on/off the road, locked/unlocked, dented, dusty, clean, messy – God forbid, bloody.

Lauren described Cassandra's silver Mini Cooper as parked, pulled onto what little shoulder existed on Carpenter Creek Road, unlocked, empty and clean. Its location and positioning would explain why it hadn't been reported as suspicious earlier. But was it suspicious? Yes, I certainly thought so, although there was little I could do about it from Europe. I rubbed my eyes. The day – especially the evening – was catching up with me.

"I'm sorry, Cade. This doesn't look good. The police are combing the brush and woods around here."

Of course, I knew what that meant. They were looking for Cassandra, sure, or anything to do with her, but they didn't expect to find her alive. Cassandra had been a thorn in my side but I didn't want her gone, at least not like that. Grudgingly, I admitted to myself that our competition as private investigators had been rather exhilarating over the past year or so. Not especially enjoyable, but mutually, shall we say, helpful, at least in that it pushed us to constantly strive to be better. I generally wanted nothing more, businesswise, day in and day out, than to prove myself a far more competent PI than the tall redhead. Besides, she had sources and resources that could benefit me, and often did. Plus my last big case had come from her.

Sighing, I said, "Yeah, I'm sorry, too. Maybe it will turn out okay." But I didn't really believe that. "Anyway, doll, would you keep me up to date on the investigation? And maybe Jim Smith can help."

Lauren, as mentioned before, doesn't especially like Jim, but she does realize that he can get things done that others can't. And she sort of has to give him some sort of special credit. He saved my life last year as I was wrapping up that big case Cassandra had thrown my way.

"Okay. I'll fill him in on what I've found out."

"Thanks." It took a lot for her to volunteer that. "Well, I'm knackered, as the Brits say. Night, doll." I made a loud show of lip smacking, my signature good-bye when touching was out of the question, then put the phone down and fell asleep, light still on, in my clothes.

Chapter 15

Waking, I noted dim light filtering in through a small window. I rubbed my eyes, disoriented for a moment before remembering the late night transfer from Le Grand Moliere to Gilles LeDuc's guest room. The French detective must have arisen early for I could hear muffled movements in another part of the flat. After putting on a clean set of clothes, I joined him in the kitchen. Fresh coffee and an assortment of rolls rested on the dollhouse-sized dining table. The coffee was strong and the breads different from any of those I'd encountered on the trip so far. It was going to be tough reverting to my normal bland breakfast of plain oatmeal when this case ended.

LeDuc had dressed in slacks and a vest, and sat looking relaxed, reading what appeared to be a local newspaper. He looked up as I approached.

"Ah, good morning, M. Blackstone."

"Good morning. Hey, I really appreciate your hospitality."

The little fellow actually blushed. "Of course." He motioned toward a chair.

Outside the kitchen window, a light snow continued to fall, batting against the panes in the wind. About an inch and a half had managed to stick on the sill. Beyond, a view of old Pezenas looked like a wall painting. Being on the fourth floor had its advantages.

My host cleared his throat, snapping me back inside his cozy kitchen. "I have business to take care of this morning. Just maybe two hours. Then I will return."

"Certainly."

"The two men in the plaza, monsieur," he began.

"Yeah, Gilles, see, I don't know." The light of morning and a good sleep had me doubting any real danger had existed at all. "Maybe it was just a pair of lovers taking a late walk in the snow. I can't swear they were both men, even. I saw two people and jumped to conclusions, I guess."

"Can't be too careful, as you Americans say." He smiled.

"Uh-huh. Speaking of that, I hate to ask another favor, but –" LeDuc held up a hand to stave off my impending apology. I ticked off a variety of items I needed, writing as I enumerated them. He looked at the list then up at me, eyebrows raised.

"It's time to change my appearance, just in case."

"Ah, just in case."

I handed him a 50-euro note and thanked him again. He shrugged.

- - -

While LeDuc took care of his business and some of mine, I unpacked the Hatif file and carried it out to the tiny dining table. I figured I'd use the time reviewing the few items at my fingertips to see if there were any clues that might lead me in a direction pointing toward the truant winemaker. And there it was: The Arrogant Frog Winery. That overlooked piece of mail from Adrien's apartment. Of course, I couldn't actually read it, but it reminded me that I had so far neglected to check out their place of business and what connection it had to the object of my search. Yvette's party and the local drug mafia had kept me preoccupied recently. And before that, there was the Chat Cachemire winery ghost that had been the cause of my hand injury, mucking up my plans for dropping by The Arrogant Frog, and then the discovery of the bum's body. Beyond that, I'd been chasing my own tail. So now, as soon as Cade Blackstone could become a bottle blonde and a drugstore myopic, with some reasonably stylish new (fake) glasses, I hoped I could persuade Gilles to drive us out to the Frog in his Saab.

Since the plans for the rest of the day were taken care of, I located the television remote and found a station that was broadcasting news. The talking heads were still updating viewers on the Amsterdam airport crash, assuring would-be flyers there were no terrorists behind it, simply a bad pilot. The aftermath of the Charlie Hebdo shootings had faded and much of Paris and its surrounds had returned to normal. At least, on the surface. Most of the stories were humdrum. The worst news came from the weather girl. I couldn't understand what she was saying, but she showed a graphic of the entire European continent. The storm currently dumping its load of snow on Pezenas was centered right over us, yes, but extended as far north as Munich and as far south as Seville. In other words, one big mama of a system. And when the meteorologist put the map in motion, the clouds swirled pretty much in place. So the simple implication: this storm wasn't going anywhere anytime soon. I clicked the TV off. That dismal ten minutes of viewing reminded me why I watch old movies almost exclusively. Or read.

Next, I placed a call to Jim Smith to get his take on the Cassandra York disappearance. It's often easier to catch him in the wee hours of the morning than later, like around dawn, when he sleeps. If he's keeping hours at all. Mostly, though, he doesn't stick to a regular schedule.

The canny old fox, he had been following the York case closely, despite it not yet being an official case. Apparently, this sort of thing fell under a subject much more to his liking than, say, babysitting Harlequin macaws with a penchant for creating songs. He volunteered to make some discreet inquiries and keep me apprised of the latest findings. If anything important should come up, Smith said he would deal with it. I had no doubt.

About an hour after ending my conversation with Smith, Gilles LeDuc unlocked his door and hobbled into his flat, toting a bag containing all of the items on my shopping list, plus a few extras. Evidently, he's a man who thinks outside the box, and very cleverly, too. There were some excellent ideas in that bag. Like a paste-on mustache. I'd never worn one, but it sounded like a dashing sort of facial feature. Also a woman's eyebrow pencil, I assumed for the application of a mole or similar kind of beauty mark.

Another hour elapsed and my hair had lightened several shades to a dark blonde and I had changed to a brown-eyed guy wearing funky round glasses. Of course, in this weather, a hat would be needed, so the whole dyeing affair might have been a waste of time and money, but it was fun if nothing else, although the mustache tickled my lip. That was going to take some getting used to.

I outlined my plan for the trip to Arrogant Frog. LeDuc was up for it, as seemed to be his pattern. He was turning out to be a most agreeable man.

"I will bring the car to the door."

It took him ten minutes to retrieve the old Saab from the car park, since the Ferrari still occupied his petite garage, and then another ten to warm up the inside of the car enough to make it drivable. The town streets had accumulated nearly an inch of snow since the last clearing, which doesn't sound like much but, on cobblestoned lanes just wide enough for a car and a donkey to pass each other, travel can prove more than thrilling.

People whizzed by us as though Godzilla were gnashing at their bumpers, while LeDuc picked his way along the roads with the care of a bridesmaid crossing a stream on moss-covered stepping stones. I thought there must be a happy medium but didn't mention it. Arrogant Frog was a fifteen-minute drive from LeDuc's apartment, but it took us twenty-five to get there with the cautious LeDuc behind the wheel. When we finally passed between the big iron gates, I noted with a large measure of relief that the tasting room was open despite the atmosphere having plunged into the deep freeze.

After five more minutes of Gilles maneuvering the Saab perfectly into a parking space, we hopped out of the car into a brisk wind that felt as though it blew directly off of a glacier. Even so, the omnipresent winery dog greeted us, an aging golden retriever with a raspy bark and bent tail. He herded us toward the door, like maybe we couldn't have found it on our own. Good dog.

A young man named Claude came forward to help us. Gilles handled the translation, although Claude seemed to understand much of my English (but little of my French). My spirits soared when Claude nodded at the mention of Adrien Hatif's name. He went on to speak for a minute or so, giving me further hope. Then, abruptly, LeDuc said, "Merci," and Claude walked away.

"What?"

"M. Hatif is not here."

"Yeah, I figured as much. But what was all that about? You talked for a long time."

"Oui, M. Blackstone. M. Hatif is not here."

"Did he work here? Apply for work here? Does this Claude know anything about him?"

"He knows little. Nothing that will help you."

I can recognize a brush-off when I hear one, and that was definitely a brush-off. What just happened?

The tasting room was small but well appointed. Not one to be easily deterred, I tried a different tack. "Okay. Well, as long as we're here, let's taste some wine."

"Sorry, monsieur, they are closing."

They advertised their hours as 10:00 to 4:30. According to my watch, it was only 1:10. Odd time to close, unless my presence and questions had something to do with that. As I pondered the implications and what my response should be, my phone jingled. Not wanting to share my business now until I had sorted out why LeDuc had turned evasive so suddenly, I stepped outside, pulling my collar up to shield against the wind. The dog came over and leaned on my leg, perhaps thinking to warm it.

The display on my phone showed a European number. Since I knew so few people in the area, I answered with a question in my tone. "Hello?"

"M. Blackstone? Cade Blackstone?"

The caller sounded male and had an accent, French if I wasn't mistaken.

"Yes, this is Cade Blackstone. Who am I speaking with?"

"Adrien Hatif. I found your card in my apartment."

I nearly dropped the phone. Here, finally, was the man I'd come to France looking for, the subject of the brush-off at Arrogant Frog, the reason Gilles LeDuc had grown close-lipped unexpectedly just now; here was Adrien Hatif calling me from out of the blue, just like that.

"Adrien! Wow. I've been searching all over for you."

"Yes? Why?"

"Wait. Where are you? I must see you, talk to you in person.

He hesitated, then said, "I am at home."

"Okay. Great. Can I come over? I mean now? Or, um, we can meet at –" I tried to remember the name of the bistro where Michel had met me but failed. Adrien seemed to want to keep his home off-limits at this point, so when he suggested a café within walking distance of his apartment, I said I'd find it, probably be there in fifteen minutes, assuming I could get M. LeDuc to drive slightly over the speed of a crippled turtle. I was forgetting the rarity of snow in those parts.

It was almost half an hour before I slipped into the café, a dull space that held all the charm of a battered shoebox. LeDuc had graciously suggested he had a need to run a couple of errands while I spoke with Hatif, affording us some privacy. To my relief, Adrien was still waiting for me.

I could hardly believe my eyes. Finally, after my long search, there they were: the dreads, the mile-deep dimples, the brightly colored clothes, the cinnamon skin. This was a guy that would be hard to miss. Someone like Adrien couldn't possibly fade into the background. People could not help but notice him. So where had he been hiding?

He stood and we shook hands. I'm sure my face beamed, like an adoring fan around his favorite rock star. "Glad to meet you, man, finally."

"Um, thank you?" His eyes narrowed. "But why have you looked for me?"

"Oh, yeah. Long story. Uh, it begins with Fou Flamant."

He smiled and cocked his head. "Ah, Fou Flamant. You are American."

I thought that would have been obvious from the very first word out of my mouth, but said anyway, "Yeah. See, the winery hired me to find you since they thought you were coming back after just a couple weeks over here. They really like your work."

The dimples deepened. "Good. Is good."

"Yes, is good. Is definitely good." We both sat and tried to get comfortable with each other. After a short silence, I said, "Pardon me for staring, but I can't believe I've finally found you."

He nodded but still looked perplexed.

"So, um, mind if I ask where you've been?"

He dipped his head slightly and looked up at me from under thick black lashes. "A little town named Passerano."

"Italy?"

"Oui."

"You went to Italy after you had a fight with your brother Rayce at Christmas?"

I think I surprised him with that knowledge. "How did you —"

"I'm a private investigator, Adrien. That's what I do. I investigate. I ask questions. I get answers." The door opened and a middle-aged couple stepped inside, bringing with them a cold burst of air. Adrien shivered. His cape apparently provided color more than warmth. "I have spoken with your family. They have been worried."

"They should not worry."

"Yeah, well, it doesn't work like that." His actions seemed beyond selfish; running off without telling anyone. Out of touch for weeks. No one knowing whether he was dead or alive. However, if I wanted him to cooperate, maybe I should reel in my moralizing. I took a deep breath to steady myself. "Okay. Okay. Why did you go to Italy?"

He closed his eyes and hugged himself. "Eve."

A woman. Of course. I should have guessed. "A woman?"

"Not just a woman. Eve."

"Eve. Uh-huh." I bit my lip. "So what about Chantal?"

He blinked several times. "Chantal?"

"The mother of your child?"

"Ah, oui, Chantal." He shrugged. "We argue. She yells. I cannot live like that."

"And your son? Pierre."

"Is nice boy."

"So you left Chantal and Pierre for Eve."

"Oui." He looked around and lowered his voice, leaning in like he was about to tell me a secret. "You see, Chantal contact me, tell me about Pierre. But when I come here, Chantal say I cannot live with her. She has roommate. So I see Pierre some days, some days not. She want me there; she does not want me there." He frowned. "It is no way to have a family. We argue. I plead.

She won't change her mind. I try. For weeks, I try, but it does not work. So I leave." He threw up his arms in a "What else can I do" gesture.

Begrudgingly, I had to admit that sounded pretty reasonable. A man will only bang his head against the wall so many times. Apparently, Adrien had reached his quota. Questions had mounted up in his absence, though. "So who is Yvette?"

His eyebrows jumped. "Yvette? How do you know Yvette?"

"I went to her party."

"Oh." His face dropped.

"Yeah."

"Yvette is fun girl. But trouble."

"Tell me something I don't know."

"Monsieur?"

"Forget it. So why did you come home?"

"Oh, because the storm comes. We are forced inside, Eve and me. Is good, but Passerano is little town. No ristorante, no cafe, no bar. Too little. And too cold. I hope it's warmer here." He shrugged again. "And I miss Lynette."

I rubbed my eyes. "Oh, bless me, I hate to ask. Who is Lynette?"

"Ah, Lynette." He shook his left hand like it was on fire. "Lynette is woman at another winery. We meet little bit before Christmas. Is very beautiful. Very sexy. Has hair down to here," gesturing low on his back. "Hair to get lost in."

"Hair the color of a gingersnap?"

"Oui! A gingersnap!" Adrien's smile widened and he clapped like a kid at a great joke.

I shook my head. Maybe some men would envy Adrien's cavalier attitude, but it came across as far too shallow for sustained living. I mean, I've sown some wild oats, but I always stuck with one woman at a time. Maybe not for long, but one at a time. And I'm pretty sure any more wild oats will be sown with Lauren from here on out.

Chapter 16

Truth be told, the French do have a different way about them. Still, Adrien Hatif's approach to women embarrassed me and I found myself wanting to apologize to every woman I'd ever taken for granted or viewed as merely a sex object. At least since I graduated from high school. Anything leading up to that might understandably be attributed to puberty and a learning curve. After that, well, some good sense should have gotten mixed in with those hormones.

Cassandra York had attracted me with red hair and breasts, all presenting fully forward and sizable. But she quickly taught me how infinitely more valuable outlook and brains are. And she did that in a negative way. Then Lauren came along and reinforced those ideals, in a positive way. As I've mentioned, Lauren has a nose for truth and a better one for bullshit. She loves the former and abhors the latter. I've quit trying to put anything over on her – well, mostly, with the possible exception of those times when she's better off not knowing the full story, like about that little chase scene with local drug czar Fabron Gauthier at Yvette's party. I mean, that would only have upset her. Now, though, we are more a team. Admittedly, she still frowns at some of my tactics, but personally I think she overdoes it.

Anyway, that's how my relationship with Lauren sits. Adrien's relationships – how can I put this and not sound judgmental? Well, Adrien's relationships with women pretty much go like this: Grab one, play with it, toss it aside and move on. Oh, did that sound judgmental? My bad. However, Jim Smith and Fou Flamant were counting on me to bring Adrien back to Oregon so I needed to shelve my attitude.

One of the documents containing info on this guy said that he had been working at the winery in Carlton for over a year, and his brother Michel concurred with that. We have a pretty small, intimate community back home and, in all that time, I didn't recall seeing him around. Not even at one winemaker's dinner, which is something high on Lauren's and my list of favorite things to do. Outside of the house, that is. As distinctive as he is, I think we'd have noticed him at some point. Perhaps he lived in the larger, neighboring town of McMinnville, did his prowling and carousing over there. Mac has many more nighttime possibilities for a young man with Adrien's appetite for, shall we say, variety.

According to Michel, Adrien had been happy in Carlton. How to convince him, though, to abandon France for the Pacific Northwest once again? What could possibly sway him now? Same thing that sways him at every turn. A woman, of course. I'd found my answer.

"So how's it going with – Lynette, did you say?"

"Lynette, oui. It goes fine. Fine."

Watching his body language told a different story, though. Maybe things with Lynette were cooling. They might be fine now, but in a day or two, not so much. An idea crept into my head. I pulled out my phone and located a picture of Lauren, a close-up, and stuck it under his nose. "Look at that. Huh? Isn't she something?"

His eyes popped. He reached out as though he'd like to touch her.

I clicked the photo off and put the phone on the table. "That's my lady. We've been together for over two years now."

Adrien smiled and winked at me. "Lucky guy."

"Yes, I am. I am a very lucky guy." I puffed my chest out in a sort of bonding gesture, or maybe more like bragging. "Uh, did you have a lady back in the States?"

He nodded, which looked more like he was rocking out to some tune only he could hear. "I did. I had a sweet lady named Elise."

"Pretty name."

"Pretty name for a pretty lady."

Where did he get these lines? I wanted to puke. "Nice. Tell me about Elise."

"Ah, Elise. The very dark hair, the big eyes, the legs…ooh la la, the legs." He laughed and I joined him.

"Is she waiting for you?"

"Maybe. Maybe not."

"Maybe? Good-looking guy like you? Sure, she's waiting. I'd bet on it."

"Ah, I don't know."

"Of course, she's waiting. Why wouldn't she?" I sat closer, as though ready to impart something important. "Hey, why not find out? I mean, what have you got to lose? You liked it there, right? You liked your job? I've already told you it's waiting for you. Elise is surely waiting for you. Surely. But if not, you could win her back easily."

Adrien pursed his lips in thought.

"The weather," I pushed on, checking my phone, "is far warmer than here in Montagnac at 2 degrees Celsius." Smiling in victory, I summarized, "Carlton: Beautiful Elise, revered winemaker at Fou Flamant, 43 degrees. Here: Cold, snowy, Lynette grows distant, no job." He hadn't exactly said that, but I can read between the lines. Besides, go for leverage, as my dad always said. I needed leverage, so I took a wild guess. And, damn, he looked just about convinced when the café door flew open again and Gilles LeDuc burst through it.

The detective looked around furtively, spotted our table in no time and headed our way, glancing over his shoulder several times as he approached. He hastily introduced himself to Adrien and added, "I apologize for my rudeness, but we must go. Is there another door?"

I started to ask why but he began gently pulling on my arm, urging me out of my seat.

"It seems M. Gauthier is in town. He appears to be looking for someone."

At the mention of Gauthier's name, Adrien was on his feet and racing toward the back of the cluttered room, gracefully dodging the few tables in his way. Gilles and I followed, squeezing by the kitchen help. At some point, I managed to slow down long enough to mutter a quick "Merci" and hand the waitress some cash. Later, when I counted, it seemed that my euros had diminished by about 30, quite a lot for two cups of coffee, even if it was French.

Outside on the street, the flakes had grown in size and volume, the wind was relentless and the temperature still plunging. Pulling my collar up and my scarf tighter, I said a silent prayer to whatever higher power had made me bring my hat and gloves.

It was a simple task to catch up with LeDuc, who was struggling in the shallow drifts. Adrien had a half-block advantage on us. It didn't matter; I knew where he lived and figured that to be his destination. We were headed there, too, since we needed a safe, dry place for LeDuc to bring us up to speed on whatever he'd seen. We encountered almost no one on the street, and none of them came close to looking like Gauthier or his henchman from last night.

My brilliant plan of changing my appearance had been a good one, but with one huge, glaring hole. While worrying about myself, I had forgotten about M. LeDuc's appearance. Gilles LeDuc, the man who could have been Danny DeVito's twin. Like he's not distinctive, right?

- - -

Adrien did not seem pleased that the French detective had followed him home, nor the American one. Ask me if I cared. For some reason, a local drug lord named Fabron Gauthier had become overly interested in Cade Blackstone, and I was beginning to doubt that it was because I had inadvertently opened the door to a room at a party and seen – well, what had I seen? As far as I knew, nothing, really. The lighting in that bedroom had been dim, the two men seated in there huddled close together, and whatever was between them appeared to be a blob of – of something. In other words, I had no clue. Anyone would guess it had to do with drugs but it wouldn't take intelligence much above that of an earthworm to come up with that, considering Gauthier's reputation around these parts.

From what I'd learned – and quite easily, too – the man wore his reputation like a crown. He reveled in it, made no secret of the fact that he sold drugs for a living, fairly dared the authorities to do anything about it. Besides, odds are that most of the other guests at Yvette's party were well aware of the goings-on in that back room. Probably most of them dropped in to purchase a little recreational material for themselves even. So why run down Cade Blackstone and his Languedoc counterpart? I could maybe understand the initial chase and their desire to ensure we wouldn't go blabbing once outside of Yvette's place. But after we'd made our escape, why press the point? Most people in Gauthier's position would simply have a good laugh, watching two grown men running like scared little girls, and return to business as usual.

All of these questions had been bouncing around in my head as Gilles and I made our way along the snowy sidewalk behind Adrien Hatif. It made no sense that Gauthier still dogged us, hunted us even. Therefore, it became evident that something else was going on. As my second favorite fictional character, Sherlock Holmes, said, "When you have eliminated the impossible, whatever remains, however improbable, must be the truth." Okay, I hadn't yet eliminated the impossible, but I had made strides toward eliminating several possibilities and had come to the conclusion that Gauthier had a far different reason for pursuing us, one having nothing to do with seeing him in Yvette's bedroom. Thus, once we'd closed the door behind us at his flat, I turned to Adrien.

"So what's going on here?" I don't like to beat around the bush and clearly Gauthier's name had sent Adrien into a panic.

Adrien, though, had no intention of confiding in this American he had just met within the past hour. Couldn't really blame him for that. However, our butts seemed to be hanging out there and I wanted to know why.

"Come on, man, what's going on?"

"There is no time, monsieur. If Fabron Gauthier is around, we should go." As he spoke, he was throwing random clothing into a suitcase he must have just unpacked. When he jammed it shut and headed for the door, Adrien's fear rubbed off on me. But instead of rushing out behind him, I grabbed his arm and gently pulled him back. "Wait, Adrien. Let's keep our cool."

I formulated a plan in my head on the fly. In a low voice, I quickly sketched out my idea for the two of them. "First, let me take a peek out into the hall. If there's no one hanging around, then you go."

My appearance had changed enough, with the new dishwater blond hair, glasses and the paste-on mustache, that Gauthier or his men wouldn't recognize me. And if one of them were lurking in the building, I had a ready excuse for being in Adrien's apartment. I'm really good at bluffing. Or at least, that's what I've led myself to believe. Fortunately, though, we didn't have to put my skills to the test that day. The corridor was vacant.

I herded Gilles and Adrien out and shooed them up the stairs. We spoke in hushed tones as I laid out the rest of my plan, loose though it was. It involved me retrieving Gilles' Saab and then somehow Adrien and Gilles would sneak downstairs and into the car and we would spirit ourselves away to Montpellier where, it being the size it is, we could disappear into the streets of the city. I mean, into cozy hotel rooms.

The plan worked rather well. Gilles had parked the Saab only about three blocks away, so my trip took a short time despite the slippery sidewalks and heightened wind speeds, which also meant few vehicles on the road. When I returned to Adrien's address, I parked on the curb directly in front of the building's door. Captain Blackstone's theory is that, if you look like you know what you're doing, people won't question your right to be there, so that's what I did. Assuming a purposeful stride, I ran inside, took the stairs two at a time, and grabbed my fugitive passengers. We pulled back onto the street a minute and a half after my arrival. No one pulled out after us. At least, not that I could discern.

Chapter 17

Montpellier, a sedate city of over a quarter million people, is sizable enough to get lost in yet small enough to retain its friendly atmosphere. Near its center sits the Hotel Des Arceaux. The Arceaux has that ornate Baroque feel to the outside but, inside, the rooms have all the mod cons, as they say, to make one's stay truly posh, an attribute I place at the top of my hotel must-haves. Plus, the name has the excess of vowels that I love about French words. So, having ascertained how to pronounce it from Gilles, we chose Hotel des Arceaux as our temporary safe headquarters and checked in.

On the downside, the staff did not appear to regard our mode of transportation very highly. Frankly, neither did I. If only we could all fit into the Ferrari, I would retrieve it along with my luggage and briefcase, which was the next task on the to-do list for the afternoon. None of us believed that Fabron Gauthier had figured out Gilles LeDuc's identity, nor his address, so we decided it would be okay for me – being the one he was least likely to recognize, with my new look – to return to Gilles' Pezenas apartment to retrieve some things. There was little I could do without my files and papers, and Gilles craved a change of clothing and a few other personal items. I'd volunteered to be the errand boy.

We secured three rooms next to each other on the top floor of the hotel, which granted us a pleasant view over the streets of Montpellier city center. While my two companions settled themselves in, I bundled up and ventured back out to make the 60-kilometer journey to Pezenas. The storm continued to quietly rage but now with a diminished ferocity and optimistically brighter skies. Once on the open road, I found myself surprised by the Saab's sturdy drivability. Surefooted, it hummed along through the snowy tire tracks as though it didn't need a driver at all, which instilled in me enough confidence to call Lauren and bring her up to date on our change in circumstances. I could probably have texted the entire conversation considering the relative lack of traffic on the highway, but even without other cars, I could still run off the road into a tree. So I instructed Siri to call Lauren. Back home, it was hovering around 1:30 in the morning. Thinking about that, I reconsidered for only a half-second and then went ahead anyway because I knew Lauren would want to hear this latest news. Plus, she wakes up far better than I do. The one difficulty would be getting Irene Adler back to sleep, so I prayed that the bird wouldn't hear the phone. It only jingled a couple of times before my girlfriend answered.

"Hello?" Lauren's voice held remnants of sleep.

"Hi, dollface."

She became instantly awake, probably realizing the reason for calling at the late hour could only be due to something momentous. She was right, of course.

"Hi. What's up, Cade?"

"Uh, it's kind of a long story. You want to brew a pot of coffee or anything?"

"Cade!"

"Okay." I filled her in on the events since we'd last spoken, leaving nothing out, although I might have painted Gauthier as a nicer guy than he really is. When I came to the part about Adrien Hatif calling me, she became as excited as I had been.

"I know! He just fell into my lap."

"So when are you coming home? You are coming home now, right?"

I hesitated, trying to gauge the best way to word my answer. Sadly, Lauren has been adopting a few of my more annoying traits, the most recent one a little thing called impatience.

"Cade, when are you coming home?"

"Well, about that. See, there's this big snow storm and we are kind of stuck here."

She chewed on that for about five seconds before playing the bullshit card on me. Technically, airplanes were flying, but Adrien couldn't leave just yet. Okay, his tether to France had nothing to do with the weather, but I had to try a little sugarcoating. Naturally, she hadn't bought it, so I came totally clean.

"All right. All right. Adrien has a few loose ends to tie up before he can come back with me, and I'm not leaving without him. I'm afraid he might disappear again unless I keep a close eye on him."

"What kind of loose ends?"

I took a deep breath. "He wants to say good-bye to his parents, of course."

"Of course."

"And, well, I'm still trying to convince him he *wants* to come back to Carlton."

"Oh, Cade. Really? That's what you're calling loose ends?"

"Yeah, they're just loose ends. You know how persuasive I can be." I let her mull that around. Come on, she'd have to agree. After all, hadn't I convinced her that I was the sexiest man alive? Well, I thought I had.

"Yeah. Uh, anyway, LeDuc, Adrien and I have moved to a nice hotel in Montpellier while we work out the logistics of how to take care of this."

I figured Lauren would see through my neutralizing terms, and she did.

"You moved? Again?"

"Just so Adrien can make up his mind without distractions."

"You moved because of this fellow Gauthier, didn't you?"

"Well, yeah, partly."

"You're calling him a distraction?"

"Well, yeah. That's all he is."

"Cade, you described Gauthier as a drug lord."

"Uh-huh."

"I'd say drug lords are a little more than a distraction."

"Yeah, sometimes, but remember, this one's French."

Normally, she limits her use of four-letter words, but a record number inserted themselves into our conversation just then, probably due to her growing fear. I assured her that I knew how to take care of myself and would be careful, yada, yada, yada, then asked to talk to Jiggs. If things went like they usually did, he would provide the soothing sounds I needed, most notably because he doesn't swear. Unfortunately, Lauren hung up instead.

A car went around the Saab, reminding me of my mission, which had become more complicated than it should have. Just a few days ago, I had been happily tasting wine with Lauren, blissfully unaware of a storm in my future, one involving unusual amounts of southern French snow and a tenacious local thug. I urged the car forward a few miles faster.

"Okay, let's get this done. Siri, call Lauren Pringle." This time, she wouldn't hang up. Or so I hoped.

It rang for a long time, so long that I feared she would ignore me entirely. My stubborn streak kicked in, though, and while I wanted to tell Lauren all the right things, a bunch of touchy-feely, smarmy platitudes, she was going to have to understand that occasionally PI work doesn't come with easy solutions. There are snags and roadblocks and, now and then, one encounters a highly dangerous person. They exist out there, often in the shadows, waiting for opportunities, and they don't like anyone getting in their way. But, hey, Capt. Harry Blackstone had taught his son a thing or two about how to survive and, if Lauren and I were going to become a long-term item, she would have to learn to handle the rough spots with a bit more grace than she was showing right now. I understood fear, but I needed support.

Merci, mon dieu, she answered. Rather, she put Jiggs on. Well, it *is* what I had requested. I listened to some Shar Pei snores and snorts for a couple of minutes while I supposed Lauren was composing herself.

Finally, Jiggs' nasal sounds faded and I heard a soft, "Hi, Cade."

"Hi, dollface." She actually hates that term of endearment, but it just slips out. "Look, I know you're scared. I get that, but I promise I'll be careful. Besides, I'm not alone. You didn't get the chance to meet Gilles, but he came well recommended." That was a bit of a stretch, since I actually knew very little about Ian, who had given me Gilles' name, except that he liked to drink at Le Vintage Bar and he told some good jokes. But he was a retired British bobby, so maybe that counted for something. "And he looks like Danny DeVito."

"What?"

"Yeah. He really does. Hey, DeVito played some tough guys, right? Seems I remember him playing a tough guy at least once."

"Hm."

"Well, anyway, he's got a hell of a mouth on him."

"Good, I guess. I love you. Stay safe."

"I promise. You, too. Go back to sleep now."

"Right." Just before she severed the connection, I thought I heard a Harlequin macaw starting up a song in the background. But it was hard to tell because there was a honk behind me as a bright yellow Renault sped around me in a swirl of snow dust. Traffic had picked up.

- - -

Rounding the last curve to my destination, a sigh escaped me. If it were even possible, the village of Pezenas looked more breathtaking in snow. With just the right balance of trees to buildings, curves to angles, brick to stone, it ticked off all the boxes as far as aesthetics, and now it was covered in a soft white meringue. I found on-street parking, although I'm not sure it was legal but no one was around to object.

Outside of LeDuc's apartment building, I noticed several footprints that appeared to belong to someone with clown-sized feet who had circled aimlessly for some time. It gave me pause, briefly, but then people do walk without purpose. Quite often, in fact. I used the key Gilles had given me and slipped inside. No telltale snow melt in the foyer, which was a good sign. I stood and listened for a few seconds, allowing myself a chance to adjust to the sounds of the building. All came across as normal. Nothing felt off about the noises emanating from behind closed doors. In other words, I didn't hear someone moving about stealthily, edging along a wall, ready to jump out and whack an American PI.

On the fourth floor (LeDuc's floor), same thing. No feeling of imminent threat. I stowed my paranoia away with my hat. That entire level was quiet, save for one of Gilles' neighbors who must have had a dog, for I heard muffled barking from down the hall. Rhodesian ridgeback, if I'm not mistaken. (Just kidding. I can't tell. Ask Sherlock Holmes, though. He'll know.)

LeDuc's door was still locked and seemingly undisturbed. Inside, my papers appeared to be precisely where I had left them on the kitchen table. I gathered them up then went into Gilles' bedroom to collect the items he'd requested. As I crossed the threshold, the hairs on the nape of my neck tingled, and I felt them stand up. A chill went down my spine but quickly passed. Had someone walked by out on the street searching for us? Or, worse, out in the hallway? Was there something in LeDuc's apartment that was dangerous? Had I missed some sign? Or was I merely shivering because of the temperature? Since the sensation was so fleeting, I had no time to puzzle out its meaning. It did hurry me up, though, and I was packed and ready to leave before another five minutes had passed. I also applied extra caution to my departure.

Tiptoeing through the foyer, eyes darting side to side, I was momentarily startled by a movement before realizing that it was an image of myself in an ornately framed mirror. The dark blond hair and moustache were still unfamiliar to me, along with the funky glasses. I barely recognized myself, and that gave me another idea.

On the return trip to Montpellier, I made a couple of unscheduled stops, one to a shop advertising what appeared to be consignment clothing. They offered a wonderful selection of old hats, scarves, costume jewelry, vintage shoes, and all manner of modern wear, too. I found several articles of clothing that would do nicely, although the clerk eyed me as though I had recently escaped an asylum for the insane.

But, see, it had occurred to me that my companions could use a change of appearance since it seemed to be helping me get around without notice. And reading Sherlock Holmes had taught me ingenious ways of accomplishing some pretty radical transformations. Gilles LeDuc would be an easy fix, relatively speaking. Adrien Hatif, however, would be nearly impossible to successfully disguise. The massive dreads alone presented a nearly insurmountable problem, unless he could be coerced into shaving his head, and I didn't want to even imagine the reaction I'd get to that suggestion. So Adrien would be mostly grounded and confined to his hotel room. Served him right for getting us all into this mess, as I was positive the blame lay with him. The specifics had yet to be ferreted out.

The second stop required a store with a bit more variety, something along the lines of a department store. There actually are such places in the south of France, although they are tougher to come by than in, say, most of suburban America. While I didn't see a Wal-Mart as I drove along – thank God – I happened upon a tiny version of a Target, which would have to do. I found everything I had in mind, and a little more, including the French version of Cheetos, a snack I'd been craving since the snow started to fly. Not sure why snow does that to me; maybe it's the shocking contrast in color. Whatever the reason, it nicely rounded out my afternoon's purchases.

Finally back at the hotel, I unloaded my packages, files and bags in my room then went to share my ideas with the other guys. Naturally, Gilles wasn't as happy with my stroke of genius as I was, but really, it was brilliant. I'd decided that he should spend a few days as Mother Blackstone, accompanying her son on a quiet trip around Europe, just the two of them. He rolled his eyes and shook his head but, eventually, my winning ways convinced him to give it a try. Or maybe he just wanted to see how crazy his new American friend really was. Either way, I got busy with my pallet of taupe foundation, light brown eye shadow and pale coral lipstick. I topped the look with a chic silver wig. Then the final touch: round wire-rim glasses. After all, Mother Blackstone's son wore spectacles, so she should as well.

Adrien watched all of this with a twinkle of glee in his eyes. I believe he was secretly pleased that he stood no chance of becoming my next victim. There, he was wrong. I had picked up a couple of blocky gray jackets and some blue jeans that I figured would fit the dreadlocked Frenchman, and a shapeless heather-toned sweater. His flamboyant days were over, at least for a while. As for the dreads, he could wrap a cloth around them like a turban, striving for the loose appearance of an Arab businessman. Keeping Adrien locked inside his hotel room didn't sound the least bit plausible. The guy didn't strike me as one to follow orders real well, so this was my best effort at taming his conspicuousness.

Finally, the *piece de resistance*: Mother Blackstone's going-out clothes. It took a lot of cajoling to get Gilles to put on the long wool skirt I'd purchased, despite it hitting right at his ankles, saving him the indignity of needing nylon hosiery, but in the end he agreed. Plus, the sensible shoes complimented it beautifully. Even he had to admit the English blazer finished the ensemble nicely, although he didn't gush about it. He really looked like a sweet, and somewhat modern, British grandmother. (Thinking back, I realize that might be why he objected so strenuously.)

Around eight o'clock, we left Adrien behind with stern instructions to stay put, and ventured out to a restaurant recommended by the hotel concierge located just a block and a half away. Gilles didn't trust his new shoes to carry him far, especially in the stormy weather. But by then, the snow was crisp and crunchy and had virtually stopped falling. The wind had died, too. It felt good to walk, even that short distance, particularly considering the alternative was the green Saab. I'd had enough of disapproving looks by then.

I hooked my arm through Gilles' to make the mother/son thing appear more authentic. He resisted at first, pulling back, then gave in, even got into character. But when he patted my cheek and said, "Such a good boy," I thought he'd taken it a bit too far.

The best part about the whole outfit is that it worked. Neither the *maitre'd* at dinner nor the waiter gave him a second glimpse. No raised eyebrows, nor frowns. In fact, the Saab got more attention every day than Gilles did that evening. I tipped my hat and gave a little bow for a job well done, figuratively speaking. Now all we had to do was pull it off during daylight hours, but I didn't think that would be a problem. In fact, I didn't think we'd be getting close enough to Fabron Gauthier for that to be an issue. I believed he had no idea that we had skipped out to Montpellier. And, besides, who pays attention to a short, middle-aged woman accompanying her 30-something son?

Meanwhile, another thought had been taking shape. Over the past few days and hours since Yvette's party, but really on the drive back from Pezenas that afternoon, I'd begun to suspect this: Gauthier wasn't looking for LeDuc nor me at all. He never had been. The two figures I'd seen outside the Grand Hotel Moliere in Pezenas after the party were just that: two figures. I'd embellished them in my own head to the point that they had grown into ape-sized henchmen out after my blood. In reality, it seemed more likely that it was a pair of lovers enjoying a nighttime stroll in the snow. Snow *is* romantic, after all. Also, my adrenaline had been racing and then I'd mixed it with some expensive and very tasty wine, which led me to several highly erroneous conclusions. All the while, Gauthier was likely back at Yvette's party having a hell of a good time, giving us no thought whatsoever.

So why were we hiding out in Montpellier now? Not because Gauthier had seen Gilles LeDuc in the streets of Montagnac while I was introducing myself to Adrien at that little café. No, my guess was that Adrien's apartment had been under surveillance since he fled Montagnac for Passerano with Eve. Because that's what I figured was closer to the truth. Adrien's trip to Italy hadn't been romantic as much as it had been fleeing for his life. That was my bet. In the meantime, Gauthier had sent men to watch out for Adrien after it seemed apparent he'd run off. The watchers hadn't noticed me when I'd gone in because they were only watching the building for Adrien. There was no one inside to see if anyone actually entered Adrien's apartment. So it was only when Adrien came home that Gauthier got excited.

We were very lucky we had suspected something like that and left his flat so quickly after the three of us had taken refuge there from the cafe. And I figured my business card had saved his butt earlier, for he had only just got home when he called me and agreed to meet at the café for coffee. He'd left again almost immediately, so Gauthier's men hadn't had a chance to swoop in on him. We didn't want to test our luck any further, though.

Now, over dinner, with these thoughts bouncing around in my head, a piece of my conscience started to poke at me. I wanted to enjoy Mother Blackstone for a while longer, but it wouldn't really be fair to have LeDuc thinking he needed to continue dressing that way. Also, I knew from experience that makeup and wigs are uncomfortable. So I shared my epiphany with him.

He popped the final bite of his truffled sole into his mouth, dabbed at the corners of his lips and said, "Good." I'm not sure, but I think he was talking about my comment, not the food, although the entire meal had been as tasty as the concierge had said it would be.

By the time dessert had been set down in front of us, we'd both decided we needed to tackle the subject with Adrien.

Chapter 18

"What you say, monsieur, it's genius. Of course, M. Gauthier does not look for us. He would not be so angry over a tiny peek at a back-room drug deal in some unimportant little party. That is absurd. He follows us to find Adrien."

"Precisely," I said, spooning a luxurious bite of silky ice cream into my mouth. "It's not like I was exactly low-profile in my inquiries about Adrien. So the way I see it, when Gauthier saw me at Yvette's, he couldn't believe his luck, so he and his ape chased after my butt in hopes I'd lead them to Hatif."

The French detective rubbed his chin. "But why does this big drug lord, as you Americans say, have such an interest in Adrien Hatif?"

I winced. "Yeah, that's the $64,000 question. I hope it doesn't have the obvious answer."

"Ah, oui."

We sat and pondered in silence for a few moments, enjoying the last of our meal before sussing out the details of the necessary confrontation with Adrien back at the Hotel des Arceaux. I felt foolish for not having seen the truth of the matter earlier. At least, Gilles hadn't beaten me to that conclusion. Looking at him now, it was obvious he hadn't beaten me to the conclusion that his new persona as Mother Blackstone was entirely nonessential either. (Not that I had ever seriously thought that it might play a crucial role in our survival. I just really love the whole science of disguises.)

Our waiter brought out a to-go bag of the lamb stew we had ordered for Adrien, and the bill. We settled the tab and stood to leave. More people had begun trickling into the restaurant by that time, and I noted with smug satisfaction that no one paid the slightest attention to the two of us, which reinforced confidence in my continued ability to work magic with make-up and wigs.

The stroll back to the hotel took longer than the trip to the restaurant had, probably due to our reluctance to bust Adrien's lies wide open, although Gilles's lack of competence with his shoes may have played into it, too. We rode up the elevator in silence. When the car stopped at our floor, a man rushed inside before we could get out, making it awkward for the two of us to negotiate around him in the cramped space. Gilles mumbled something that sounded grumpy. I just glared at the man over my shoulder as we extricated ourselves.

I thought about suggesting that Gilles change into something more comfortable, but decided to just forge ahead and get the conversation with Adrien over and done with. M. LeDuc stood to my left as I knocked on Adrien's door.

"Adrien! Hallo, Adrien, it's Cade. We are back." Sounded friendly enough, right? My upbeat tone shouldn't clue him into any impending pissed-off state I might be working up to. Well, I didn't think so, but then he didn't answer.

"Hey, M. Winemaker, come on. Open up. We brought you something."

Gilles looked at me with a dubious expression.

"I thought maybe it would lure him out." Hearing nothing from inside Adrien's room, I knocked again, with more force, force possibly borne of a newfound panic. Why had we left him alone, especially since we were familiar with his penchant for running off? I know, we'd told him to stay put, but this guy wasn't exactly good at obeying commands. So he'd probably decided not to hang tight in his room. Then a more ominous thought occurred to me: Had he run off again, or had someone snatched him? Or was the silence inside the room an indicator of something far worse? My mind flashed back to the man in a hurry to get into the elevator. The pleasant buzz from the dinner wine wore off almost immediately.

"The guy in the elevator!"

Gilles's eyes grew huge. I readied myself to kick in Adrien's door, but LeDuc grabbed my arm. "Wait, monsieur. I will get the key from downstairs." His short legs carried him off toward the elevator at a remarkable pace, cane clicking alongside. Having no other good choices, I pulled out my cell phone and scrolled through recent calls, finally locating the one from Adrien. I hit "Call Back" but it went to voice mail without ringing even once.

"Damn."

I knocked on Adrien's door again and pressed my ear to the smooth wood of the panels, straining to hear any sign of life inside. A family of four walked by, giving me a strange look as they passed. I smiled back, silently cursing Hatif under my breath. I hate looking like an idiot, and this guy had made me look like one more than once, all in under a day. If he wasn't dead in there, I might kill him myself.

In less than five minutes, Gilles returned, swinging a silver key from a leather loop in his left hand. No plastic key cards for the Arceaux. Classy.

"How did you do that? And so quickly?"

"I have some tricks, monsieur."

"I guess so."

He bent slightly to insert the key into the lock and twist it. As he straightened up, we heard, "Arrete ca!" (*Stop that!*) from behind us.

I jumped and we both whirled around to see Adrien striding toward us wearing a big grin on his face, dimples deeper than ever, arms spread wide.

Before saying something I might regret, I stood biting my lip and did the proverbial count to ten. Yet my voice still quivered with anger. "I thought you were going to stay in the room."

"I got hungry."

"We told you we would bring you something to eat." I held up the bag containing lamb stew as proof of my statement.

He shrugged, his endlessly annoying answer to all uncomfortable questions.

"Adrien, we are trying to keep you safe. Don't you understand that?"

That shrug again. And he looked at his shoes, as his brother had done, and his uncle. Another Hatif gesture of avoidance.

Gilles pushed the door inward. "Let us get out of the hallway, shall we?"

He nudged Adrien forward and I followed them both into the room. Two of us sat in the chintz side chairs, while Adrien perched on his bed. I dropped the bag of food on the floor next to me. If he wanted it later, fine. I didn't care whether he ate it or not. This gig was turning out to be as bad as babysitting some spoiled, rich brat.

We sat, not speaking, while I regained my good temper, which had taken a trip of its own. Being stalked by guys with violent reputations in a foreign country will do that to me. I don't know how Gilles kept his cool except that maybe this case didn't mean as much to him. He was just the second string, after all.

I took several deep breaths and ran my hands through my newly dyed hair, which sent me into a new bout of pique. Why had I gone to such lengths? Changing hair color, pasting on a false mustache, bothering with fake glasses. This kid clearly had no clue how much danger he'd created for himself. He just merrily went about his life as usual, callously ignoring his own security.

"Okay. Adrien," I spoke slowly, to help him understand and to help me avoid flying into a rage. "This is come-to-Jesus time."

"Pardon?"

"We need to talk. Fabron Gauthier is not the kind of man you want to be on the bad side of. However, for some funny reason, you are. Tell us why."

Adrien apparently wanted to play dumb, though, so we danced for a while until he understood that his game wasn't getting any play. After a few minutes, his shoulders slumped and he rubbed a hand down his face, neutralizing those dimples and lightening his skin a full shade. A genuine look of worry finally appeared in his eyes.

"I may have done something stupid."

LeDuc groaned, and we both let out the breaths we'd been holding.

"What stupid thing might you have done?" I didn't want to hear whatever he had to say but, if we were going to get Gauthier off our trail, we needed to be able to come up with a good strategy and, for that, all of the facts and the ugly truth would be key ingredients.

And the truth was ugly indeed, although not a particularly unique truth. Adrien Hatif had gotten himself in deep with Gauthier. It had begun as recreational drug use, a little cocaine, just for his own amusement. Soon, he started sharing with a close friend or two. Then he discovered the, shall we say, interesting effects on his libido. Being a man who appreciated a healthy libido, that attribute by itself kept Adrien going back for more, and then more. Not long ago, he realized that he had run up quite a balance with the man, who now had a nonmonetary suggestion for paying off his debt. Bottom line, Adrien simply couldn't clear himself with Gauthier. So he'd taken the coward's way out and fled.

Gilles and I made a couple leaps of logic from what Adrien had said: While Gauthier was steaming about his chicken flying the coop, rumors had likely started up about one dark-haired American detective with a Cajun accent also searching for Adrien Hatif. Then some info had gotten back to him that this selfsame PI had allied himself with a local private eye looking like the movie actor Danny DeVito. And the duo had then dropped into Gauthier's lap at a party given by one of Hatif's friends.

"Yvette is some friend," I said, maybe a touch snidely.

"Yvette is no friend."

"Yeah, I was catching onto that."

"Why did you go to her party, monsieur?"

I wouldn't have blamed him had he said *that* a touch snidely. After all, it wasn't my name on Yvette's invitation. At the time, it had felt like a good lead. Really my only lead. Trying to explain that became complicated, though, and it didn't exactly clear anything up.

Fortunately, LeDuc decided to play arbitrator. "Pointing fingers now does no one any good. We must make a plan where to go from here."

Adrien and I nodded, for once on the same page.

A disturbing thought occurred to me. "Does Gauthier know about Chantal and Pierre?"

Adrien shook his head, eyes downcast. "No."

"Are you sure?"

"Oui." He raised his head and looked at me straight. I studied his face for signs of deception, which I had come to recognize in him even over the short duration of our acquaintance. There was none.

"Okay. Tell me how you know." He had to be positive. Otherwise, his child and his child's mother could be in jeopardy.

"Yvette."

"Yvette?"

"Oui."

"I thought you said Yvette is no friend."

"Oui. Yvette introduced me to Fabron Gauthier. He is her friend."

"Ah. So you became involved with Yvette. Yvette wanted to enhance your sexual experience with drugs, so she introduced you to Gauthier. He was happy to help out, and you started an account with him."

"Oui." He had argued with Chantal, as he'd said earlier, about not being able to be around for Pierre because of Chantal's roommate. He sought solace in the arms of Yvette. Once he'd hooked up with her, he never visited Chantal and Pierre again, nor did he mention them. Whether that was brilliant or selfish, it was fortunate. Neither Yvette nor Gauthier had any idea of their existence nor of their importance to Adrien. At least, we did not have to worry about those two innocent souls being in harm's way. Or so we believed.

Chapter 19

By the time Gilles and I left him, Adrien had already opened the bag of food and started eating. Didn't he say he'd gone out because he wanted something to eat? If true, that must be a constant state for him. Whatever, we needed to plan a strategy, and soon, but my brain had quit working. I suggested we start fresh in the morning. I took a small amount of comfort in Adrien's assurances that his halcyon days of cocaine bliss were over. In fact, according to him, the getaway to Passerano had been more about cleaning up than about the beautiful Eve. When pushed, he admitted that she served as his sobering coach instead of his lover. Fortunately, for him, he had a constitution that didn't easily form addictions, so he had been able to enjoy his fun on occasion with less in the way of the ensuing cravings. But fewer cravings didn't mean they were nonexistent and, although he swore Eve had gotten him off of the stuff entirely, I had trouble trusting his word. Drugs can be tricky, and their hold on a person unpredictable. I know; I'd watched a friend go through hell.

Back in my own room, I called Jim Smith to fill him in on the latest developments. As one might guess, he was less than pleased about Adrien's confession and the pickle it left him in. Me, too, Jim. Even though I had found the winemaker, during his lost months he'd become a (hopefully recovering) addict with a huge IOU outstanding to the local drug cartel. That was sort of a big problem.

All I'd come up with as a solution was, if Fou Flamant still wanted him back, maybe they ought to think about advancing a large sum of money, like a major chunk of his upcoming salary – with heavy strings attached – and then we could try negotiating with Fabron Gauthier. That could turn out to be tricky, though, because drug dealers aren't generally fond of the give-and-take idea. Well, we'd cross that bridge when we came to it. First, we had to get the money. Smith promised he'd have an answer by the end of his day, whenever that might turn out to be.

Next, we talked about the Cassandra York issue. He didn't have any news on that subject. Still missing. His sources had informed him that her car was wiped clean. Nothing to be learned there. I didn't like what I was hearing. More and more, I wished I was home. Of course, Lauren was the major factor there, but this Cassandra problem really ate at me. Even a drama queen of her caliber wouldn't take things this far. The likely outcome was probably going to be bad. Real bad.

I clicked off and called Lauren. We exchanged some X-rated words, and I promised to wrap up the Hatif situation quickly, then I hung up without talking to the bird or the dog. In the ensuing quiet, an unreasonable feeling of loneliness settled over me. I wanted to go back to Le Vintage and hang out with English Jack and Ian if I couldn't be with Lauren, but the roads were frozen and, even in the Saab, treacherous. It took less than half an hour, though, before the emotions of the past several days caught up with me and I surprised myself by dropping off to sleep. In my clothes again.

- - -

Things looked better in the morning. For one, the sun broke through the clouds, giving me (possibly false) hope that the storm had moved on. My weather app showed the temperature as 0, which sounds cold but that display was in Celsius. Once converted to Fahrenheit, it brought the outside heat all the way up to freezing! Okay, that's not warm either, but with the sun out it had to start melting the snow soon.

Adrien showed us where he'd eaten the night before, which was a cubbyhole of a café attached to the northwest corner of the hotel. We ducked in, the three of us, and grabbed a quick breakfast of, yep, pastries and coffee. Ah, the French. They do have eggs, but their pastries are hard to pass up.

I'd received a text from Jim Smith during the night which said that Fou Flamant was still interested in getting Adrien back. (The kid must have one hell of a talent with those grapes.) If he would agree to a one-year contract, without further vacation days aside from the statutory holidays, they would advance $20,000 to help get him out of his debt. Seemed generous, even considering his salary. Adrien, though, hung his head.

"What?"

"Is not enough."

"Good lord, man, you've only been here a matter of months. How much fun did you have?"

He looked up from under those thick lashes, his eyes deeply troubled.

"How much, Adrien?"

He mumbled a number that I didn't quite catch. Or hoped I hadn't.

"How much?"

"60,000 euros."

"Sixty? *Thousand*?"

"Oui."

It was my turn to hang my head.

Gilles groaned.

Both men looked at me. What, did they think I was some sort of miracle worker?

"What?"

"Monsieur, what to do?"

What to do, indeed?

"How should I know? Sixty thousand. That's a – a crazy huge number!"

Adrien looked about to cry. Gilles sat still as a statue. We remained like that for a matter of three or four minutes.

Finally, I sighed. "Let me think."

While I thought, Gilles went and got more coffee.

"Thanks. I needed that." When he went to fetch a third cup, I had an epiphany.

"Okay. How about this?"

The two men leaned in closer as though my idea might sound more brilliant that way.

"We give Gauthier the $20,000 Fou Flamant will advance. He won't like it but it's what we have. Then we promise twenty more in six months and twenty more as soon as possible after that. We'll probably have to sweeten the pot with a bit of interest. Say you dangle another ten maybe in three more months and, voila! Paid off."

Adrien shook his head. "No, he will not like."

"I said that, but it gets him paid off."

"He will not accept."

"Why not? It's better than nothing."

"No, not to Gauthier."

"Why?"

"Because he does not care about the money so much as what he wants me to do for him."

I'd forgotten Adrien had mentioned Gauthier suggested paying off his debt with something other than money. A favor?

Taking a deep breath, I asked, "Okay, hit me with this little favor."

"What?"

"Yeah, sorry. What does he want?"

He looked at his shoes, which were sticking out from under the table.

"Come on, Adrien. What did he ask you for?"

"He wants me to get Fiers Cygne for him."

"Fiers Cygne?" I tried to recall the name. Suddenly, it came to me. "He wants your uncle's winery?"

"Oui."

"That's absurd!"

"Gauthier wants to branch out, get into a new business. He wants to try the winemaking. He has to start somewhere, and Fiers Cygne is doing well."

"But you can't give it to him."

Adrien shrugged.

That complicated the situation. How could Fabron Gauthier expect Adrien to convince his uncle to part with a thriving winery? Vicente wouldn't want anything to do with a buyout, especially for such a low sum. No, there was little likelihood he'd consider letting go of Fiers Cygne. So Gauthier stood no chance of getting his hands on that winery. Unless Adrien was in line to inherit, in which case I didn't want to go where that thought might take me – or Gauthier. There had to be another solution. We sat there, sipping our coffee in silence, trying to come up with one.

After ten minutes, I suggested we set aside the question of where to get the money and figure out the rest of the details. "First off, Gauthier can't have Fiers Cygne. No way. That's not going to happen. So you pay him off. Let's assume we have the 60,000 euros. Euros, right?"

"Oui."

"Okay. We have the 60,000 euros. Another thing: You, Adrien, continue to stay away from Chantal and Pierre. Actually, you continue to stay away from everyone."

He nodded and I hoped that meant he agreed. With Adrien, one couldn't be sure.

"Gilles, do you have a contact at the bank so we can get the 60,000 in cash?"

"Piece of cake, as you say."

"Good. We need to arrange a drop, or rather a transfer of the money into Gauthier's hands. I absolutely will insist Gauthier himself show up for it. From what you've said, he does not keep a low profile."

"A low –"

"He goes out in public."

"Oui. All of the time."

"Good. I think I know the perfect place for the meet." I had explored the blocks near our hotel and thought I'd found the ideal location. "We will suggest Montpellier, calling it neutral territory, and we will suggest the Plaza de la Comedie specifically. It is well known, wide open, many people milling around, although in this weather maybe not so many, but easy to stay visible.

"You, Gilles, will be sitting in one of the cafes on the square, watching to be sure it goes down as planned. I will give Gauthier a briefcase containing the money. Immediately after that, Adrien, we will board an airplane for the U.S. You will already be at the airport. You will go nowhere near the plaza. You will wait for me at the airport, and, after the money drop, we just leave. Got it?"

When Adrien didn't answer, I tapped him on the arm. "Got it?"

There was a moment's hesitation, then, "Got it."

"Good."

I started to rise, but Adrien wasn't finished.

"Wait, monsieur."

"Yes?"

"Please, first, I must say good bye."

"Yes? To who?"

"My parents, my brothers. Chantal, Pierre."

"No, absolutely not. Not Chantal and Pierre. Didn't you listen? It is too risky. If Gauthier really doesn't know about them, we must keep it that way. Adrien, promise me you won't try to see them."

Gilles said a couple sentences in French which I could only assume were strong words in support of my position. Thereafter, Adrien agreed to stay away from his son and Chantal. That had to be a tough decision to make, but he couldn't afford to gamble with their lives.

"Your parents and your brothers, I don't see a problem. Gauthier already knows about them."

"Merci. Thank you."

I started to get up again, but heard a flurry of French from Gilles once more. After what appeared to be a slightly heated exchange, LeDuc explained, "You need to understand which brothers he means."

"Great. Okay, Adrien, which brothers? I thought you had an argument with Rayce and Patric. Yves and Chanler live in other countries, so – Michel?"

"No, I wish to see Chanler before I go. Michel can come to Maman's and Papa's place. We will have a party."

"Chanler? Doesn't he live in Figueres?"

"Oui."

"That's in Spain!"

"Oui," he said, with a broad smile.

"And what's this about a party?"

"Oui. A going-away party. Maman will love to do it."

"Damn." Just when I thought I had all of the loose ends pretty well worked out, the guy throws a monkey wrench into the middle of things. He wants to run down to Spain, and he wants to have a big going-away party. Terrific. So much for a low profile.

When I stopped to think about it, though, really, having Adrien take off to Spain would keep him out of our hair for a while, and keep him out of danger, but I didn't want to give in too easily and have him suspect an ulterior motive. So I groused a bit, but only argued for about a minute, winked at Gilles, and said, "Well, that's settled then."

The three of us left the table, all, I believe, happy with our victories. If only things had turned out the way we had envisioned.

Chapter 20

Now that we had a rough plan in place, it fell to me to work out the details, although Gilles would be instrumental in the implementation of them, considering my limitation with French laws and language. Adrien's assignment was to make contact with Gauthier to let him know of the impending payoff. We all hoped he would be happy about that. Once we had all of the steps choreographed, the final arrangements would be between Gauthier and myself. Adrien and Gilles could listen in, but I wanted total control. I wanted to personally lay out the ground rules and, later, personally hand off the cash.

At the end of the day when the three of us met to report on our progress, things were looking up. At least, on my end. The most important aspect of the plan would be for Gauthier to agree to it. Adrien gave nothing away by his expression as he approached the table. This was to be a celebration, so we had chosen one of the top restaurants in the area. Despite it being a weekday, Chez Jolie had been almost completely booked, so we ended up with a reservation at 7:45, on the early side for dinner. Nonetheless, by the time Adrien joined Gilles and me, we had already ordered a bottle of wine and I'd gotten halfway through my first glass.

As he sat down, he puffed out his cheeks. A bad sign?

"So?"

"He is not happy."

"You told him you will pay him everything you owe him, right? The 60,000?"

"Oui. He is not happy."

"And?"

"He wants more."

"How much?"

"He says 90,000 euros. Nothing less."

"What? That's robbery!"

"Merde." Gilles echoed my sentiment.

"He says for his trouble."

"Yeah, right." I took a large sip of my wine, then poured more into my glass.

"M. Cade, I don't have the money."

"Yeah, I sort of guessed that. What about your parents? Can they loan you some?"

Adrien shook his head vigorously. "No. Papa invest all his money in the business."

"Your uncle? Brothers? Sister?"

"No. Aimee has money, maybe, but she will not help."

From what little I'd seen of Adrien's sister, he was right; she would not help. Aimee did not strike me as the type of woman to get all weepy about a sibling's self-made predicament, even if it was potentially fatal.

"What is it with you and Aimee?"

He shrugged. "We were close as children. We grew apart."

"You grew apart? That's all?" It didn't ring true. Sure, I had a falling-out with my sister a few years ago, but that was because I blamed her for the loss of my niece. Of course, Becca's death wasn't actually my sister's fault, and I finally faced that fact. After that, we cleared the air between us. Mostly. But just growing apart? How does that even happen?

"Aimee is jealous."

"Jealous? Of you?"

He blushed. "Yes. She always wanted children, but she cannot have them. It ruined her marriage."

"Ah." Adrien was the one brother in the family who had a child, the one thing Aimee wanted most, and he blew it off like it didn't matter. That sort of attitude could tend to drive a wedge between siblings, I suppose.

"There must be someone you can turn to." I mean, if his old employer in the States was willing to put up $20,000 to get him back despite his demonstrated unreliability, it seemed like someone actually near and dear to him should be willing to do the same thing. It sounded like the problem was that the only one with the possible resources to spare was the only one with no desire to help out.

Adrien looked miserable, slumped and defeated. The gray clothing I'd forced on him added to the picture of glumness.

"How about if your mother and father mortgaged Cinq Chenes?"

Gilles explained my question to him in French. The two bantered back and forth for a couple of minutes, ending with a more distressed-looking Adrien.

Gilles said, "It is not possible. They have taken loans to keep Henri's winery going. It is just now becoming profitable, but wineries, you know." He grimaced. Yeah, wineries, I knew.

I wiped my hand down my face. "We have to think of something."

In a situation like this, you might think my appetite would shrivel up and die. Not so. It is always robust, and I thank my father for a good metabolism or I'd be at least a hundred pounds overweight. So I suggested that we order hors d'oeuvres. I think better with food. At least, that's what I tell myself.

A large bowl of clams arrived for sharing and we ate and tossed around possibilities. It was agreed that nothing could proceed without the funds for Gauthier's payoff. So far, we had a commitment for $20,000 from Fou Flamant. The exchange rate was pretty close to par at that point, so that meant we only needed another $70,000. *Only.* In the world of the Hatifs, it might as well have been the moon. I pried open another clam before heading into forbidden territory.

"Okay, look." I hesitated, giving myself time to reconsider. "I'll probably regret this, but say I advance the $70,000."

"You, monsieur?"

"Yeah, me, I advance the money." I quickly pointed out, "But it's a loan. With strict payback terms. Ironclad, in fact. You won't spend a frivolous dime for years to come, Adrien."

He stared at me, blinking rapidly, as though trying to comprehend. "You can do this?"

I nodded. "Oui, I can do this." All sorts of alarm bells were going off, but no other solution had presented itself. Someone had to step up. "I can loan you the money, yes. We will have loan documents drawn up though. It will be all formal and legal, and you will pay me back." I stressed the words *loan* and *will*.

Adrien reached out and grabbed me around the neck. When he drew back, he smiled widely and a tear slid down one cheek.

"Oui, M. Cade. I *will* pay you back."

"Yes." I looked over to Gilles, who wore his lopsided smile. I said, "Quit that." Of course, that smile only grew wider. "Do you know someone who can handle the papers?"

He nodded. "I do."

A dozen escargots arrived then, swimming in a rich garlic butter. One minute after that, a loaf of crusty bread was placed upon the table. Gilles and Adrien each tore off a thick piece and delicately maneuvered a snail atop the bread. My offer seemed to have made them ravenous. It had the opposite effect on me. I mean, I love escargots but my outburst of generosity had sort of chased away my appetite. As I said a moment ago, that rarely happens. I reached for my wine. Maybe the alcohol would numb the enormity of what I'd just done.

- - -

Chez Jolie lived up to its reputation, if you judged by my two companions. They downed four courses and might have ordered more if I hadn't put a stop to it. After all, we had work to do – and maybe a little money to save. Adrien was to call Gauthier with the good news about having found the funds to settle the score with him. While he did that, Gilles and I would be packing. I'd decided to move back to the Grand Hotel Moliere in Pezenas the next morning and hang out there for the remainder of my time in France. I know, it would be more convenient for the hand-off if I stayed in Montpellier, since we'd set it up for the Plaza de la Comedie in the city center, but Gilles needed to get back to his agency and, truth be told, I missed Le Vintage Bar and the gang there. Pezenas beckoned.

Meanwhile, it was going to take a few days to get the cash together and have the legal papers drawn up. Plus, Adrien had a train trip to make to Figueres to see his brother, Chanler. Maman and Papa Hatif had a party to put together, and I had airline reservations to make. I figured I'd be home in a week, tops. Sounded great. Lauren was less pleased, though. Apparently, she had counted on a far shorter stay in the Languedoc for me. Jiggs seemed a bit distant, too, and Irene Adler wouldn't even speak to me. Was everyone against me? Hell, I was trying.

Chapter 21

The days had all begun to blend into one another. European businesses keep odd hours anyway, so it made it all the harder to keep track. Fortunately, Le Vintage seemed to never close, and English Jack, Ian and various of their friends drifted in and out such that I could almost always find a sympathetic ear. Or at least someone to drink with. Without Adrien to search for or keep an eye on, it became almost relaxing to hang out and do an occasional bit of business. He had gone to stay at Cinq Chenes for a few nights to help his mom plan his farewell party, since we still deemed it best that he not return to his apartment, just in case. Gauthier had said he agreed to our terms, but why take the chance that his word wasn't worth squat? And Gilles had discreet eyes watching Cinq Chenes, just to be triple cautious.

Maman Hatif had begun preparations for the big send-off as soon as she'd heard, and invited both Gilles and I to attend. The party was to be this Friday evening at 8:00, so two or three days from now. I'd have that figured out before then.

A couple of days after that, on Sunday, Adrien would catch a train to Figueres, Spain. Assuming he left early in the morning, he'd be there in time for lunch with Chanler. He and his brother could reminisce about old times all day, have some fun that night, and Adrien could be back in Montpellier by mid-day Monday.

Meanwhile, back in France, Gilles' guy at the bank figured he'd have the cash scraped together by Monday morning, so my meeting with Gauthier at the Place de la Comedie had been set up for one o'clock on Tuesday, giving us a little wiggle room in case something didn't go quite the way we hoped. Airline reservations had been made for around seven o'clock Tuesday evening. Adrien would be waiting at the airport when I arrived. The idea was to keep him far from the vicinity of the Place de la Comedie or anywhere near the center of Montpellier.

So that pretty much summed up my plans for the upcoming week. Plans which involved paying off one of France's most notorious drug dealers and stealing one of their most revered winemakers. Well, okay, that last bit is a stretch, but there had been weeks I'd looked forward to a whole lot more. Besides, I really missed my bird, my dog and my girlfriend, not necessarily in that order. The up side was that, at the end of that week, I'd be in the company of all three.

Wednesday or Thursday – still hadn't gotten a handle on what day it was by then – I ambled over to Le Vintage around half past six. The snow remained only in patchy piles and shaded areas, the temperatures having risen above freezing by about ten degrees and hovered there. The forecast told of a nice warm-up, which meant that the Ferrari would see some road time again soon. Probably tomorrow. Gilles had already reclaimed his garage space, and I wanted nothing more to do with the Saab.

Typical of mid-week at the Bar, many tables were empty, especially at that time of evening. However, I didn't mind a little solitude. I ordered my usual bottle of St. Hilaire, and shrugged off the idea of tapas for a while longer. Within the hour, here came "the lads". I loved calling them that. It made them sound immature and full of mischief, which they were. They swarmed my table, slapping me on the back, like old friends. Felt nice. If they wondered what I was up to, they didn't ask. Gilles stopped by each evening, too, and he never let on about our big meeting with Fabron Gauthier.

English Jack seemed most interested in the discovery of a body at the abandoned Le Chat Cachemire winery building. In fact, he bought a round of drinks as though entertaining heroes returning from a war. If only he'd seen me skulking around in the rubble, there would have been little doubt about the courageousness of my nature, at least at that point in time. The good thing was, though, that the police had seemed satisfied with the statements they'd taken from Gilles and me, and had okayed me for travel home.

Anyway, the two or three days passed pleasantly. Gilles and I had engaged people to take care of what needed taking care of, so he could get back to business and I could do whatever struck me. I found myself with time on my hands, a rarity which I used touring more of the Languedoc countryside. I mean, the Roquefort caves are only about an hour from the hotel, and the fabulous Millau bridge leading into the Gorges du Tarn takes about the same amount of driving. The Ferrari loved the roads in the Gorge along the river Tarn. They're just twisty enough to be fun but not so severe as to become troublesome for a driver unfamiliar with them.

One of the mornings – the first one, I think – Adrien called me with what I considered an odd request. While staying with his parents, his sister Aimee had dropped in unexpectedly. Apparently, she does that with some regularity.

"M. Cade, she has offered to draw up the loan papers free from charge. Is good, no?"

Probably not, but I couldn't think of a reason to argue. She hadn't struck me as wanting to slant things her brother's way, but then I didn't know her well. Not well at all. I'd only met her the one time when I had coffee with Michel. Were I a betting man, though, I'd have laid odds that she had a personal reason masquerading as generosity hidden in there somewhere. I advanced weak dissent.

"Um, are you sure that's a good idea?"

"Monsieur?"

"Well, I mean, does Aimee practice contract law?"

"She is lawyer."

"Uh-huh."

"Lawyers make agreements."

"Okay."

"So we meet her today. She can make the agreement."

"Yeah, okay. What time?"

He told me when Aimee expected us at her office and clicked off in what sounded like an excellent mood. Me, I had a bad feeling about Aimee's involvement, but it was probably nothing to worry about. She'd had some sort of fight with Michel; that was evident that day in the cafe, but that didn't impact her relationship with Adrien. Did it? He acknowledged that they had grown apart, but she could still have fond feelings for her littlest brother, right? It would be only fair to give her the benefit of the doubt. I called Gilles to let him know so he could cancel the appointment with the attorney he'd set up for the job, and laid aside my unease.

- - -

Aimee had her law offices set up in a middle-of-the-road building in downtown Montpellier. It had seen better days, and the area was just a smidge to the right of a good one but, still, it emanated an air of mild success. Her situation on the first floor, though, proclaimed her as an attorney yet waiting for that big case to come along and elevate her in the legal world.

Adrien ran his fingers over his sister's name on the door, as though it might not be real, then beamed. Maybe the mere fact that she was a lawyer made him proud. Funny, at home we cracked jokes about lawyers, but this guy held them in some sort of high esteem. At least this particular one. I supposed growing up around five boys who had not really gone very far in their careers and then one little sister who had managed to claw her way into a man's profession, well, that could make one's heart swell. It could, except that this was Aimee we were talking about, and she didn't seem the type to make anyone's heart swell. Tremble, yes; swell, no. Anyway, it was sort of nice to see Adrien show a soft spot for his sibling.

Inside the meager suite, the waiting room was nearly nonexistent, with one chair for clients – make that client – and a sickly plant in desperate need of watering. There was no secretary nor a receptionist, just a tiny bell to announce the arrival of Mlle. Hatif's appointments. She made us wait five minutes before emerging from the back room.

"Bonjour, Adrien, M. Blackstone. Come in." As at the café where I'd first met her, Mlle. Hatif turned on her heel and walked away, with supreme efficiency. We followed.

I noted, with relief, two chairs in front of her desk. Adrien sat in the one on the right; I took the other. Aimee reached into her top drawer and pulled out a legal tablet and a pen. Her laptop was open off to the right of her blotter. She looked across at us expectantly, pen poised for information. It fell to me to explain what sort of papers we wanted drawn up, mostly because I would be the beneficiary of them, or the one to get screwed if they were done improperly. That remained a concern for me, considering these two were family. I was trying to keep Adrien happy, though, and alive at the same time, so I'd decided to go along with this idea. Aimee said she could prepare the documents in English, so what could they hide?

She didn't ask Adrien why he needed the money. Actually, her demeanor came across as very professional. Her questions pretty much stuck to the facts. All of which gave me tremendous relief. It appeared that we would get an agreement prepared that assured me of repayment, and a provision for collateral – what little collateral Adrien had – in the event of failure to repay, with as much in the way of consequences as the law would allow. I couldn't find fault with anything, but I still had a few niggling doubts.

"This will take a day or two, monsieur, to finalize."

Really? At home, it's pretty much a matter of filling in the blanks on a form. I didn't say as much, just nodded. Whatever.

"Come back on Friday. These will be ready." She turned to Adrien. "Will you be in town?"

I thought that a peculiar question. He had just returned to town. Why would she think he might not be here? Sure, he had plans to go to Figueres, but she hadn't been told of those. Or had she? How much was Aimee kept in the loop about Adrien? Maybe Chanler, down in Spain, had spoken with her and mentioned that Adrien was coming for a visit.

Anyway, he answered, "Yes, of course."

Oddly, that reassurance made me even more nervous. It must have something to do with my trust – or lack – of attorneys in general, and this French one in particular. Well, we had set things in motion. Now we'd see how they played out.

Our business complete, I stood to leave. Expecting Adrien to do the same, I turned toward the door, ready to thank Mlle. Hatif – actually, Mlle. Hatif-Purdue, for that was the professional name displayed on her office door – when I heard Adrien blurt, "I am in trouble, Aimee. Something bad may happen. Please don't let Maman and Papa know."

My mouth must have hit the floor, I was so stunned. We had agreed to keep the reason for our visit to an attorney quiet, but I'd forgotten that I was dealing with one of the Hatifs. Two of them, actually. The two youngest. Maybe they had a special bond because of that. There was something I hadn't thought of. And it was a little late now for an epiphany of that sort.

Aimee sat calmly behind her desk, pen at rest on the blotter. She folded her hands and looked at her brother. "Adrien –"

"No, please." He glanced at me, then rushed on in rapid French. An awkward three minutes passed while I stood looking at the walls of Aimee's office as the two of them carried on a private conversation. Then it got worse, with Adrien wiping away tears before hugging his sister and walking out. I gave a half wave to Aimee, who didn't acknowledge it, and hurried after him.

Despite my pleas, Adrien would not explain himself. I had a pretty good notion of what had passed between Aimee and him, but, as I've said before, I really like specifics. Details, details, and more details; the lifeblood of a detective. Unfortunately, this kid wasn't sharing.

Adrien and I parted out on the street. Even though he had ridden to Montpellier with me, he said he had other business in town. He'd get a ride back to Cinq Chenes. Fine by me. I wasn't sure I could sit next to him without grilling him – or choking him. Going our separate ways at that point would be best. It would be all too easy to say something I'd regret later.

With my newfound freedom, I took the long way home. It was a beautiful day, and a drive along the Canal du Midi gave me a chance to mull things over without interruptions, except for the occasional traffic. Thankful that the temps had risen to mid 40s – Fahrenheit, even – I cruised along in the Ferrari at a sane speed (somewhere around 60 MPH, which is super sane for me, especially in a Ferrari, but then I was on those Languedoc two-lane highways) and enjoyed the intermittent groves of eucalyptus and stately stone gates announcing grand wineries behind them. In my deep-thinking state, I overshot Pezenas and ended up in Beziers, a splendid midsize city famous for its bullfighting festival and capped with a grand cathedral, but spirited driving felt so good that I took back roads through mature vineyards, green fields and stone villages with names like Coulobres, Espondeilhan and Roujan. The car needed the workout, and my head needed the clearing. By the time I reached the car park opposite the Grand Hotel Moliere, the sun had just set. There was no more perfect time for Le Vintage Bar. Some St. Hilaire and some Brits to lighten my mood. You might be catching on that I enjoy a bit of routine.

Chapter 22

By Friday, my time in France was winding down, although with the cast of players involved, the end game promised to be a thrilling one. So I was looking forward to this party almost as much as if Maman Hatif were throwing it for me. Gilles had generously offered to drive us out there and I'd reluctantly agreed, since we couldn't get three of us into the Ferrari and it seemed only polite to offer Michel a ride. So I found myself back in the green Saab for one more slow journey along the rural roads between Pezenas and Montagnac and Cinq Chenes. Even without snow on the pavement, Gilles exhibited an extraordinary amount of caution, some would say an unbearable amount. I mean, come on, push down on that accelerator already!

Finally, we got there, surprisingly only about fifteen minutes late. I was coming to realize that Gilles simply went about the business of life at his own pace. Now, seeing Cinq Chenes again, which had captivated me from the first time I'd laid eyes on it, all the tensions of the day fell away. The Hatifs' miniature estate looked even more welcoming dressed up for an occasion. In fact, everyone looked festive tonight. Even Chirac had on a party hat and neon what we at home call a kerchief. Not sure of the word in French. The Hatifs certainly did know how to show off their flamboyant side, even the canine member.

Mme. Hatif was stunning in a caftan-like drapey dress thing. Henri, wearing a tri-color billowy shirt, beamed at her side as they led us into their home. Most of the family had already arrived, and many of their friends, too.

Aimee stood out for her lack of color. She still looked like a lawyer, dressed in a gray suit and low boxy heels, her one nod toward a girly look being a slouchy butterscotch turtleneck under the severe blazer. The rest of the family positively flounced in their bright capes and loose trousers, and, of course, madame's caftan.

I myself had found a poet's shirt with flowing sleeves to wear with my black jeans. I felt very Dali-esque, although I doubt that Dali ever wore anything of the sort. Jeans, though, I'd learned, had originated in France (the south, as a matter of fact) so I considered myself quite appropriately attired.

About an hour into the evening, two more men showed up. They could only have been the twins, Rayce and Patric, for they were undeniably Hatifs and nearly identical in every way except for their shoes. The latter gave Adrien a broad smile and a bear hug. The former haltingly approached his youngest brother, looking at the floor – or maybe his shoes, as the Hatifs were keen to do – and held out his hand. The two shook, although it came off as something that had been more Maman's idea than either of theirs. Let's say they didn't exactly link arms and hang out together for the duration of the party.

"Well, that showed a lot of brotherly love."

Gilles arched an eyebrow at me. I returned a sly grin and motioned for him to follow.

We ambled over to the libations table and found some red stuff that looked wonderful, most likely one of Henri's special vintages. I poured a splash for us both.

"Are you worried about M. Hatif's trip to Spain?"

"No," I said, although I was. "He is going to visit his brother. What's to worry about?"

"Coming back maybe?"

"No problem. He'll be back." I swigged some of the wine. It was excellent. "Yum."

"Oui. I told you he makes the good wine."

"You weren't kidding."

"No. Henri studied very well. He studied the chemistry of wine like Toulouse Lautrec studied color. He paid close attention to the harvesting times and the brix."

Well, now he was getting into murky territory for me. I know a little something about winemaking, but my expertise lies mostly in wine tasting. Once you start talking technical terms like brix and terroir, you lose me. I'm more of a nose and mouth kind of guy.

Guest of honor Adrien worked the room like a politician, making sure he didn't miss anyone. This was his big chance. Who knew when he'd be returning? Watching him made me feel almost like a kidnapper, seeing many of his friends and relatives as they fought off tears.

At one point during the evening, Maman Hatif discreetly drew me aside. Pressing an envelope into my hand, she said, "Take this, monsieur. Adrien would lose it. You keep it for him, help him get a good start." Her eyes looked deep into mine. "Take care of my son, M. Cade. Please."

I almost got misty. It's not that I'm terribly emotional, but Simone Hatif could do that to a fellow. I understood why Gilles LeDuc had spoken of her with such passion. Peering into her face, I saw raw, honest emotion and doubled my inner promise to keep Adrien on track. Crap, I didn't need that responsibility hanging over my head. I'd just planned to get us both home, deposit him back at Fou Flamant, and that would be that. Now, well, things had blossomed into more than I'd bargained for with Maman Hatif's personal appeal. But there was no resisting those eyes.

"I will, Mme. Hatif."

"Simone, please."

"I will, Simone." I gave her hand a little squeeze of reassurance. How I was going to live up to this one, though, was anyone's guess.

The conversation turned to Adrien's plans for visiting Chanler in Figueres.

"Oui. He goes tomorrow."

I couldn't conceal my surprise. "Tomorrow?"

"Oui."

"Oh. I thought he was going Sunday."

She looked over at him across the room. "He *was* going Sunday. He changed his mind."

"Ah." I wondered what else he might have changed his mind about. Before I could explore that subject further, Aimee appeared at her mother's elbow, almost as though conjured there in a puff of smoke. Stealthy, that one.

"Ladies." I bowed my head slightly. "I should be getting back to M. LeDuc." Folding the envelope, I turned and went across the room to tuck it into my jacket pocket. I could feel Aimee's eyes following me. How had she sneaked up on us so easily? She was like a cat, so silent, and probably just as cunning.

LeDuc spotted me and came over, carrying his wine glass and a small plate of Simone's hors d'oeuvres, which smelled wonderful. He pointed at my jacket.

"Mme. Hatif gave you something?"

"It's for Adrien. She doesn't trust him not to lose it."

"A wise mother."

"Yes." We strolled again toward the wine table as we spoke. Henri's cabernet was so good, and I wanted more. While pouring a new glass, I said, "Did you know he is leaving for Figueres tomorrow?"

"Who?"

"Adrien."

"Yes?"

"Yes."

"No. I did not know this."

"This wine is fabulous."

"Oui. The Swifts, they do make the great wine. Do you worry about him coming back?" He asked for the second time that evening.

"No," I lied again. "He will come back."

Gilles studied my face, probably seeing the skepticism there as heavily as it sat on me. "Okay. Maybe it is good he goes a day early. Maybe it keeps him out of danger."

"Maybe."

We stood there avoiding each other's eyes, sipping on the wine. Finally, Gilles asked, "Do you worry why he did not tell you he goes a day early?"

"Maybe."

"Maybe, monsieur?"

"Okay, yes. Why didn't he say something?"

"Perhaps he has been busy." He nodded toward Adrien. "Look at him, a busy man."

Adrien moved from one small group to another, shaking hands and back-patting his friends, throwing his head back and laughing often.

"I think he will come to tell you soon."

"Now you're making excuses for him?"

Gilles shrugged. "Devil's advocate, as you say."

Gilles was wrong. Adrien did not come to tell me. At no time during the evening did he mention the change in his plans. In fact, he barely spoke to either of us. It almost felt like he was trying to avoid us altogether. But why would that be? We were the ones who had figured out a solution to the very nasty predicament he had gotten himself in.

I wondered whether his parents had a clue about the trouble their son had caused himself. My bet would have been no, they did not. I suspected Aimee knew because her brother had told her in his little outburst at her office, and she might have heard even before that, considering that her position in the community was one that could put her in earshot of rumors shared between shady street types. But the rest of the family probably thought the baby of the family was living an enviable life, a dream life even, the lucky fellow. It wouldn't be me that burst their bubble on that front. I was left wondering, though, about Rayce, one of the twins, who I caught watching me several times during the evening. His expression appeared unfriendly bordering on hostile. Or maybe I was reading something into it that wasn't there.

The party promised to continue long into the wee hours of the morning. Not for Cade Blackstone, though. He had plenty to do that would require a clear head, so I coaxed Gilles out of there shortly before midnight. To be honest, it didn't take much coaxing, just a suggestion really. We thanked our hostess and slipped out into a dark and balmy night, an unexpected change considering the climate of just two days before.

Chapter 23

The weekend drew out into an agonizingly long period. Had it not been for English Jack and friends at Le Vintage Bar, I might have gone bonkers. As it was, the days stretched into what seemed like weeks. Sure, I had the Ferrari to help pass some of the time, but there are only so many hours one can whiz around in a sexy red sports car touring ancient stone castles and cute hill villages. All right, I understand not getting a lot of sympathy on that, but I don't handle waiting well. Action suits me far better. In reality, I liked the whole France trip much more when Lauren was here, too. Way better action.

Aimee had had the loan papers ready for signing early Friday, so we'd taken care of that important step. Gilles had his man at the bank working to secure the cash, which he assured us again would be ready first thing Monday. Fou Flamant Winery had already transferred the promised $20,000, so everything on the money front appeared to be under control. Prior to Adrien leaving for his visit with his brother in Figueres, he had gone shopping for a nondescript bag to stow all of the cash in; a piece that was not too big and definitely not showy. It seemed that we'd thought of everything. Still, I couldn't help but worry over a missing detail or overlooked piece of the plan.

Since the night of the party, Adrien had dutifully checked in at least once a day and, since Saturday afternoon, claimed to be having the best time ever with his brother Chanler down there in Spain. I found that hard to swallow, but chocked it up to the innate Hatif enthusiasm, which always came across like it was on steroids.

Two or three times, I traveled over to Montpellier, to the Place de la Comedie so that I could familiarize myself with the pay-off area. It served a couple of purposes: one, pass a few hours in a pleasant manner; and, two, learn every inch of the plaza so that Fabron Gauthier wouldn't have even a microscopic advantage over me. Each visit, I'd spent something like ninety minutes ambling around, memorizing the plaza, considering every facet of things like layout, bench location, light posts, even street vendors (who it appears have proprietary stakes on certain spots in the square). Come Tuesday, I wanted to know where exactly to position myself for maximum visibility and safety. Mostly for that last bit. Lauren had actually suggested this whole recon idea, reminding me that you can't be too careful, and by retracing your steps ad nauseam – over and over and over – you will prepare yourself as well as possible. Or so we hoped.

Anyway, by Sunday evening, when I popped into Le Bar, I breathed one colossal sigh of relief at nearing the conclusion to my case and another at seeing that head of white hair at its usual place in the restaurant. It was an evening that, more than all the ones before it, I needed the company of good friends. And, yes, I'd come to think of these guys as good friends. Also, I'd decided to run a hypothetical situation by them, see if they had any words of deep wisdom to share. Within thirty minutes, we had a full table, of men and of drinks. By now, we numbered four, five when Gilles joined us, but something had kept him away this evening.

With the requisite greetings and small talk out of the way, I launched into my query. "Hey, guys, I've got a little question. A theoretical scenario I'd like your opinions on."

"Excellent."

"We love a puzzle."

"Bring it on."

At least I think that's what they said. It was a bit hard to untangle individual sentences, as they all talked at once, loudly and with profuse animation. I took a deep breath and pushed ahead. "Okay. Here goes. Say you had a sandwich you needed to hand off to your boss."

"Seriously?"

"Yes, seriously."

"This is the question?"

"Yes."

"Sounds like a bunch of rot, but okay."

"Okay."

"First, what kind of sandwich is it?"

"Huh?"

"What kind of sandwich?"

"Doesn't matter."

"Course it matters. Is it pastrami? Because I hate pastrami."

Jack. He had to be messing with me. But I'd play along. As I've mentioned before, these Brits were like a gang of immature teenagers.

"No, it's not pastrami. It's tuna."

"Oh, well, all right then. Go on."

"Okay. So you need to get this *tuna* sandwich to your boss. Now at one o'clock, he's going to meet you at the Place de la Comedie in Montpellier."

"Why on earth would he do that?"

I groaned. Maybe this wasn't such a good idea after all. "Because he works close by. Okay?"

There were several moments of grumbling, but they finally settled down again.

"Anyway, he's meeting you in the Place de la Comedie. You've all been to the plaza, right?"

Each one nodded and waved me off as if to say, "Pish. Of course."

"Good. Now, your co-worker Sam is going to be watching from one of the cafes on the plaza."

"Oh, bollocks. That's daft. Why?"

"Because your boss is a dickhead, that's why. He's the kind of guy that's likely to claim he never got the tuna sandwich at all and you want a witness to prove that you handed it off to him. Okay?"

"Okay. Whatever."

"Boss is a dickhead, all right. Got it."

"Geez. Play along a little." I ran my hands through my hair, recalling once again that it was still blond. At least, I had managed to ditch the itchy paste-on mustache and fake glasses. "Okay. Here's what I want to know."

They leaned in as though afraid they might miss out on a crucial piece of information.

"Where should I tell my boss to meet me and which café should Sam be sitting in so that he has the best view when I hand off the sandwich?"

English Jack sat back and folded his arms across his chest, Ian stared down at the table, and Kellen chewed on the inside of his cheek. Looking at the three of them, I'd no idea I'd posed such a tough one.

Finally, Ian cleared his throat and spoke. "Well, sir, I've got a hunch that this isn't really about a tuna sandwich hand-off at all, but then that's not our business, is it. Whatever it is that you need to drop off in that plaza and have a witness for, I'd say to put your Sam in La Maison, and you position yourself on the north side of the Three Graces Fountain, standing just below the cherub that's sitting halfway up the side in the moss."

Jack and Kellen argued about whether Chez Prisse or Bistro Jardin was a better restaurant choice for Sam, but in the end deferred to Ian. Retired police usually won out when it came to matters criminal, and they had all come to the correct conclusion that there was something decidedly less than lawful lurking in my hypothetical.

"Thanks."

"Do you think you'll need any hot sauce with that tuna?"

I looked at Ian to see if he was toying with me. He looked deadly serious.

"No. Sam is all I need."

"Does your boss usually carry his own hot sauce?"

Taking a deep breath before answering, I said, "Yeah, he carries his own."

"How about Sam; does he have any hot sauce?"

"No, I don't think so."

Ian studied my face, then raised his glass to his lips. Finally, he took a drink and nodded. "Okay then. If you change your mind, though, I have a good selection of hot sauce."

I said again, "Thanks." The conversation was starting to take on a weird tone, and one a little bit scary. Fortunately, Jack changed the subject.

"Well, all this talk of tuna has made me hungry. What say we order a charcuterie plate and some cheese?"

Happy to have moved on from imaginary tuna sandwiches and hot sauce, we all sounded our assent to the suggestion. Then the conversation turned to some English sporting event, probably Manchester United since Man U always seems to be part of whatever English sporting event is going on. The rest of the evening passed in a very congenial manner. Later, I slept better than I had in days. Something about talking your problems out with friends will do that. Plus, I was convinced that I'd sewed up all the loose ends in our plan. Of course, I didn't take into account the one big wild card.

Chapter 24

The next morning, Monday – never my favorite day of the week, and for good reason – started smoothly. I didn't question why, just enjoyed every second that didn't present a problem. First off, Gilles' man at the bank came through with the cash, even a few minutes ahead of schedule. The bulk of the 90,000 euros was just about what we'd figured size wise, and it fit nicely in the bag Adrien had purchased. Carrying it around, though, made me immensely jumpy. I couldn't get it into the hotel safe fast enough.

Once the money was stowed behind their heavy-duty combination lock, I could relax. The next step was to call Adrien to give him a progress report, and to find out when his train from Figueres would be getting in. That's when the smooth part of the day ended.

"I have decided I come back tomorrow instead. I take the train directly to Montpellier airport. We can meet there."

This did not make me happy. Not at all. I don't like sudden changes. Actually, I don't like changes, period. They usually spell trouble. So, now, there had better be a good explanation.

"And why is that? Why not stick to the plan we spent so much time working out?" I carefully modulated my voice in order to keep the anger from bleeding through.

"I am having very much fun with Chanler here. Besides, I am not needed in Montpellier."

It didn't matter to me that he was right about that. I still had my suspicions that he was hiding something; call it an intuition. My nerves had become frayed just thinking about the meeting with Fabron Gauthier. I'd set up things like this before, but – well, no, actually, I hadn't set up anything quite like this, not ever. Gauthier was way out of my league. And the last hostile guy I'd arranged to meet in a place of mutual consent had not exactly played fair. In fact, he'd played real dirty. He brought along a buddy who tried to run me over with a car. (That's where Jim Smith came in to save the day.)

Now, I'm not saying there was much chance Gauthier could try running me over with a car in the Place de la Comedie. Frankly, I don't think cars can get anywhere near the Three Graces Fountain, the spot we'd agreed on as the hand-off of the cash. But you never know; he might wax creative and bring a knife, a nasty tool used in silence, allowing the wielder a pretty good chance of getting away before people catch on that anything's amiss. So, yeah, I was already a tiny bit on edge. And Adrien's news didn't help.

"Call me when you're on that train. The nanosecond you get on. And no more changes in plans, Adrien. Your life is at stake, man. Got it?"

I could almost hear him smiling. Wouldn't it be nice to live in a world where everything is carefree like that and unicorns scamper around with fluffy bunnies? "Oui, M. Cade. Got it." The phone went dead in my ear. I massaged my temples before placing the next call to Gilles. I wanted someone to share my outrage with, and also we needed to run through tomorrow step by step. For my comfort, if nothing else. Gilles suggested we meet for a late lunch at a bistro half a block from his office.

It was a frou-frou place called Chartre, and it had one large window nearly obliterated by an overflowing planter box and a bright yellow door with the knob in the center. It also had many enticing aromas flowing from inside. I wondered why Gilles hadn't shared it with me before.

The French detective sat at a small table to the left of the door, sipping a thick liquid from a demitasse. He waved when he saw me.

As I joined him, he advised, "Order the clam chowder. It's the best in Pezenas."

"Thanks for the tip."

While waiting for the chowder, we ran through the plan once more. In almost no time, Gilles began to look bored, as though I'd rehearsed it one too many times. Maybe I had. Maybe I was being over-cautious. Maybe. But it gave me a more solid sense of security. So it was worth whatever eye rolling he wanted to dish out. Finally, I moved on to the subject of Adrien staying in Figueres a day longer than expected. His reaction was disappointing.

"M. Blackstone, you must not worry. He will come tomorrow."

"What if he doesn't?"

"Then he doesn't. You can do nothing to change it. If he does not meet you at Montpellier airport, you go on home. You have done what you can." He shrugged. The French and their attitude. I wanted to get good and worked up about Adrien and his lack of responsibility, his inconsideration and immaturity, but Gilles was having none of that. In the end, we sat in that warm, cozy bistro eating the most incredible clam chowder I'd ever had, making small talk. I'll admit, it felt pretty good. Still, it didn't stop me from fretting about the next day.

- - -

Despite Gilles' assurance that I was overthinking the meeting with Gauthier, I drove up to Montpellier and did one last dress rehearsal, just without the key player present. I had to turn the Ferrari in anyway, since I'd be flying out the next day, so why not make the best use of my time? After my final run-through, I took a taxi from the car hire to the Grand Moliere and called Lauren to share my excitement. After all, I was on the verge of wrapping up the case. Tomorrow we'd be on the home stretch. Adrien and I would get on a plane bound for the U.S., and that would be the denouement. Lauren sounded happy and weary at the same time. Weary? Why weary so early in the day? It was only about seven a.m. at home.

"Oh, Cade, it's been so hectic here. This Cassandra stuff, well, it's keeping me running."

Her job as crime reporter rarely kept her "running" since crime in Carlton and the surrounding communities usually consists mostly of speeding, jaywalking and, when it gets really nasty, a rash of brazen shoplifting. Yes, we did have a murder a couple of years ago, but that was way out of character for our wine country. I figured things must be heating up.

"So what's going on that's got you running so much?"

I heard a little intake of breath and could almost see her shake her head, almost see her blonde hair brushing those luscious tanned shoulders. God, I missed her.

"Sorry. It's not important. I'm so thrilled you're coming home. This other stuff can wait. But you need to talk to Jim Smith when you have a chance. He has inside information that even I can't coax out of anyone. For now, just concentrate on tomorrow. Stay safe, Cade."

"Yeah, I will, dollface."

She groaned.

"Give yourself a hug. And tell Jiggs he's a good boy."

"What about Irene?"

"Um, yeah, teach her a new song."

"Right, funny man." She lowered her voice, "I mean it, Cade, stay safe." And she clicked off. I air kissed a good-bye to a dead phone.

A quick glance out of the hotel window showed a string of three figures walking along the far side of the small plaza, the lead one bearing a head of white hair. Show time! The evening's entertainment had arrived. I grabbed my jacket and headed out.

- - -

English Jack and friends had put together a hasty good-bye party for me at Le Vintage Bar de Vins that night. It was to be my last time there, as tomorrow was the big day, as they say, and as soon as Gauthier had his cash, I'd breathe a sigh of relief, grab Gilles, and have him drive me to the airport in the green Saab. All the rest of my business had been taken care of, the final task being the return of the Ferrari to the rental agency, where I'd said a fond farewell. Not a bad car, but my Lamborghini could drive circles around it any day. In my mind anyway. Still, it was worlds better than the ugly Peugeot had been, and ten times that for Gilles' Saab.

With the Brits in control of the bar tab, though, I had to be super cautious, because they had a sneaky habit of ordering drinks at times when I wasn't looking, like during a trip to the gents' or sometimes even when I just blinked. I figured, if I wanted to stay alive, I had to keep my wits about me tonight so that I had them when I met the drug lord in the plaza tomorrow. Gilles sat close and kept me sober, and for that I was grateful.

At one point, Ian said, "So did you get that tuna sandwich to your boss?" LeDuc's head swiveled toward me and I could feel his eyebrows rise.

"Um, not yet."

Ian nodded, then offered, "A toast!"

There were shouts all around the table, "A toast!"

Jack asked, "What are we toasting?"

"M. Blackstone and a successful delivery of his tuna sandwich."

"Hear, hear!" We all clinked glasses and drank.

Ian's gaze lingered on me. "And a safe journey home."

"Thank you, Ian."

The evening did not stretch out like the ones before it, at least not for Gilles and me. Saying good-bye was bittersweet. I wanted desperately to see Lauren again. Yes, Jiggs and Irene Adler, too. But I had never had a circle of male friends quite like these guys. There was something to be said for that. I liked it, and leaving them was going to be more than just a little bit difficult. If I'd had more wine, I might have gotten all sappy, possibly even shed some tears, so it was good that Gilles dragged me out of there shortly after eleven.

As we were leaving, Ian offered "hot sauce" once again, and I'd swear I heard him say, "Good night, Sam," to Gilles, but my ears must have played tricks on me.

Chapter 25

D-Day had finally arrived, the day that would get me out of there one way or another. No surprise to say that I'd slept poorly. But, when my feet hit the floor, all I wanted to do was get it over and done with. Well, mostly. Part of me wanted to just forget the whole business and go on home. If only that had been an option. I may be green, but I'm not a quitter.

Gilles and I met for a leisurely – as leisurely as possible with a day like that one facing us – brunch type meal. We didn't talk about what was going to happen at one o'clock. Gilles had made it clear that I'd already overthought it. Go with the flow now. Really, it was so simple, he was right. I'd be in Montpellier at the appointed hour, bag in hand, positioned near the cherub on the Three Graces Fountain. Gauthier would come by and take the bag, and Adrien's debt would be forgiven. Gilles, meanwhile, would be standing by to make sure it all went down as it was supposed to.

The day was sunny, which meant there should be a reasonable sized crowd flocking to the Place de la Comedie during the mid-day break, and that sort of added a modicum of safety. With everything set and so well thought out, what could go wrong? Never ask that.

I stowed my luggage in the trunk of Gilles' Saab, then retrieved the bag with the money from the hotel safe, thanked the staff and took care of my final checkout. Then we began the slow trip to Montpellier, a trip I knew would take awhile. After all, Gilles was behind the wheel.

Even so, we reached the center of the city a full hour and a half before I was due to meet Gauthier for the payoff. Gilles tucked his car into an underground lot, took meticulous care positioning the ticket stub on the Saab's dashboard, and we started off toward La Maison. I noted that Gilles seemed to be leaning more heavily on his cane today. Stress? He generally didn't show stress. Well, with the possible exception of the night of Yvette's party, when Gauthier took out after us. Oh, and I guess maybe he displayed a small amount of panic that day in the café when Adrien first came back and he thought he'd seen Gauthier on the street. So, okay, he sometimes showed it, especially when Fabron Gauthier figured into the equation. And today stress looked to be weighing him down quite badly.

One thing we hadn't bargained on was La Maison being as busy as it was. They don't take reservations for lunch and none of the tables overlooking the plaza were available, so we had to wait for one to open up. Gilles smiled broadly and said some gracious words to the hostess, which gained us some sort of priority, and we scored a prime spot in just under fifteen minutes. We ordered enough food for six people, and then merely pushed it around on our plates. Not that it didn't look and smell divine, but our anxiety overtook our appetites.

The fountain was getting a lot of attention, despite the season being winter. The sun brought out whatever tourists were in town, and it seemed that the plaza became their focal point. I'd come often enough in the past few days, though, to know that the actual spot I had chosen for the meeting, the one near the cherub, was generally ignored by the masses. And today, nothing appeared to be different. At exactly 12:45, I picked up the bag like any ordinary businessman would do, and tipped my hat to Gilles as I exited the bistro.

I had only to travel about forty yards from the façade of La Maison, which gave Gilles a clear view. There I perched on the lip of the fountain, trying to appear casual. Wishing I smoked to further the nonchalant look, I groped for something to disguise my nerves. Getting out my cell phone, I pretended to have a conversation with an imaginary friend. Then I made a show of hanging up, looked around and started snapping off pictures. It was a ploy that allowed me to both concentrate on faces yet remain alert. After that, I kept the phone to my ear for several minutes, muttering occasionally and shifting my feet, always keeping the fountain to my back and my eyes roving the plaza.

I consulted the photo album on my phone for the pictures of Gauthier that we'd managed to scrape together. Assuming he hadn't done a chameleon job like I sometimes do, I thought there would be a good chance of spotting him from quite a distance. His hair, if nothing else, along with his ghostly pallor, made him a standout character. Those albino characteristics are about as difficult to disguise as Adrien's dimples and dreads.

I'd gotten there early, and now Gauthier was late, a combination which makes for a very tense Cade Blackstone.

At 1:10, I called Gilles. "Any sign of him from where you sit?"

"No, monsieur. Relax. He keeps you waiting. It puts you on edge."

"No shit."

"Do not let him make you nervous. He does it to bother you."

"Okay." I rang off, trying but failing to not let it bother me. Waiting for anything, good or bad, is the hardest part. Always has been. I remember my parents telling me they were going to take me to Disneyland for my ninth birthday. Unfortunately, that was a whole month away. To an eight-almost-nine-year old, that was an eternity away. The wait nearly killed me. Now, Gauthier was almost fifteen minutes late. Another eternity. Where the hell was the man? Didn't he want his 90,000 euros?

I'd no sooner disconnected from my brief chat with Gilles than I saw a man coming toward me. He smiled and asked for a light. Was this one of Gauthier's scouts? I mean, the guy spoke English but with a French accent. Of course, if he'd been in earshot when I was talking to Gilles, he'd have picked up that I was an English speaker. Still, it made me nervous. But, by then, everything did.

By 1:25, I'd begun pacing. I called Gilles again and he sounded less sure of himself. Almost half an hour late. That's really pushing the envelope. Nonetheless, I remained at the fountain.

At 1:40, I thought the mood of the area had changed. People in the plaza seemed jumpy, but I decided I was projecting my feelings onto them. A few of them suddenly covered their mouths like surprised; some changed directions abruptly. I looked around, thinking Gauthier must be approaching. That would explain the displays of fear. And, yes, someone was approaching. But when I took care to focus, it wasn't Gauthier coming my way, but Gilles. What the hell was he doing? I tried to wave him off discreetly. The deal was that I meet Gauthier alone. The instructions were explicit. Any variation and Gauthier would abort the rendezvous; I was sure of that. His tardiness could be a test. Why would Gilles take such a chance?

"No! Go back," I hissed, glancing around to see if anyone was paying the slightest amount of attention to us. "Get out of here!"

He slowed but kept limping toward me. I motioned him away again.

Then Gilles stopped and slumped against his cane, looking down as though defeated. "M. Cade, please, come with me.

"No. I know he's late, but I have to wait. It's our only chance. Go back to the cafe!"

But he struggled forward, getting close enough to touch my elbow. Quietly, he said, "M. Cade, listen. Something has happened. We must go."

At first, I resisted. This was not part of the plan. It hadn't played out as it should, but I wasn't ready to accept that something had gone wrong. Gauthier could still come. I tried to tell Gilles that. "What are you talking about? He's not even an hour late. He might be testing me. I must wait for him. This is our only chance."

He tugged gently on my arm. "There has been an accident. Gauthier is not coming. He is dead."

"Dead?" Dead. So that's why he hadn't showed. "How? Car wreck? How do you know?" Imagine the irony, being killed on your way to collect a ransom.

"No, not a car wreck. Please, come with me. I will tell you, but first we must get out of here." He led me toward the car park, now limping badly. I kept glancing over my shoulder, yet unable to believe that Fabron Gauthier would not appear beside the fountain at any second.

Once in the Saab, Gilles released the breath he'd been holding, but still didn't talk. We rode through the streets of Montpellier to a neighborhood of older stone buildings flanking narrow alleys. Gilles abandoned his car haphazardly at a crumbling curb and motioned me into a grimy looking establishment named Coogan's Irish Pub.

Inside, it was as dark as my mood. Gilles placed our orders before guiding me to a booth in the rear of the bar.

There, he sat down hard, listing to one side. His cane clattered to the floor. He placed his phone on the table, screen side up. It showed a news flash from some app he used, and was running a banner alert across the screen. The story was in French so I could not read it. The detective took a deep breath and looked at me, his brow knitted together in what looked like pain.

"Okay. Tell me, Gilles. Tell me what happened now."

"Gauthier was killed while riding on a train.'

"A train."

"Oui. He was shot." He watched me digest this piece of information. Living the kind of life he did, I could understand Gauthier dying by the gun. But what was he doing on a train when he was supposed to be in Place de la Comedie meeting me?

Gilles went on, looking at his phone screen, "There was an attack. Shots were fired." He shook his head. "It is very confusing. The authorities are trying to sort it out. Reports are early yet, but they say it might be terrorists."

"Terrorists?"

"On the train. Especially after Charlie Hebdo. But they do not know. Fortunately, two American soldiers were aboard and they subdued the gunman before he could kill any more people."

"Wow. Good for them." I swallowed, trying to understand yet why Gauthier had been on a train. "Subdued?"

"Oui, the soldiers killed the gunman. But he shot several people." Gilles waited until he had my full attention before continuing. "M. Cade, he shot Fabron Gauthier and Adrien Hatif."

That hit me like a slap. "Adrien?"

"Oui, monsieur."

"Adrien? What was Adrien doing on that train? What train?"

Gilles shook his head. "I don't know. This happened only about an hour ago. The police, as you can imagine, are working very hard to figure it out."

Adrien had been on a train, the same one as Fabron Gauthier, right about the time that Gauthier should have been in la Place de la Comedie meeting with me? None of this made sense. Then Gilles' sense of urgency about leaving the plaza came into focus.

"Are you worried about Gauthier's men coming after us?"

"I do not know what to think, monsieur. But better safe than sorry, as you Americans say."

"Is Adrien going to be okay?"

Gilles shook his head. "No, monsieur. Adrien will not be okay."

The noise level in the pub seemed to have ratcheted up tenfold. It all felt suddenly chaotic. Waiters bustled around like children at a backyard birthday party. Our pints finally arrived. I took a large gulp. It went down like tepid dishwater. Looking around, I noted that the few patrons in Coogan's were riveted to the television set mounted above the bar. Footage of a train behind a reporter showed on the screen, with an info banner running across the bottom. I couldn't read the text, of course, once again, but it must have not said much for Gilles dismissed it with a disgusted shake of his head and didn't bother to translate. We watched, hoping to see real news, for another hour, nursing our beers.

At intervals, Gilles got on the phone to whoever he knew that might know something and gathered information like he was herding sheep into a pen. By the time I finished off my second Guinness, he set his phone down and gave me that lopsided DeVito grin.

"Interesting day, monsieur." LeDuc sat up straighter, apparently more in his element than just a few minutes earlier. Before going on, he adjusted his sleeves. "A friend tells me that Adrien boarded the train in Beziers this morning around 11:35. It is a forty-five minutes ride to Montpellier. Witnesses say he carried a bag and met a man looking like Gauthier. The two men sat in seats at the rear of the first class car, which was half full at that time of day. About thirty minutes into the journey, passengers saw a man walk toward the back, then heard pops. Of course, there was much panic. Two soldiers were sitting ahead of Adrien and Gauthier and took action to subdue the gunman."

"The Americans who saved the day." I needed something to sound positive.

"Oui, monsieur."

LeDuc wasn't finished.

"The interesting part is that the gunman is a street thug from Montpellier named JZ Durand."

I listened, still numb and having a hard time understanding how the day had gone so terribly wrong so quickly.

Gilles frowned and leaned forward. "Here is what puzzles me, monsieur. JZ Durand is a petty thief. He has been in and out of the jails since he was a teenager. He is no stranger to crime."

"Yeah, like at home. We don't keep the bad guys in jail, and this is what happens."

"But he did not ever use a gun before."

I mulled that over for a second. "What are you saying, Gilles?"

"It is odd, no?"

I had to admit it did seem odd.

"Something else is odd."

"What's that?"

"Witnesses say Adrien carried a bag."

"Yes, you mentioned that already."

"Police found no bag with the bodies."

"The witnesses were mistaken." I shrugged. "Happens all the time."

"Maybe."

"What are you suggesting, Gilles?"

"Nothing, monsieur. Just giving you the facts."

"Speaking of the facts, how did you find all of this out?"

"I have friends." He sat there with that sly smile spread smugly across his chubby little face. I knew he wouldn't explain himself further. Indeed he had friends, really good ones if they could tell him all of this before the media – always clambering to one-up each other – had even begun speculating about it yet.

"Was Gauthier alone? I can't imagine he wouldn't have a bodyguard along, even a secret one."

"Oui, monsieur, there must have been one. JZ shot three men. Maybe the third man killed was a bodyguard. There were maybe more bodyguards, too, but none will come forward. Especially after failing to protect their boss. Whoever was with Gauthier is probably somewhere in Italy by now." He chuckled.

"So how did the shooter get a gun onto the train?"

"I don't know, monsieur. A slip-up maybe. Or somebody pays somebody off. It can be easier than you might think. There is corruption." He rubbed his thumb and forefinger together. "Slip some euros to the security. They look the other way."

"Yeah. And the two soldiers?"

"Oui?"

"What about them? How did they get guns aboard?"

"Oh, no, they did not have guns. They killed the shooter, but not with a gun. I think it was a broken neck, but my friend says he is not sure."

"Wow." You have to love those soldiers. Their training doesn't leave them a whole lot of middle ground. That was lucky for the other passengers on that train, really. JZ Durand may not have been ready to stop shooting once he'd finished off Adrien and Gauthier. Heat of the moment and all.

It had turned into a very bad day, and we wanted to make sure it didn't get worse. We debated the possible repercussions to ourselves. Might Gauthier's thugs blame us for a part in their boss' death? After much back-and-forth, we came to the conclusion that we didn't think so. I know, not a very definitive conclusion, but it's the best we could come up with. Criminals are hard to gauge sometimes.

I snapped my fingers as a thought occurred to me. "Aimee."

"Monsieur?"

"We should go tell Aimee. Her office isn't far from here. Maybe we can get to her before she hears about it on the news. Or at least be there to comfort her if she's already seen the story." The odds were on the side of her already hearing about it, but we felt compelled to give it our best shot anyway. Despite the personal distaste I felt for the woman, she was Adrien's sister and deserved a bit of human care. I helped Gilles to his feet, after retrieving his cane from where it had fallen, and we exited Coogan's.

Unfortunately, the awful Saab was right where we'd left it. Fifteen minutes later, we turned onto the street which housed Aimee Hatif-Purdue, Esq.'s law office. Parking in the neighborhood around her building could be sketchy but sometimes luck won out, as it did that day. About the only piece of good luck we had.

Chapter 26

Fortunately, for Gilles, the parking spot we scored was just three spaces from Aimee's building; fortunate because his leg didn't look like it could hold up much longer. He had never told me what caused the injury. Knowing him for even this short time, my imagination couldn't help but run wild. One day, I would ask for the story behind it and hope he would tell me.

As I rounded the front of the green Saab, I noted a man coming out of the building in somewhat of a rush. It's my business to pay attention to things like that. And, while my senses were deadened quite a bit by the day's barrage of events and emotions, the guy's hostile body language and angry expression struck a chord with me. In fact, with Adrien Hatif freshly dead, a sudden worry for his sister momentarily flitted through my mind. I quickened my pace.

But, inside, all appeared normal. There was nothing so dramatic as the door to the attorney's office hanging open with a body crumpled behind her desk in a congealing pool of blood. No, a very alive Aimee walked out into the reception area when we rang the tiny bell, wearing her customary charcoal suit and stony expression. She looked from me to Gilles and back to me before speaking.

"Monsieurs. We did not have an appointment, did we?"

This was the difficult part. LeDuc and I had flipped a coin and I'd won – or, rather, lost. I had the task of delivering the death notice. I took a deep breath.

"No, mademoiselle, we did not have an appointment. Please pardon us for the intrusion, but we have come with sad news." Obviously, she knew about the loan to Adrien; she'd drawn up the legal papers for it. And she may even have known why Adrien needed the cash, since he had decided to have a private tete a tete – in French – the day we had Aimee draw up the papers. I was still pretty put out about that. Okay, I was pissed, but I held that in check now. "We are very sorry to tell you, but Adrien has had an accident." That always sounds so inadequate, and more so today as it did not seem to be an accident at all. But this was the victim's sister, so I soft-pedaled. Aimee, though, stood stoically before us.

"Adrien is dead, Aimee," I said, as kindly as possible.

"Ah, oui."

We waited, looking everywhere but at her. Soon, it would sink in. Neither of us wanted to be here, but someone should be with her in this time of tragedy. But as seconds stretched into minutes, I began to wonder whether we were wrong. She exhibited no emotion. No tears. No questions. Nothing. In fact, I couldn't tell whether she'd already heard. None of her responses had given us a clue. Finally, she turned to walk back inside her office.

"Thank you for coming to tell me."

She didn't want to know what happened? Had the situation been reversed, I'd be full of questions. Maybe shock had dulled her senses. I volunteered, "Adrien was shot. By a man named JZ Durand."

Aimee stopped and dipped her head. "JZ Durand."

"You know him?"

"Who does not know JZ Durand? Everyone in my business knows JZ Durand." She came back toward us, closing the door to the inner office behind her.

This woman was Adrien's closest playmate in their childhood, at least at home, since they were nearest in age. They spent many days laughing and giggling, and he probably watched out for his only sister, played her brave protector. He was her valiant knight. He made sure she was treated right all her life. Whenever her name came up in my company, he had spoken of her with great affection. And the day he and I came to have her prepare the loan documents, he'd shown huge pride in seeing her name on the office door. Just from that small gesture, you could tell he adored his sister. So I had expected more grief from her. Hell, I had expected *some* grief from her. But, I told myself, everyone handles loss in their own way. Not all of us react in a textbook manner. Plus, Aimee was a lawyer, and lawyers often hide their true feelings well.

Gilles must have been on the same wavelength as me, for he cocked his head and asked, "Did you ever represent JZ?"

Aimee looked toward him, scrutinized him for about ten seconds, then gazed over his shoulder to a spot on the wall. "I believe I did. Once."

"Did you win his case?"

"I don't remember."

"If you lost, I think you would remember."

Aimee glared at LeDuc. "I don't remember."

I had a couple of questions. "Was JZ acquainted with your brother?"

She squinted at me. "How would I know that?"

"Maybe he mentioned some connection between you? Your names? It is not a common one, after all."

"No."

"Can you think of any reason he would want to kill Adrien?"

"Drugs maybe?"

So Adrien had told her the reason for the loan. Once again, that puzzled me, since I thought he didn't want anyone in the family knowing about his problem, but he had blurted out *something* emotional the day of our appointment, and I'd feared it was a confession.

"JZ was into drugs?"

"JZ was into whatever made JZ money."

"And Adrien? Was Adrien into drugs?"

She looked at me with ice-cold eyes. "You know very well, monsieur, that Adrien was into drugs. Why else would he be meeting Fabron Gauthier?"

How did she know he was meeting Gauthier? Neither Gilles nor I had mentioned it and I didn't think that was part of what he'd confessed to her that day. Had he called later to tell his sister what his plans were? Somehow, that didn't ring true either. But how else would she know? Maybe she had heard from someone else. So why the charade now? The implacable facade of a moment ago showed the slightest waver before Aimee regained control of herself.

"Now, if you will pardon me, monsieurs, I must call Maman and Pap."

- - -

After Gilles and I left Aimee's office, we ducked back into Coogan's. We had been comfortable there just an hour ago, so we knew we could be comfortable there once again, and we wanted a place to hang out and have a conversation without being scrutinized. Coogan's was one of those off-the-radar spots that doesn't make waves and doesn't try to make a name for itself. Good or bad. So no one would look for us there, our guys or theirs. Plus, we knew the gendarmes would likely want to talk with us sooner or later, and we preferred to make it later.

We reclaimed the booth we'd vacated a short while before. Gilles heaved a sigh of relief as he slid behind the table. He reached down and rubbed his knee. I took a chair opposite him.

"Was it just me or did you think Aimee wasn't very broken up about her brother's death?"

"Her reaction did seem strange, monsieur."

"*Strange* – nice way of putting it."

"Monsieur?"

"Well, I thought her reaction was more along the lines of didn't give a shit." I realized I was acting like an adolescent, but my nerves were shot. The whole day had revolved around me handing off 90,000 euros to a drug dealer in order to save a French winemaker's life, and none of it had gone down as it should have and the winemaker ended up dead, along with the drug dealer. Then, for some reason totally unknown to me, the dead winemaker's dear sister didn't seem to care at all. Plus, my travel plans were canceled for the foreseeable future, and I was homesick. So, yeah, I said it just like I thought it. Bluntly.

Gilles seemed to understand and he nodded. A dark-haired waitress dressed in a wench's costume (they still do that?) brought the pints we'd ordered on our way in. We both thanked her before taking the first step toward drowning our sorrows. Actually, we didn't drown anything, but it wasn't what you'd call a happy afternoon. Trying to unravel Aimee's demeanor sort of left us cranky. It would have felt so much better had she wailed and cried and gotten hysterical – something closer to what we'd expected. Something closer to what a grief-stricken woman would do.

Not only did we come to the realization that Aimee obviously didn't love her brother, but we were left wondering whether she might have actually hated him. But if so, why? Sure, not many sisters want to admit they have a drug user in the family, but that doesn't mean they stop loving that person. Right? Besides, Adrien had not been a chronic problem, only recently having become involved with drugs. Or did I miss something?

I asked LeDuc about JZ Durand, but he had little to add. The profile he painted of the guy depicted him as a two-bit crook who had terrorized Montpellier for a couple of decades, and that would be overstating his reputation. Pretty much a big schoolyard bully who, this time, had stepped out of character and used a firearm. We both got hung up on that, since he'd never gone in for guns before. Criminals have a modus operandi, MO, a way they do things, like artists have a style or musicians have a genre. It would be out of character, say, for Yo-Yo Ma to put on a rap concert or Vincent Van Gogh to paint a battle scene between cowboys and Indians. So JZ using a gun was sort of a big deal.

Maybe soon we could get some answers, but for now, we'd have to settle for simple speculation. Gilles' friend or resource or whatever one calls it must have run out of information, for we were receiving no more updates. Even the television was showing a loop of repeat footage.

Meanwhile, something else bothered me. Why had Adrien been on that train at all? It wasn't the train from Figueres. So it had to do with something else. Obviously, he'd changed the meet with Gauthier. But what did he hope to accomplish? I still had the money. Did he think he could reason with the drug kingpin? Was he planning to try and fake it, hope Gauthier didn't look inside the bag Adrien was carrying? Another puzzle: reports so far said the police found no bag with the bodies. Then I thought of Gauthier's bodyguards. There had to be at least one of them on that train with him. The man didn't move without bodyguards. How did none of them get involved in the gunfire, or was that the third victim? And if not, where had he/they gone after the dust settled? The idea that any surviving bodyguards might have fled to Italy wasn't holding water with me. Gilles offered the corruption solution again.

"Yeah, maybe." That wasn't all that felt off. My mind couldn't bring it into focus quite yet, though. Finally, we tried to relax and nurse our beer, stretching it out for as long as we dared before it was time for Gilles to drive us back to Pezenas. The authorities would find us soon enough.

Chapter 27

As you just learned, I didn't fly out that Tuesday evening. After Gilles and I left Coogan's Irish Pub, we drove to his office where we could await the latest bulletins, and probably the police. Plus, I could call Lauren with the bad news. She took it about as well as I had, and she'd not even gotten the chance to meet Adrien. My stay would have to be extended for a time yet to be determined, and we both understood that but neither of us was happy about it. The French police wanted to have a polite chat with everyone remotely connected with the dead men on the train, especially after they learned that one of them was a man they had long sought to put in prison.

Adrien Hatif had not been on their radar at all, but police types like to tidy up every loose end, Adrien being a very big one. His presence brought up a lot of questions. Like, what was he doing in the company of a drug czar such as Fabron Gauthier? First, though, they had to establish that he actually *was* in the company of Gauthier and not just an unlucky passenger in the adjacent seat. In talking with Adrien's friends and family, to a man, they swore there was absolutely no chance of Adrien having any connection to an underworld drug czar. Gilles LeDuc and I remained neutral on the subject. Finally, the cops tabled the idea, finding no way to tie the unfortunate victims together. Of course, the investigation would go on for days.

Meanwhile, Gilles offered me his guest room once again but I declined, thanking him profusely and suggesting that it might be best if I checked back into my old room at Le Grand Moliere. So it was that, late Tuesday evening, he pulled the green Saab up to the hotel door and I unloaded my bags from his trunk. It felt like old times, just not in a good way.

I waved as he drove off, grateful to the heavens – and Ian – for hooking me up with Gilles LeDuc. Maybe he didn't look like much, but the man had an incredible stable of resources and a network to rival Verizon's. And he had a heart that was even bigger than that. Staying in his flat held an appeal, certainly, but he had put himself out for me far beyond the call of duty already. The guy could use some legitimate rest, which would be accomplished much easier without Cade Blackstone underfoot. So there I was once again at the Moliere.

I was greeted at the front desk by a night clerk with the unlikely name of Molly. A lovely young lady with a quirky sense of humor, I'd found her quite captivating during my earlier stay. Always full of clever banter, amusing without being flirty, she fairly defined the term "welcoming". This time, though, when she saw me, her demeanor changed from friendly to distraught bordering on intense unease. I didn't know what that was all about but my first concern was to get the bag with its cash back into the hotel's safe. I'd been holding it close to me all afternoon, afraid to let it out of my sight. Now, though, nothing sounded better than to stow the bag securely away and hit the hay.

When I approached her with it, Molly stared at the bag as if it were a snake coiled to strike. Her eyes grew as big as saucers. Okay, I'm not super tuned into women's body language but even I thought this was something to comment on, and so I did.

"Mlle. Molly, are you all right?"

"Ah, oui, monsieur." She still didn't take the bag.

"What is it?"

"The valise, monsieur."

"Yes? What about the valise?"

"Adrien – M. Hatif, he came in to look at that valise." Big tears had started to roll down her cheeks. "M. Hatif was so nice."

What was she talking about? She was making no sense. "Pardon? Molly, what did you say about Adrien – M. Hatif?"

"M. Hatif came in to see the valise, monsieur. He said you had forgotten to put something inside and you had asked him to put it in the valise for you." She shook her head. "I am sorry. I know I should not have let him, but he said it was very important."

All at once, my head started to spin. I needed to think and my mind wasn't working well. Let's see, I had brought the bag to the hotel safe Monday morning, shortly after getting the money from the bank. I then called Adrien to let him know everything was going along smoothly, and that's when he dropped his change-of-plans bomb on me, saying that he was staying in Figueres an extra day. That was Monday. Then, Tuesday – today – I got the bag out of the hotel safe first thing in the morning for the meeting with Gauthier in the Place de la Comedie. Adrien should have still been in Spain at that hour. The timing didn't add up.

"When was it that Adrien came in, Molly?"

"Last evening, monsieur."

"Last evening?" Monday evening? That's when I celebrated the wrapping up of my case with the Brits at Le Vintage Bar. Did Adrien change his plans once again and sneak back into town? Did he then come to the hotel, chat up sweet, naïve Molly after he saw me leave? But why? What would he have wanted to put in the valise? Suddenly, I had a sick feeling.

Molly wiped the tears from her eyes and tried to regain her professionalism. "Monsieur, would you like me to take your bag?"

"Merci, Molly, no. I think I will keep it a little while longer."

"Oui, monsieur." She blinked several times. "I heard about M. Hatif. It is so awful. I will miss him." Her voice had lowered to a whisper. I assumed Adrien's deep dimples and mocha skin had worked their charms on this young lady, too. He did have a certain *je ne sais quoi*, as the French say, about him. A great sadness descended on me.

"Me, too, Molly. Me, too."

Up in my old room, I placed the bag on the bed and stood back, hands on my hips. "So what do you have to tell me?" Almost afraid to open it, I stood looking at it for a full two minutes before I summoned the courage to release the latch. Spreading the mouth of the bag wide, I held my breath as I peeked inside.

"Shit." As I had begun to suspect, it did not contain 90,000 euros. In fact, there was mostly just paper. Shredded paper. Lots of it. But on top of the heap sat some envelopes, and one of them had my name on it.

I picked that one up, ran my finger under the flap and took it to the chair by the window. I opened it and read: *M. Cade, Thank you for all of your help. I am sorry to have deceived you, but I cannot have you put yourself in more danger for me. If you read this, things did not go so well. I have messed up much in my life. But no more. This is my problem. I will handle it. What kind of man would I be to let another man risk his life for me? I want for my son to have a good memory of his father. Please, would you tell him that I love him? And Chantal, too. Adrien.*

I stared at the paper until it blurred. What felt like half an hour passed before the emotional numbness wore off. This young man had gone to a great deal of trouble to protect me. Huh. Much of what I'd previously thought about him would have to be viewed in a new light. His dalliances with women took on a more mature feel, and the fact that he put little Pierre first above all spoke volumes as to the man's blossoming character. Yes, he'd made mistakes, but in the end he hadn't hesitated to try to put things right.

Adrien had somehow managed to take the money from the bag I'd stowed so carefully in the hotel's safe. How? Maybe he had bought two identical bags and switched them? That took a lot of forethought. How, though, had he gotten the fake one in under Molly's nose? I tried to picture scenarios, played several through in my head, and here's what I concluded: His cape. Sure, that colorful, flowing cape could conceal a whole lot, including a valise of this size. Besides, Molly was primed to see the absolute best in Adrien, so she would believe almost any story he told her, making it a breeze for him to get by her.

The sheer scale of Adrien's scheme was slowly dawning on me. Obviously, he had called Gauthier and changed the entire plan: place, time and players. That much I'd guessed before. But what I hadn't realized was that he'd come back from Figueres early – if he'd actually gone at all – snagged the money out of the safe, and run off to buy his life back. Only it hadn't worked out quite the way he'd expected. Instead of a seamless hand-off of the money to Fabron Gauthier on the Beziers-to-Montpellier train, a local hood had hopped aboard with a gun and spoiled everyone's day.

Was the encounter between JZ Durand and Adrien on that train simply random? That sounded too convenient. A small-time hustler takes out both Gauthier and Adrien on the very day they are carrying a bag with 90,000 euros? Too big of a coincidence. I don't believe in even *small* coincidences so this one was setting off every kind of alarm. And the other burning question was what had happened to the money? So far, there had been no mention of a large sum of cash nor of any bag being recovered in any of the reports. Somehow it managed to walk away from that train. Which meant, to me, that there was someone else at the shooting scene who knew about the money. My suspicion was that the shooter had a partner, one that no one else on the train knew about, one that got off with 90,000 euros in a plain bag looking a lot like the one lying open on my hotel bed.

And suddenly I realized what it was that had been nagging at me during the afternoon. I called Gilles to share my epiphany. When I told him, he was as stunned as I had been.

Chapter 28

Exhausted or not, Gilles and I both knew that neither of us would sleep until I shared my news. We agreed to meet at Le Vintage in fifteen minutes. That gave him barely enough time to get there from his apartment. I'd have volunteered to pick him up but I'd become wheel-less by that point, a condition that would have to be remedied first thing in the morning. (You might have picked up by now that I'm a car guy.)

Naturally, I arrived at the bar ahead of LeDuc, having only a quick stroll across the plaza from the hotel. I handled the drinks by ordering a bottle of cabernet sauvignon and acquiring two glasses. Due to the late hour, the bar was pretty much empty. Even Jack and the rest of his British gang had long since departed. Maybe the news from earlier in the day had been instrumental in clearing the place out, too, for tragedies of that sort tend to send loved ones grouping together.

Gilles came in looking more haggard than ever, as though he'd been up for three days straight. It appeared that the pain from his leg was taking its toll in addition to everything else.

"M. Cade." He stuck out his hand. I grasped it, noticing how cold it was. "I wish you had had your epiphany in the morning."

"Yeah. Sorry."

"So tell me what has happened since I dropped you off an hour ago."

Had it only been an hour? I glanced at my watch. Sure enough, slightly more than sixty minutes had elapsed since Gilles drove away from the front of the hotel. I poured him a glass of wine, then recounted the conversation with

Molly, the night clerk, and my subsequent discovery of the contents of the bag.

"No money, monsieur?"

"None."

"It is all gone?"

"Yes."

"The bag had only paper in it?"

"Yes, and some letters." I handed Gilles the one with my name on it.

His face slackened as he read it, and he dropped his head into his hands once he'd finished. "That is very sad, monsieur."

"Yes."

"M. Hatif, he did something noble, no?"

"Yes, Gilles, he did indeed do something noble."

"You will, of course, visit the little boy?"

"Yes, I will visit Pierre. In fact, I will visit Pierre tomorrow, right after I rent a car."

"Good." He paused for a drink of his wine. "You had remembered something else?"

This was the part I still had doubts about, but I'd mulled it over since calling Gilles, most especially while waiting for him to arrive at Le Vintage, and had become even more convinced. "That man this afternoon."

"Which man?"

"At Aimee's office."

"There was a man at Aimee's office?"

I shook my head. "No, not *at* her office. When we arrived, as we got out of the car, a man came out of her building."

"Okay."

"Something about him bothered me but then he was scowling so I thought that was it. But I was wrong. That wasn't what bothered me about him." I chewed on the inside of my cheek, building confidence. "It came to me tonight in my room. I'd seen him before."

"Oui, monsieur?"

"Yes, Gilles, I'd seen that man before." I took a deep breath. "He was the other guy in the back bedroom with Gauthier at Yvette's party."

Gilles scratched the side of his head. "Monsieur? What are you saying?"

"Yeah." What was I saying? I sort of knew how it sounded. Aimee pissed me off so I was finding a way to implicate her. But I knew I was right. That had been the same man. I was more certain than ever, and it wasn't certainty brought on by the red stuff in the bottle on the table or a desire to lay blame on a person I'd come to dislike. I laid out my argument, and it took me less than five minutes to convince Gilles. Once I had, he picked up his phone and set about putting people in place to ensure that Aimee didn't make a move that we didn't know about.

Between LeDuc and his old pal Ian, Adrien's sister was under surveillance by two a.m., both at her residence and at her office, plus everywhere in between. Nothing would be moved without being reported back to the French detective and myself. We only hoped that nothing had already been disposed of.

If my theory held water, then the man I'd seen leaving Aimee's office building was one of Gauthier's bodyguards. Furthermore, I figured he'd been on the train when the shooting went down. He had to have been the one who spirited away that bag full of money. And I was absolutely positive he'd delivered it to Aimee. That's why he'd been in her building. The connection between them wasn't clear yet, but then little was.

The wine and the day's events emboldened me to ask Gilles about his leg. Maybe I wanted a diversion, too. We had much to figure out in the days ahead, but for now a story that had a concrete conclusion sounded good. He looked at his folded hands for a long time before answering.

"An old injury, monsieur."

"I'd guessed that much. It didn't look like arthritis. So what happened?"

For a second, I didn't think he would tell me. Then he tipped his head back and laid it all out. Well, laid some of it out anyway.

"I was a detective."

"You still are."

"No, monsieur, I was a police detective. In Marseille."

"Huh."

"That is how I know Ian."

"Ian wasn't a French policeman. He's British. Scottish, to be exact. And Scotland's a long way from Marseille."

Gilles shrugged. "Different country, same brotherhood. We met, became friends. We worked together on a case. That was a short time before I moved here. It was me that convinced him to retire in Pezenas. Him and some of his other buddies." He took a deep breath. "Anyway, Marseille is a rough place, monsieur. Even for policemen. The streets can be very dangerous. One day, there was a shootout. Two bullets hit my leg. I spent weeks in hospital. I didn't recover so well. My superior wanted to put me behind a desk. I decided maybe private work would suit me instead, so I moved to this little village."

I watched him as he spoke. A veil had come down over his face as he related the critical moments. He was leaving out at least part of the story, maybe a great part of it, but he had opened up this much. For now, I'd leave it, but the man's history intrigued me even more with that little teaser.

He drained his glass and struggled to his feet. Clearly, the last fifteen hours had nearly depleted his energy. Mine, too, when I thought about it.

"Monsieur, shall we meet at Chartre, ten o'clock? That is good, n'est-ce pas?"

"Sure, Gilles. Chartre, ten o'clock. Thank you."

He looked at me quizzically.

"I mean it. Thank you, Gilles. For everything."

He leaned on his cane, reached out with his free hand and patted me on the shoulder before walking out onto the quiet streets. I had a cab waiting for him.

Chapter 29

The last week in France was memorable, and that's an understatement. Sure, I was anxious to get home to Lauren (yes, and Jiggs and Irene Adler, too) but was having mixed feelings once again about leaving my new friends. While I thought Lauren would love the "lads" and really wished she could join us, in truth there was no place for her at the table the nights we devised the final set of plans. A lot of women wouldn't have understood, Lauren among them. Their sensibilities are just too pure. The five of us guys swore a blood oath not to tell what we cooked up over cocktails, right down to the pricking of fingers and swapping of blood. Okay, we didn't go that far, but pretty damned close.

I'll tell you what, that English Jack has a great head on him, and I'm not just talking hair. Living up to his impish looks, the man can tweak the best of schemes and find the holes in plots where no one else even senses their presence. Ian, being retired police, naturally knows a lot about crime, so his input was invaluable in a myriad of ways. We've already seen how connected and inventive Gilles is, so he took care of what Ian couldn't. It fell to the two of them to round up the cast of characters to play the roles. That left Kellen, the quiet one. Kellen is an enigma, but an enigma with fill-in skills, meaning he picked up the slack wherever any of the rest of us fell short. My job, you ask? Well, I came up with the plan, at least the skeleton of it. Boiled down, I was kind of the what-if guy. Once a glimmering of the plot was hatched, perfecting it didn't take long with that crew. After that, we set it in motion and it hummed along like a well-maintained engine.

We didn't know how long we had before the police would release me to travel. Of course, once the cops discovered my relationship to one of the dead guys on the train (particularly when they also noticed my connection to a dead guy at Le Chat Cachemire winery), their interest in me took a sharp uptick. Fortunately, though, it quickly waned. Gilles vouching for me helped – to a point. They still wanted me to hang around for a little while, I guess in case they thought of more questions. What could I tell them that I hadn't already done, at least twice? I mean, I wasn't on that train. And if I ever found the money, I sure as hell wasn't giving it to them. In fact, none of us even mentioned it. Assuming the cops had initially heard of the mysterious bag – and they surely had – they might as well have dismissed it as fantasy since nothing further was said about it and no proof existed that it had ever been on the ill-fated train. At least, that's what we thought. But it was early days yet.

Possibly, if we had come clean up front with everything we knew, the police might have arrested Counselor Aimee Hatif-Purdue right away, but we didn't want to take the chance that she might go free. Besides, that would have tied up the 90,000 euros, and I had a use for that money if we could recover it. No, we decided to trust ourselves over the French police. Maybe that was wrong, but we were the ones who would have to live with that decision.

The days went by quickly. Of course, the first priority was for me to go rent the Ferrari again. Aside from just wanting my own wheels, I needed a car to get myself over to Chantal's little garden apartment. I had a message for her, and one for little Pierre. Adrien had written notes to both of them, sealed them in a couple of the envelopes that were in what I'd come to call the decoy bag. (I'd become convinced that my initial theory about him buying two identical bags was spot on, as English Jack would say.)

Now, on the heels of Adrien's death, the notes he'd left might be small comfort, but comfort was precisely what his family and friends needed, in whatever measure. And I wanted a somewhat impressive way to deliver them, thus the Ferrari, especially for the child. Besides, I thought maybe little Pierre needed to take a countryside ride in a fun sporty machine. We'd see; that would be up to his mom. The boy had not known his father, but he was catching on to the concept of love, so when I told him his daddy loved him but couldn't be there to tell him in person, he giggled and then hid his face. Maybe he'd do that with everything I said, but I chose to believe he understood.

I made a habit of stopping by every day, because Adrien's message to his son seemed so important and I took my duty as messenger seriously. It was still hard to accept that the guy was dead. There would be no more of his colorful flamboyance and carefree shrugs. Those excellent dimples had been neutralized, and that reckless charm silenced. He probably never realized how many lives he'd touched or how many people would mourn his passing. But, then, he probably never thought about his passing at all, not at his age. I understand, because, at 36, I still consider myself pretty much invincible.

Chantal seemed to appreciate the visits, too. She had taken Adrien's death especially hard. I came to suspect that she'd held out hope for some sort of reconciliation. But now even that small hope had died.

Chantal and her roommate, Marie, were doing a wonderful job with Pierre, though. The kid got a ton of TLC. Marie worked a different shift than Chantal, so Pierre essentially had two moms, one of them at home with him all of the time. An ideal situation for the almost-one-year-old. Yeah, Pierre would soon turn one. It was tragic for both father and son that Adrien wouldn't be here to celebrate his child's first birthday, a giant milestone in anyone's life. Partly because of that, and partly because Pierre had his daddy's dimples and full-face grin, I never arrived without an armful of toys. This kid was not going to want for anything by the time I left. And, no, don't go thinking I was beginning to get all domestic and wishing for a little one of my own. Pierre was cute and all, but fatherhood could wait awhile longer for Cade Blackstone. The boy had started to grow on me, though.

Each day, after I'd leave Chantal and Pierre at their tidy apartment in Montagnac, I'd make the drive over to Montpellier to check out what was happening at the law offices of Aimee Hatif-Purdue, Esq. (I hate hyphenated names, which was another reason to dislike Adrien's scheming, dissembling sister. It was almost as though Aimee had taken a husband for the sole purpose of acquiring another name to put after a hyphen. I mean, she'd dumped the guy quickly enough after the wedding yet kept the name. What better proof is there?)

The day after the train shootings, Gilles and I had returned to Aimee's office, our excuse being once again concern for her in her grief, but in reality we were just nosing around. The conversation went something like this:

"Monsieurs, you are back?"

"Oui, mademoiselle, we wish to express our sincere sorrow for your loss and bring you a small token of our sympathy." On cue, I'd handed her a bouquet of flowers we had purchased before leaving Pezenas.

"Merci." We had expected that she might go in search of a vase and some water to put the flowers in, but she plunked them down on the tiny table in the reception area, thwarting our chances for snooping, the actual purpose for our visit.

After a short awkwardness, Gilles started speaking some soft words in French while I stood with my hands behind my back and let my eyes wander around. The door to her inner office stood ajar only about six inches, allowing almost no view of its contents. Aimee shifted from foot to foot and sniffed, her impatience palpable.

Once Gilles had finished speaking, I flashed my most charismatic smile at Aimee and said, "If there is anything at all we can do, please do not hesitate to call," then motioned to Gilles, who handed her one of his cards.

She had taken it, said a brusque, "Merci," and walked into her office, slamming the door behind her.

"Well, I think she appreciated our condolences, don't you, M. LeDuc?"

He'd shaken his head and turned to leave.

Back outside, I'd stopped and done a slow, sweeping view of the narrow street. Everything had appeared normal and no one looked out of place. Gilles' man was hard to spot but I'd finally picked him out about half a block down.

"That your guy at the café there?"

"Oui."

No one would guess the fellow was sitting there for the sole purpose of observing Aimee's building. He looked like any young man with a phone glued to his ear, a pose the bulk of Europeans spend most of their day in. I'd merely pointed him out because he was the only other fellow within eyesight. He was barely noticeable, though, tucked behind one of the café's potted plants.

Gilles and I had walked back to the car. A real car that day, the red Ferrari. I'd decided to drive. Gilles' leg was giving him a lot of trouble, which gave me a good excuse to offer my services as chauffeur. And it made the ride back to Pezenas much more fun. And much more perky. I'm not sure Gilles appreciated the extra fun, though.

- - -

Several evenings later, at Le Vintage, our gang of five gathered, as usual. We discussed our progress, and pretty much agreed it wasn't really progress at all. We were going to have to go out and make something happen rather than sit around and wait for it to occur. Problem was what?

Naturally, Kellen sat by, quiet, awaiting suggestions.

Oddly, Jack seemed to think all was humming along quite nicely. "Gilles' guy is doing a brilliant job."

Ian disagreed. "Gilles' guy is sitting at a café table all day having an imaginary conversation on his phone. What about that is brilliant?"

"Nothing is getting by him. That's brilliant."

"We don't actually know that, now, do we? What we do know is that the money is still missing."

"Yeah. Bollocks about that."

Gilles defended his man in the café but did not dispute that things weren't moving fast enough. In reality, if you were honest and thought about it, Aimee could leave the cash hidden wherever it was for months. And I, for one, believed she would do just that. Only impatience would compel her to tip her hand. Or panic. So a panic is just what I intended to create.

The five of us once again put our heads together to work out a new, better strategy. By the time I drained the last of my wine, we had a variation on the original plan we were all proud of. Next on the agenda, Cade Blackstone would place a call to Aimee Hatif-Purdue in the morning.

- - -

Early the following day, Gilles and I met his surveillance guy at the café down the street from Aimee's law office. Everything about the place was awful except for the view of her building. I had to admire the man for sticking it out with no complaints. He probably would be happy to see this job end soon just so he could get a decent cup of coffee.

Once the three of us had situated ourselves around a wobbly table (one that appeared sketchy in the cleanliness department, too), we waited until we saw Aimee arrive at work. We gave her just three minutes to ensure she'd gotten completely inside and maybe plunked down her suitcase of a purse. Then I placed my call to her.

"Mlle. Hatif-Purdue," I addressed her by her full formal name since this wasn't a friendly call.

"Mr. Blackstone. What do you want now? I have a busy day." She countered with an iciness to her voice that made me believe we were getting under her skin, at least a little.

"Yes, I am sure you do, so I will get right to the point. We are not certain of your reasons for wanting your brother dead —"

She made a noise that might have been a gasp. I think I'd surprised her.

"– but we know you were involved, and we know you had the bag with the 90,000 euros in it."

"A bag of euros?"

"Oh, come on, mademoiselle, don't bother to deny it. It only makes you sound silly. We know you *had* the bag. This we know. But do you know where the bag is now?"

I listened to her measured breathing for a few seconds.

"I only ask because Adrien's Facebook page shows a picture of that bag, recently posted, like this morning. We have no idea who posted it – obviously not Adrien, since he's *dead* – but it's definitely a picture of that bag." I paused for drama. "Go ahead, take a look. You can call me back if you'd like."

Kellen, the loose-ends member of the team, had managed this small feat. Don't ask me how; that's why we had Kellen do that part. Of course, it wasn't the actual bag containing the money. That's the bag we were trying to get our hands on. The picture on Facebook was of the decoy bag. But, if Aimee had the money in her office in the original valise, odds were good that she'd be checking on its safety this very instant, looking to see that it was exactly where she'd left it, and there wouldn't be any sign of panic. If, on the other hand, she had stowed it elsewhere, Gilles' guy observing from the café should see her running out of the building any second.

I realized Aimee had gone silent but had not hung up. Checking Facebook on her office computer? Or making sure the bag was where she'd last put it, just a few steps from where she was sitting? Did her silence mean she was on to me or just a really cool cucumber, as my dad, Harry, used to say? I waited her out.

"You waste your time, monsieur. I do not know what you are talking about."

Well, she had delayed her response by about three clicks too long to be believable. However, this ploy wasn't getting the definitive response I'd hoped for. Now I needed to seriously rattle her cage, so I decided to use Auxiliary Plan A.

"Ah, so you are going to stick to that story? You disappoint me. But okay then, I should let you know that we also have Silvie's cell phone." Silvie, it turned out, was the guy Gilles and I saw leaving Aimee's office shortly after the attacks on the train, so we figured him to be the guy who delivered the bag to her. We also knew that he was one of Gauthier's bodyguards who'd been with the drug lord on the fatal train trip. I counted five long seconds before she replied.

"Who is this Silvie you speak of?"

"Now you're sounding silly again. Silvie is the fellow who brought you the bag of money."

"I do not know a Silvie."

"Well, then, there's no reason we would find any record of calls to or from your number on his phone, is there?"

"Of course not."

"Okay. If you refuse to be open with me, I will take my information elsewhere. Au revoir, mademoiselle." I disconnected before she had a chance to protest. We had given her plenty to think about. Now we just needed to wait and watch while she stewed. Hopefully, she would stew. And hopefully, she would tip her hand.

After that, Gilles and I left the observation of her movements to the people tasked with surveilling her.

One of the tactics was employed shortly after I called her that first day. We sent Kellen in to see her with a trumped-up story of a land deal he was working on. That got him into her inner sanctum, as hoped. But his observations weren't very helpful. He said her office was quite cluttered (I already knew that from my earlier appointment), with piles of files stacked on the floor and boxes of what looked like evidence in columns as high as three feet. Despite Kellen's keen familiarity with the appearance and dimensions of the bag that contained the money, he said it might have been behind any number of things and he'd have been unable to see it. That was disappointing, but not surprising. We didn't really expect that she would keep it out in the open.

He did report, though, that Aimee seemed distracted during the entire time he was attempting to engage her services. She rushed him along as though she had someplace to be off to. That sounded promising. Maybe we were about to catch a break. But, by the end of the day, we had no word of any discovery, and no overtly suspicious movements on her part.

Gilles' connections at the bank had done some checking, too, but no one had reported a deposit of 90,000 euros by a Montpellier attorney. Wherever Aimee had the money, there didn't seem to be an official record of it, which could only work in our favor. We wanted it back so, if no one officially knew it existed, no one could officially complain if it went missing. Again. The trick would be flushing out its whereabouts. Once located, retrieving it shouldn't present more than the smallest of efforts.

We kept prodding at her, though. One of our tricks was bound to push her over the edge. We knew we had spooked her. She'd break soon; we were sure of it. We had a great team working every conceivable angle.

Each night, our little group met at the bar in Pezenas to report on the day's activities. We'd go around the table, hissing and booing at any setbacks we'd encountered and cheering every stumble that Aimee made. On the third evening after my phone call to her, Ian came in carrying a large plastic bag.

"What have you got there, Ian?"

"Well, sir, I have myself a bag here."

"Yes, so it seems. And what's in the bag?"

"A tuna sandwich." He winked.

My jaw dropped. Not that I hadn't expected this, but why had it taken so long?

"A tuna sandwich! Oh, my. I can't tell you how much I like tuna sandwiches. I've really been looking forward to this." I peered inside the plastic bag, and stuffed down toward the bottom of it was the valise that Adrien had carried onto the train. It looked a bit worse for wear but intact. Although I harbored a secret fear that there might be blood spatter on it, I kept that thought to myself and just hugged the bag close to my chest.

"How did you manage to get this sandwich?"

Ian winked again. "A couple of my friends are experts at sniffing out lost lunches. When they catch wind of them, let's just say they don't let a closed door stand in their way."

So, sometime during the night, Ian's friends had "sniffed out" the money and "recovered" it. I could almost hear Aimee's screams when she discovered the bag missing. Imaginary music to my ears. I sighed, long and slow.

"Thank you, Ian."

"Quite welcome, sir." He motioned to the waiter. "Garcon, a round!"

Being regulars has its perks. The fellow didn't hesitate for an instant, nor did he need to ask what to bring us. He simply knew. So drinks were on the table in short order and we toasted our success. It had taken a wild amount of deception, lots of surveillance, clever maneuvering, much legwork and probably a few things that could technically be called illegal, but the 90,000 euros were back where they belonged. Well, most of them. Several had gotten spent along the way, probably some in a payoff to Silvie was my guess, and possibly some went to a quick spree that Aimee indulged herself in. Happily, possession of that fortune had been short-lived for her.

Now it was time to gear up for Part Two of Operation Snag Aimee. Getting the money back had been the easy part. But no way were we going to let her get away with murder. And there was no question in our minds that she had had her brother knocked off. For some reason, she'd grown to hate him. A misguided anger stemming from her personal inability to have children and his uncaring attitude toward his own, we figured. Plus, she knew he would be carrying a lot of money. She'd drawn up the loan papers, for heaven's sake. She must not have been able to believe her luck. 90,000 euros, that's quite a sizable motive.

Then Adrien had gone a step further the day of our appointment and indulged in some kind of private chat with her; a confession, I guessed, but it was all in French so I had just stood there like a third wheel while he spilled his guts. My bet now was that he'd told her pretty much everything. So she saw an opportunity to take out her brother and get her hands on a tidy sum of cash. Gauthier was just a nice piece of collateral damage. We didn't know all of the details yet but they were slowly emerging.

So, next, we had to ensure that this cold-blooded killer went away for a long time. This part of the plot might be a bit trickier, but, hey, the devil is in the details, as they say. And Aimee, nasty little devil that she was, deserved a well-thought-out scheme. The five of us – Le Vintage Five as we'd begun to call ourselves – were just the ones to dream up the scheme that would take her down. Of course, she was sure to know who had swiped the money, so, angry as a stepped-on rattlesnake or not, she probably thought we were all square now. Boy, she couldn't have been more wrong. But we'd need to tread carefully because a stepped-on rattlesnake can be extremely dangerous.

Chapter 30

Each of Le Vintage Five was looking forward to setting in motion the Aimee End Game, or Part Two of Operation Snag Aimee. I had finally been released to travel, so we stepped up our timetable. Really, though, once we had completed Part One, it would play out better the faster we got it done anyway. Besides, being away from Lauren was starting to affect my brains, or at least one of them. Lately, I'd begun to have frequent dreams about her silky blonde hair, green eyes, long, slender toes and, um, a few other parts.

But back to the plan. We were getting ready to set the trap. However, first, we had to figure out our resources. The task of counting the recovered money fell to Kellen. The total came to 67,786 euros and change, a slightly disappointing amount, considering it started out life as 90,000. Aimee must have paid Silvie close to 20,000 of it, which should have been enough to ensure his silence and maybe his loyalty, if he had any. I wouldn't have bet on it. In fact, given the chance, we would test the limits of that loyalty.

Ian and Gilles had been gathering intelligence from as many police sources as they had around the area (a lot), and discovered that the idea of the missing valise was still alive and kicking out there. Apparently, multiple witnesses swore that they'd seen one of the victims carrying a bag matching its description, and there was a possible sighting on surveillance tapes from the train station in Beziers of a man in a cape with dreads and a bag. Those closed circuit photos are notoriously blurry but folks who know what they're looking for can suss out the details pretty well. Sort of like ultrasound techs, I guess. Besides, a dread-headed figure wearing a cape is not real typical of the train-riding public in the south of France. Then you add in gorgeous mocha skin and cavernous dimples, and narrowing down the ID becomes a whole lot easier. From the rumors we'd heard, the cops had formed an opinion that sort of paralleled actual fact. Now we just had to figure out how to use that to our advantage.

Meanwhile, the men that we had watching Aimee reported that her routine had become erratic and she was keeping odd hours. Well, if she was searching for the purloined bag, that could go a ways toward explaining it. But, of course, we had a constant guard on that bag. No chance she'd be getting it back. At least, not until we were ready. It must have been driving her mad to think that she'd gone to the trouble of having Adrien killed and then lost the money, too. Murder's a bitch. And then comes the payback. If we had anything to say about it, Aimee's happy days were over. Forever.

The night before The Big Trap, I returned to my suite at Hotel Moliere a couple of minutes before midnight, or late afternoon at my home in Oregon. That's a time of day that would find Lauren out interviewing some victim of petty crime or possibly putting the finishing touches on a story for the *Community Press*. Didn't matter, I had to talk to her.

When she answered, she sounded breathy. Rushed? Tired? Neither?

"Hi, doll."

"Hey, Cade."

"Is this a bad time?"

"It's fine."

Fine? What does it mean when a woman says that? I waded in cautiously, just in case of a misinterpretation on my end. "Well, doll, tomorrow's the big day."

"It is? Because I've heard that before."

Okay, now I was catching on to what *Fine* meant. In this case, pretty much *not fine at all*.

"Yeah, well, this time's for sure. Got everything set. I realize you don't know these guys – well, except for English Jack – but they're the best of the best. Incredible, actually. And we've worked out all of the details. Timeline has been checked, double-checked and even triple-checked. It's a definite go."

"Uh-huh."

"Honest. Anyway, I'll be on a flight in two days, three tops."

"Uh-huh."

"Can't wait to get home." I paused, but apparently she had no response. "Any word on Cassandra?"

"No."

Maybe I shouldn't have asked that, especially considering Lauren's chilliness. I had to, though. Cassandra York had not been heard from now, by my reckoning, for over a week. Maybe longer. Maybe a lot longer. I'd lost track. That kind of disappearance absolutely screamed that something was crucially wrong. Ex-girlfriend or not, I had a right to be concerned. The *entire county* had a right to be concerned. One of their residents appeared to be in serious jeopardy, or worse. It was time for everyone to pull together. Cassandra York needed to be found.

"I'll look into it when I get home."

"Have you spoken to Jim Smith?"

"Not yet. I've been too wrapped up in recovering this money."

"Oh, yes, the money. You have it now, right?"

"Yes, but – well, it's complicated. I'll explain when I see you. "

"Complicated. Uh-huh."

I hate it when she repeats words from my sentences. It never bodes well.

"Hey, gotta go. Love you, doll." Shit, had I just said the "L" word? I hung up before she could get all mushy, although it hadn't sounded like that's the direction she was heading. Anyway, I had a lot to think about without Lauren muddling my brain – either brain. Tomorrow was game day, and the end game promised to be highly entertaining. Also, I knew, from past experience, that game day has a way of not always working out exactly as one envisions. I had my fingers crossed that, this time, it would.

- - -

Part Two of Operation Snag Aimee was indeed trickier. It involved a lot of finesse and even more luck. Much of its success depended upon good street info and French police who didn't question too strongly the appearance of some sort of new evidence this late in the game. And then, we'd need a jury down the road that didn't mind a few blurred lines. Tricky, as I said. Still, we had to try.

Jack kept us all on track, making sure we didn't miss those loopholes that can bring down the best-laid plans. Kellen did his normal filling in. But it was Ian and Gilles who were positively invaluable. They recruited the exact perfect individuals for the jobs. What jobs, you ask? Well, I'm not sure the guys would want me detailing the whole operation. That blood oath and all, remember. But the highlights went something like this: Two highly proficient B&E specialists returned the bag of money – minus several thousand euros (okay, minus all but 20,000 euros, sort of what we figured her payoff to Silvie had been) – to Mlle. Hatif-Purdue's office. The bag and its contents had been carefully handled since snatching it from Aimee, to keep from leaving any new fingerprints behind.

Next, a tip was strategically – and anonymously – phoned in to the Montpellier cops once Aimee had settled into her office. If the timing came off the way we hoped, the police would arrive about the time Aimee discovered the bag, realized something was up, and attempted to get the hell out of Dodge with it. Of course, it didn't happen quite like that, but it did work out so that she was caught red-handed. Good enough. Score one for Le Vintage Five.

Now, the next tricky bit comes into play. We had our fingers crossed that Aimee had, indeed, made at least one, and hopefully several, calls to Silvie. We knew that his fingerprints would be discovered on the bag. (He wasn't smart enough to wear gloves. No, huh-uh.) So naturally, the cops would want to interview him. And, once they did, we couldn't see any reason for him not to roll over on Aimee. She'd already paid him his hush money, but he wasn't going to admit that. If he had even half a brain, he would claim all he did was deliver the bag. He knew nothing about a planned hit on his boss or her brother. "Seriously? It was a hit?" Gasp. Go the wide-eyed innocence route.

And, really, there wasn't anything tying him to the killings. JZ Durand was the one with the gun, the one who walked up to Gauthier and Adrien and pulled the trigger; there was no dispute about that. And, as far as we had been able to ascertain, no connection between Silvie and JZ existed. At least, scuttlebutt on the street hadn't found any.

So the 20,000 that remained in the bag should look like the payoff to JZ, the small-time hoodlum-turned-hit man. Gauthier's bodyguard, Silvie, would claim he had simply rescued the bag when JZ shot his boss and then was killed by the soldiers on the train. He'd take the story further and say that, being the upstanding citizen that he is, he peeked inside and found an envelope addressed to Aimee Hatif, immediately put aside any thought of personal profit and took the money to Mlle. Hatif. Even if the cops discovered that Silvie had some cash from that bag in his possession, he could persuasively argue that it was a reward for the return of the money.

So that tricky bit might not be so tricky. On to the next one, and it definitely was more iffy: A French jury. Any jury is iffy. There is no telling how a panel of one's peers will interpret the evidence put before it. In this case, there was no telling what they would think about an otherwise upstanding attorney, pillar of the community (sort of) being accused of hiring someone to murder her own brother. People don't like to think of murders within families, so they try to find a more palatable explanation. We prayed the jury on Aimee's case would see the truth.

That's why we had come up with the last tricky bit, which some might call manufactured evidence. Well, so be it.

Chapter 31

So what was this manufactured evidence, you ask? Well, we had come to the conclusion that, in order to cinch the noose even more tightly around Aimee's neck, we needed what we at home call proof beyond a reasonable doubt. The bag and its monetary contents had already been taken care of. The cops had found the 20,000 euros in Aimee's possession, which should raise eyebrows all on its own. Also, the cash was found in a bag that they had a pretty decent picture of on surveillance tape at the train platform that was the departure point for one of the shooting victims. And the bag was slung over that victim's shoulder at the time the tape shows him boarding the train. This by itself gave them a nice direction in which their suspicions could run wild and ultimately form themselves into a fairly solid case. So what else had we come up with to seal the deal? Pay attention now, because I think we did a pretty cool job or, as English Jack would say, a bloody bang-up job.

Over the course of several evenings, Le Vintage Five had agonized about how to trap Aimee securely in a web of her own making. In the end, we decided we had to weave a few strands of that lethal web ourselves. So, after much discussion and many ideas that we kicked around and ultimately booted, I came up with the ingenious strategy of using Adrien's words against his sister. Really, the idea had been staring us in the face all along. I mean, he'd left several envelopes containing plenty of his words. Yeah, I know, he had written those notes as special last messages to the people he loved, but I thought he would forgive me hijacking them for a short while. It was for a good cause, after all. In fact, the best: catching his murderer.

For this, Ian had a guy – yes, yet another guy – that was flawless at forging. That's the wonderful part of having men with a police background on your team. They know all sorts of super competent shady types who lack much in the way of a conscience. Between Ian and Gilles, one had only to mention it and a guy would appear who could handle whatever one wanted done. Anyway, this guy just needed for us to feed him the words and he'd look at Adrien's letters – the ones written to me, to his mom and dad, the ones to Chantal and Pierre, even the one to Aimee herself – and pen a new missive. I'd made copies of each one of the notes before delivering them to the addressees. Why? That's just the detective in me. And the part of me that loves details. I realized the letters were private, but I couldn't help it. You just never know when something might come in handy. And, sure enough, these came in handy. More than handy, in fact.

Since we already had an envelope that Adrien had addressed to Aimee, we used that one to carry our manufactured note, figuring that any handwriting expert employed by the police – in addition to probably many other forensics types – would begin there. The handwriting would easily be validated (because it was real, for heaven's sake), which might lead the experts to overlook an inconsistency or two while attempting to authenticate the envelope's contents. But Ian's guy was flawless, as I said, so we didn't worry about inconsistencies. He could duplicate any of Adrien's printed letters and numbers simply by studying the selection of notes. We had him practice writing several messages, using wording we played with until we got just what we thought sounded most damning without coming across as phony. So we composed a message from Adrien to his sister that went something like this, as I remember:

Dear Aimee, I hope you never see this because if you do it means I am dead. My friend will ensure that this is delivered to you. Please reward him for his risk. I will try to pay off Fabron Gauthier the 20,000 like you asked, but if you are reading this now, something has gone wrong. I am sorry. Tell Maman and Papa I love them. Your brother, Adrien.

"Now that's a nice little hors d'oeuvre for the French police," Ian remarked.

"Do you think it's enough?" I asked. A worrier by nature, I always wanted assurances. And then assurances on top of those assurances. True, we were confident that Aimee had already disposed of her office copies of the original loan between Adrien and me, an effort on her part to erase any evidence that she'd known about it. If she had not, *c'est la vie*. We figured it still would be hard to explain away this note in her brother's handwriting, especially when found in a bag with 20,000 euros that had been at the scene of a shooting.

And as a nice little bonus, it turned out that there was some blood on that bag, which we viewed as God's little contribution to our trap. And, while it tied Adrien to Gauthier – a fact we sincerely regretted, especially if it sullied the memory of their son in the minds of Maman and Papa – well, there's a yang for every yin. This might have been a pretty good-sized yang, but if it meant catching a killer, Adrien's reputation would have to take the hit. And possibly, if looked at in a different light (a light Le Vintage Five was striving to emphasize), it might suggest that Adrien was merely assisting his sister, who was the one with the connection to Gauthier, not himself, which would be easier to understand. Besides, I'd read the note he left to his parents. (Nosiness is another trait of us detective types.) In that note, he said some pretty powerful stuff. After reading his beautiful words to them? I figured he could be forgiven his fall from grace, if that's how they saw it, especially considering how brief the fall was. Frankly, he'd had me sobbing.

So now, when I asked the question, "Do you think it's enough?" and Ian answered, "Absolutely; it's even better than the tuna sandwich," I heaved a giant sigh of relief. Jack slapped me on the back and said, "Bloody good job, mate," which left me beaming, too. Kellen smiled enigmatically and nodded. Gilles dipped his head and raised his glass. All in all, those were some pretty strong votes of confidence. We had yet to see everything fall into place and play out the way we hoped, but a conviction looked promising, thanks to these four guys – and the guys they knew, and the guys those guys knew. I suggested we get the entire cast of players together for a celebration to show my appreciation.

Ian grinned. "Lovely idea, that, but I'm afraid they've all faded back into the landscape. I'll tell them you thought of them, though."

Well, indeed I had thought of them. I'd thought of them plenty. And I'd paid them plenty, too. Everyone who had helped pull this off had been compensated. Very well compensated, as a matter of fact. Fortunately, money was still left over, even holding out Fou Flamant's original $20,000, which would have to be returned to them. Actually, quite a decent sum was left over. And I had one last errand to take care of before I left France for the States. It was another thing that Gilles' man at the bank could help me with.

I'd never had an account in a foreign country, so this was new territory for me. I deposited close to 22,000 euros in the account that Gilles' man set up for me. I signed as co-owner, with one tiny fellow named Pierre Hatif as my other account holder. (Yes, Chantal had given her son Adrien's last name. I supposed she held out hope they might eventually become a family in the traditional sense.)

In time, I would let Chantal know about the money. But not for a while. That amount could tempt even the purest of mothers to dip into the account, and I wanted it to grow for Pierre. And it would, especially with the type of fund the banker had chosen. As for monitoring their future, I have my ways of keeping track of people. In fact, Pierre's Uncle Michel had volunteered to help however he could. It seemed he'd taken quite a liking to his nephew, and he placed great trust in me, which felt good. I really had tried to save Adrien, a fact at least he wholeheartedly believed.

Anyway, Chantal's whereabouts – and her circumstances – would be reported to me periodically over the upcoming years. And I'd know when the time had come to turn over control of the account. Adrien's son deserved some stability in his future, even if it was mostly financial. After all, he had lost any chance at a relationship with his father. That's a huge loss for any child. Here I had a chance to do something to help fill that hole. This would be my small contribution. Hey, my Uncle Cliff left me this money to do with as I pleased. Somehow, I thought this might make him happy that he had.

Chapter 32

The earliest flight out of Montpellier that connected to anywhere near where I wanted to go was headed for Seattle. Fine by me. I love France and all, but I'd had enough of it by then. And, while I'd become immensely fond of the guys during our evenings at Le Vintage Bar – and I believe the feeling was mutual – I think they were ready to get back to their daily norms, too.

The attack on the Charlie Hebdo offices was what had originally brought Lauren and me to France, and it had been a wretched reason for the visit. And now the visit had a wretched ending, too. My other purpose for crossing the pond – to find Fou Flamant's missing winemaker – had seen brief success before spectacular failure. Sure, I'd located Adrien Hatif, and I'd even convinced him to come back to Carlton with me. But there was a huge flaw in the execution of that whole plan, and winemaker Hatif ended up dead.

It hadn't needed to be that way. His sister, once his closest playmate and greatest ally, had turned into his deadliest enemy. It just goes to show how thin the line between love and hate. Aimee's bitterness over her inability to have children and Adrien's seeming lack of interest in his son planted a toxic seed of resentment, and her resentment grew into a spreading malignancy, aided by other jealousies that festered over the years. Ironically, she had been deeply wrong about her brother's paternal instincts. Adrien's last thought was of his son, at least judging by the notes he left behind. If you ask me, there was no doubt that he dearly loved little Pierre. In fact, he loved him with a fierceness that was magnified tenfold by his role as an absentee father. He might have even made a go of family life eventually. But Aimee killed any chance of that when she killed her brother. Now that little boy will grow up without ever knowing his dad.

I had been fortunate to know Pierre's father for even the briefest of times. And Pierre's father was the reason that I had gotten to know English Jack – and Ian, Kellen and Gilles LeDuc. What a journey the past few weeks had turned out to be. I'd at least made some invaluable friends, friends that would last for a lifetime, and I'd learned a lot more than I ever wanted to know about the French laws and their legal system. The beautiful Languedoc region has a less attractive side than I'd seen before, but that wouldn't keep me from returning. I wanted Lauren to see the Camargue horses yet. I mean, from the windows of a carriage being drawn through the marshes. And I wanted her to experience Montpellier in snow, a rare and wonderful sight. And share another bottle of St. Hilaire with me, at Le Vintage Bar. One day, we would come back. First, though, I'd need time to recover from this trip, for the losses to me were still open wounds, raw and emotional.

My sympathies went out to Henri and Simone Hatif, losing essentially two of their brilliant children in one year. That had to be tough. Worse, they would never know what a hero their youngest was in the end, but some things are best left alone. Maybe time spent with their newly-discovered grandson would help ease their pain. As I've said, there's a yang for every yin. And Pierre was one hell of a yang, if you asked me.

There was one more thing about Gilles LeDuc that I found out right before leaving. It happened on the eve of my departure. Naturally, Le Vintage Five met for a final toast to one of its members, Cade Blackstone, as he prepared himself for the trip home. I've already mentioned that parting was bittersweet. Indeed it was. Ready to head back or not, leaving the guys I'd been through so much with turned out to be more difficult than I had dreamed possible. We vowed never to lose touch with each other, and I'm sure they meant it as much as I did. They were four more reasons to bring Lauren back to the Languedoc. I know she'd absolutely love The Lads, as I'd taken to calling them. Actually, they started it.

At half past midnight, everyone had trickled out except Ian, Jack and I. It seemed obvious that Ian had something on his mind. I'd come to recognize a certain thoughtful look that he wore whenever he needed to clear his head. That look had settled on his face. So I waited for whatever it was he would tell me. Jack sat by, humming as he did when he'd gotten more than three glasses of wine in him, before realizing, I suppose, that Ian's posture signaled a request for privacy.

"Oh, bollocks, would you look at the time." Jack stood and held out his hand. "Say there, M. Blackstone, it's been a bloody great pleasure."

I shook that hand and did the three-cheek air kiss. I was really going to miss Jack, probably most of all. "Yes, a bloody great pleasure, Jack. You come visit me in Carlton. You know you're welcome anytime. I have lots of room." I slapped him on the back, although I could have pulled him into a big bear hug. It would be a long time before I'd see him again, and he'd never be in this good of shape. He nodded and ambled off. I hadn't said half of what I'd wanted to, and what little I'd said seemed so inadequate. He'd understand, though. Guys have a hard time saying good-bye. I watched him until he was out the door, then sat down again.

Ian leaned forward with his elbows on the table and said, "Great week, this."

Had it been just a week? I supposed it might have been. A week, maybe ten days. I'd lost count. But so much had been crammed into it, how could anyone keep track? Anyway, I agreed. "Yes, the entire time I've known you, however long that is, has been great. And I can't thank you enough for recommending Gilles. He's quite a guy."

"You don't know the half of it."

"I suppose I don't." Ian clearly had more to say. "Why don't you tell me what I don't know?"

"Gilles should do that."

"Yeah, probably." I waited, then nudged him with, "Gilles told me he was a police detective in Marseilles and that a couple of bullets essentially ended his career. Some kind of street shoot-out."

"Some kind of street shoot-out, yes. That it was." He took a deep breath. "That it was."

"Tell me, Ian. Please."

Ten seconds passed while he considered my request, I suppose. At last, he said, "Yes, well, Marseille can be very beautiful. Very beautiful indeed. But Marseille has a dark side, a dark and very dangerous side."

"I have heard that."

"It is no place for folks who don't know their way around it."

I nodded.

"One minute, you're in safe territory; the next, you've crossed a line."

"Chicago is like that."

We both smiled.

"Gilles knew his way around. He knew where the line was."

"I've no doubt."

"Have you heard of La Castellane?"

"No."

"La Castellane is a neighborhood in Marseille – or should I say on the outer borders of Marseille. More properly, it is a slum, a notorious place, known for its drug trafficking. Remember the American film *The French Connection*?"

"Of course. It's a classic."

"That film was based on a true story, a story about smuggling drugs from Marseilles to New York. In the movie, a big heroin shipment came from Marseille. Very likely the connection was in La Castellane. It's a hotbed of crime. Drugs are rampant at La Castellane. And not just drugs. There's smuggling of guns and also prostitution. Everybody steers clear of La Castellane. Everybody that can help it, anyway."

"Sounds like a nice place."

"No, that it is not. Even the police try to stay away from there." Ian pursed his lips. "Sometimes it cannot be helped, of course."

"Of course."

"But on this day, Gilles had no plans to go anywhere near La Castellane."

I nodded. "Wise decision, I'd say."

Ian agreed. "Ah, aye. Gilles wasn't going near La Castellane. But La Castellane spilled over into Marseille proper. It brought its violence downtown on that day. And on that day, Gilles was taking his lunch break downtown. Gunfire erupted near the café where he was eating. It was a beautiful day, so he was outside, on the sidewalk patio. Of course, he jumped up to protect everyone around him. But two Castellane gangs were vying for new territory and they don't take over anything without a fight. And they don't care who gets hurt when they do it." Ian sighed. "Gilles pushed people to the ground, shielded them with his own body, helped them to safety, all while firing at the gangs." Ian paused. "He got the shooters."

"Good."

"Aye. He even got a medal for it. But the gangs got him, too."

"Yeah, obviously I've seen his limp. And he told me about the shots to his leg, the tough recovery and the loss of his position."

"The position wasn't all he lost."

I looked up at Ian. His eyes had dropped to the table and his voice had become almost too low to hear. "Two people died that day, in addition to the gang members."

"Oh, no."

"Oh, aye. Two people. A waiter at the café and a young lady named Cheri. Cheri was Gilles' fiancée."

"Oh, damn."

"Aye. He'd asked Cheri to meet him for lunch. He had big a surprise for her: tickets for their honeymoon cruise on the Danube. He told me she'd dreamed of a Danube cruise since she was a tiny lass."

I swallowed, my throat suddenly dry. "Damn. That's awful."

"Gilles was devastated. Cheri's death was as much the reason for his resignation as his disability was. He did not step foot inside the department ever again. He moved to Pezenas before that year was out."

"Wow." Gilles hadn't even attended the medal ceremony. Once released from the hospital, he'd spent the weeks sequestered at home, refusing visitors, until Ian had broken through his depression. He wouldn't tell me how he did it, just that he did. Ian didn't say in so many words that he'd saved Gilles' life, but that's what I took away from the conversation.

I tried to envision how I'd feel if that had happened to Lauren, and I found that I could totally understand Gilles' reaction and subsequent decision to leave the job and Marseille. I shook off the thought of losing Lauren. "And has he never met anyone else?"

"No. No one will ever take the place of that lady love."

- - -

When the pilots set us down at Sea-Tac, I was the first person off of the plane, and I hastily made my way to the Enterprise car rental desk where I chose a Ford Mustang, a white one with a blue racing stripe. Not the best color combination, but it was far better than the green Saab I'd ridden to the Montpellier airport in and it would get me home in some sort of style, although I would sorely miss my French driver. It was shortly after 4:30 p.m. when I merged onto Interstate 5 a few miles south of Seattle. As usual in that area, traffic was a monster.

Portland lies about three hours south down the freeway (considerably less when *I'm* behind the wheel). Then to get on over to Carlton takes another half an hour, give or take ten minutes, allowing for pokey farm implements traveling the roadways. That evening, as soon as I took the turn onto Highway 47 just outside of Forest Grove, I punched it. The driver of the Mustang knew he was on the home stretch.

At straight up eight o'clock, I shut off the engine in my driveway and unbuckled my seat belt. As the motor ticked in the cool evening air, Lauren's face appeared in the kitchen window. The side door opened shortly after that, and out came my dog and my girlfriend. I hugged Lauren first, having gotten my priorities well straightened out, then Jiggs. I could hear Irene Adler screeching inside the house. Sounded like even she was happy I was home, although with Irene it can be difficult to tell. We had a lot of catching up to do in the coming days, but for now, a hug, a face lick and an ear peck were the most welcoming of gestures. God, how I'd missed them.

Chapter 33

When I awoke the next morning, I had no idea what day it was. That had been happening a lot recently. Jet lag didn't help either. My brains were scrambled, and I mean both of them. But Lauren was happy to see me, and she'd thought up some very inventive ways of showing it. I couldn't complain.

The calendar said February but the weather looked more like May. Sometimes it does that here in the Pacific Northwest. I'd left several weeks ago, early January as a matter of fact, when the weather was gray and dismal. Lauren and I had found ourselves in France, honoring slain journalists and showing unity for a country in shock. We'd tried to make something of a holiday of it, too, but that part didn't work out so well.

When we left for Paris, I'd been facing a search for a missing person, and I'd come home now empty handed but facing the same task. Wrapping my mind around Cassandra's disappearance was proving difficult. So I did the only thing I could right about then. I took the four of us on a day trip to the beach. February often has a couple weeks of unseasonably clear skies and calm winds, especially at the Oregon coast, and sometimes it even warms up like a late spring month. Surprising, really, and a little secret I've tried to keep to myself.

At the shore, Irene Adler stayed in the car, but Jiggs tore away from the Jeep as though spring loaded. He had enough fun romping through the surf for a dozen animals, at least. Frankly, he looked possessed. Lauren ambled along the sand like a waif, dressed in loose pants that billowed in the light breeze, and a wide-brimmed hat. I stood, watching the scene for a couple of minutes, amazed at my good fortune, then trotted to catch up. I slipped my hand into hers and we walked along, listening to the waves break, for about a mile and a half before turning back. I'm not sure either of us spoke a word. The murmur of the ocean and the dog's blissful splashing was all we needed.

At the car again, I wiped the sand and salt water off of Jiggs and he leapt into the back of the Jeep, panting and drooling. Irene tuned up with a song she must have been practicing while the rest of us walked. Eyes rolling, Lauren slid into the passenger seat. Yeah, I'd missed all of that while away setting my trap for Mlle. Aimee Hatif.

The beach trip went a long way toward clearing my mind, elevating my mood and paving the way for the next case, which I would need to face soon. Cassandra York had been missing for something like sixteen days by that time, and it couldn't wait any longer. Her current boyfriend, Rollie Hansen, used to be a deputy sheriff based in our fair town, but he'd proved himself too incompetent even for a community of our size, so he'd moved on. Considering his penchant for keeping a critical eye on me, especially when I'm driving my Lamborghini, that had made me exceptionally happy, but still, I felt for the guy. Cassandra could grate on even the most mild mannered of people, but I'd come to believe that Rollie had genuine feelings for her, feelings bordering on the "L" word, feelings deep enough that he tolerated not only all of her crap but also that nasty pugahuahua creature she called Pedro, or something else Mexican sounding. Apparently, it's a kind of designer dog, a skinny piece of bug-eyed fur with a tendency to yip incessantly, an annoying little creature that girls swoon over, cram into their purses and carry with them everywhere they go.

Anyway, even Lauren had started urging me to contact Rollie and see what help I could give him. The local police were doing what they could with their resources, but they were stretched somewhat thin, a state of affairs that Oregon law enforcement has been experiencing more and more over the past decade or so. My connections with the local police were stretched even thinner so I'd have to rely on other sources and try to keep a super low profile, as in wear an invisibility cloak.

Jim Smith had found some disturbing clues, clues that were pointing to foul play, but then going missing for sixteen days sort of pointed that way, too. The cops had towed her Mini Cooper and then subjected it to all kinds of forensic testing, the results of which had not been shared with me. In the upcoming days, I'd need to think of some ingenious ways to wrest information out of Sheriff Belanger and his gang of merry men. Sometimes they felt like sharing, but, most often, they didn't.

I already knew that Cassandra's car had been found out on Carpenter Creek Road. While that road branches off of some major routes, it peters out in a fairly remote area. No one goes out there without a reason. What reason had Cassandra had? Did she simply want solitude? Well, that was definitely a reason, and a pretty good one, too. It can be tough finding privacy, a place to just sit in peace, in the hundreds of square miles that comprise the Portland metropolitan area. So, yeah, I could understand hungering for that. The closest I get to a little privacy is when Jiggs and I take the kayak out for a spin on Henry Hagg Lake during the off season, notably those times that the kiddies are in school. So had Ms. York gone out Carpenter Creek Road for a break from the hustle bustle? Was it simply a case of searching for a quiet place to collect her thoughts?

Probably not. My gut told me she'd been lured out there. Cassandra is a PI, like me. Grudgingly, I'll admit that she's a pretty savvy one, too. So logic led me to believe a case had taken her to Carpenter Creek. So where had she gone from there? Especially without her car.

Had I learned anything in trying to coax Adrien Hatif home that might help me find the tall redhead? In truth, the French detective – Gilles LeDuc – had imparted several years' worth of experience condensed into a couple short weeks. Ian and the other Brits had had a hand in furthering my PI education, too. Now we'd see if I knew how to put it to any sort of practical use.

I'd really come to care about Adrien. Maybe too much. Maybe because of that little boy of his, Pierre. Yeah, Pierre might have clouded my judgment. His dimples and those eyes that were heading for deep, dark brown like his papa's. The kid was killer cute. What a pity his Aunt Aimee wouldn't get a chance to know him. Hiring a hit man to take out his dad kind of ended that possibility for her. And why? All because of a burning envy and a misreading of Adrien's love for his son. A double tragedy, stemming from a grave misunderstanding.

I do know about misunderstandings between brothers and sisters. I'd irrationally blamed my sis for the death of her own daughter. And at a time when she must have been at her most vulnerable. She must have craved sympathy, hungered for it even. But I was too immersed in the pain of that loss to see beyond my own selfish needs. We didn't speak for over a year, but at least I finally came to my senses. I'm still trying to make up for it. In fact, it's probably time to call her again, let her know how much she means to me, let her know I care. I'll give Aimee credit for unwittingly reminding me of that.

Once upon a time, I cared about Cassandra, too, but that time has long since passed. She and I were a happy item for a grand total of about a day and a half. Other than that, I've described our relationship as an extended wrestling match. That it was, as Ian might say. That it was. So I should be able to tackle this problem without emotions messing with my head. We'll see. I have a tendency to wax emotional at times, and the Hatif case has brought many raw feelings to the surface. What I'd really like would be time to put the last few weeks into perspective, overcome my lingering jet lag, and generally enjoy being home. It would have been nice to ease into the York case, to have time to carefully pore over the clues that filter in and gradually follow up leads, but the latest discovery sort of crushed dreams of doing that. The urgency has been stepped up.

I never liked Cassandra's dog Pedro or Pancho or whatever she called him, but he was still a dog. (I guess.) Not my kind of dog, but Cassandra loved him. Sorry, I'm stalling. There's no sugarcoating this. Jim Smith just called. He said Pedro had been found, out on Carpenter Creek Road, close to where Cassandra's Mini Cooper was discovered. His tiny throat had been cut. He'd been tossed into a bush by the side of the road. What kind of person would do that? Nasty little nipper that Pedro was, he hadn't deserved an end like that. Yeah, he was a dog, an ugly one at that, but he was a living creature. No living creature deserves to die like that. Much like Adrien hadn't deserved to die like he did. His death keeps haunting me. Maybe one of these days, I'll find the missing person I'm looking for – I mean, alive and well. I fear, however, that it's not going to be Cassandra.

Epilog

A couple of weeks into my new investigation, which did not seem to be going too well if you really want to know, I came home late, worn out, and thoroughly discouraged. As I shut off the Lambo's engine, the fragrance of garlic and onions wafted out of the house and into the garage. Ah, two of Lauren's favorite things to cook, which works out pretty well because they are two of my favorite things to eat, especially when paired with a massive rare steak. The aromas brought a weary smile to my face, and I wished I had more of an appetite. The damned thing had deserted me sometime during the day as my suspicions pointed toward more bad news looming on the horizon.

I rubbed a hand down my face and took a deep breath, trying to remember why I'd chosen to become a private investigator. Oh, yeah, it had something to do with thinking that it would be a cakewalk. A nice, easy way to write off my office building, some fancy furniture and an expensive car. Also, I'd figured that, hanging my shingle out here in wine country, I'd have very little real business, leaving a ton more time to take Jiggs over to Hagg Lake for leisurely paddles on free afternoons. In the event I actually did have a case, I planned to contemplate clues in my floating "outside office". Boy, was that a pipe dream. I mean, people have been taking my "Blackstone Investigations" sign seriously. Too seriously.

I levered myself out of the car and plodded toward the side door of my house. Irene Adler squawked out a raspy tune from wherever she was perched deep inside. She's a vocal one, that Irene. Jiggs met me at the threshold with a look on his mug that said, "Feed me." Lauren leaned against the doorjamb between the mudroom and the kitchen. A smudge of butter glistened on her left cheek. Face cheek, that is.

"Hey."

"Hey back at ya." She ambled over and gave me a kiss while Jiggs pushed in to paw my leg. Frankly, I preferred Lauren's approach.

"Don't let him lie to you. He's had his dinner."

Jiggs snorted and looked up at her as though she were a traitor. Well, she sort of was, at least in his eyes. He put his head down and slinked away.

I followed my girlfriend through the doorway into the kitchen, letting the aromas guide me. As I passed by the little telephone desk at the end of the counter, an envelope with "Par Avion" caught my eye. It evoked memories of the day I'd snatched Adrien's mail from his sofa table when we had kind of broken into his flat, making me feel momentarily sad, knowing that Adrien would never wow me with that wide, sparkling smile again.

The envelope was of expensive stock, with a return address that read "Gilles LeDuc Agence". I hadn't heard from the French detective since the day he'd dropped me off at the Montpellier airport. We'd all needed a bit of time to catch our breaths. The whole affair surrounding the Hatifs had turned into quite a whirlwind, one with an exceptionally distressing outcome.

Lauren slid a glass of wine into my free hand, glanced at the envelope I held in the other, and said, "You have about half an hour before the Bolognese will be ready."

"Thanks."

Lauren had taken to cooking mainly Italian dishes since I'd gotten home, which seemed odd, considering we'd traveled to France, not Italy. Odd but fine, as I do love the Italian stuff. Food, wine, shoes, cars, you name it; if it's Italian, I love it.

As I passed into the family room, Irene Adler screeched a flurry of words. "Hello, Irene. Lovely to hear from you." Her answer really wasn't lovely at all. Besides, it may have included a curse word or two. She tends to sulk when a case takes up too much of my time in her opinion. It affects her attitude in ways bordering on bipolar behavior. Right then, she seemed to be angling for another road trip in her near future.

Standing before the fireplace, I tore open the envelope and pulled out the contents. A piece of paper on which Gilles had dashed off a quick note tumbled out. I unfolded it and read: *I think you will find this article interesting. Maybe your belle femme will translate. Jack says she speaks wonderful French. By the way, the lads send their hallos.*

A half page from the *Midi Libre* newspaper, Montpellier's daily, slipped out of the folded sheet. I confess confusion, yes, because everything was, naturally, in French. The hairs on the back of my neck tingled, though, when I focused on the article's two pictures. One showed an angry-faced woman standing in a rigid posture before what appeared to be a courthouse. I couldn't read the caption and the picture was blurry, but the words "Aimee Hatif-Purdue" were clear enough that the woman's features became recognizable as those of Adrien's sister. Mlle. Hatif seemed to be baring her teeth – and was probably growling, if I remembered her customary pissed-off state. I'd bet that none of what she was saying would have been pleasant. Some words jumped out of the article, ones like *chamber de mise en accusation*, which sounded ominous even to me, and *ministere de la justice*, which definitely sounded official and legal. I caught a glimpse of Silvie's name, which led me to believe his loyalty to Mlle. Hatif had indeed been tested, and he'd decided to defect to the other team.

But the larger picture under the headline that I couldn't read was of a mangled motor scooter. It looked like someone had run it into a wall, which I thought absurd as the road split in two at that point and seemed clearly marked. I called Lauren in to read me the article, most importantly the part pertinent to that photograph.

She took the clipping, cleared her throat and began, in her best journalist's voice:

"In a stunning turn of events, Montpellier attorney Aimee Hatif-Purdue, currently under investigation for the death of her brother Adrien Hatif, died last evening in a one-vehicle accident. It appeared that she was riding a Vespa and failed to stop at the intersection of rue Aspirant Lebaron and Avenue Pierre Sirven, running into a stone wall across from Bouscary Andre Winery at high speed. There were no witnesses to the crash, but a German couple returning to their hotel from a late dinner spotted the scooter around 1:15 a.m. and stopped to investigate. They found Hatif-Purdue lying about fifteen feet from the motorbike. Apparently, Hatif-Purdue was semi-conscious and tried to communicate something to them, but the couple could not understand what she was saying because they do not speak French. Medical personnel called to the scene pronounced Hatif-Purdue dead upon their arrival."

The article went on to quote friends and family of the victim, as the reporter called her, a word I would never use in the same sentence with "Aimee Hatif" but, again, *c'est la vie*. Her parents said she'd been highly distraught over her legal troubles and extremely depressed, leading the writer of the article to speculate about the causative nature of the accident. Accident or suicide? I knew which way I'd vote. And Gilles left no doubt about his opinion on the subject either. At the bottom of the clipping, he had penned, "Aimee did something noble, no?" Well, on that we disagreed. Gilles was giving her a salute for saving her parents the misery and heartbreak of a public and protracted murder trial. Yeah, that was a decent thing to do, and I'd give her my salute, too, if I believed she'd given a single thought to anyone other than herself.

But me, cynic that I tend to be, I leaned more toward the "accident" being a defiant thumbing of her nose at the courts. An escape clause of her own making. A rebel to the bitter end, Aimee was making sure no one took Aimee Hatif down but Aimee herself. This was the big middle finger aimed at the rest of us. One more victory in her column. She made sure that she would not be convicted of her brother's murder. Damn.

But I do wonder what she tried to convey to the German couple in her dying moments. Do you suppose, at the bitter end, she had a change of heart? That she saw the error of her ways and confessed? Personally, I hope so, because that meant she wasted her last breath. Her final words fell on deaf ears.

*

About the Author

Kate Ayers spent much of her early career as a court reporter in the Pacific Northwest, taking up the writing of mysteries in just the last dozen or so years. She's the author of *A Murder of Crows* and *A Walk of Snipes*, the first two books in the Mysteries With a Wine List series, which allows Kate to continue her research into fine wines and fast cars, plus – the real motive – legally kill anyone who fatally annoys her. She has also written *Eyes & Ears: The SetUp*. She lives in Oregon with her husband of over three decades and her slightly imbalanced dog.

Visit her website: www.kateayers.com
Email her at kate@kateayers.com
Follow her on Facebook at Kate Ayers, Author

Acknowledgments

Thank you to Bobbie Berbereia, Yamhill, Oregon, for the exquisite cover photo.

And my gratitude goes out once again to Ken Morrison at K&M Wines for his continued exposure of my titles on the shelves of his tasting room. Also, to Roselyn Mostafa at R.R. Thompson House B&B, and Karen Choules, proprietress of The Carlton Inn, for including my books among their other guest offerings.

Thank you also to Sally Weber for advance reading and critiquing comments.

And to my husband Jim, as always, for his endless support and patience.

Made in the USA
San Bernardino, CA
18 June 2016